BLIGHTSLAYER
A GOTREK GURNISSON NOVEL

BLIGHTSLAYER

A GOTREK GURNISSON NOVEL

RICHARD STRACHAN

BLACK LIBRARY

A BLACK LIBRARY PUBLICATION

First published in 2023.
This edition published in Great Britain in 2023 by
Black Library, Games Workshop Ltd., Willow Road,
Nottingham, NG7 2WS, UK.

Represented by: Games Workshop Limited – Irish branch,
Unit 3, Lower Liffey Street, Dublin 1,
D01 K199, Ireland.

10 9 8 7 6 5 4 3 2 1

Produced by Games Workshop in Nottingham.
Cover illustration by Anna Lakisova.

A CIP record for this book is available from the British Library.

ISBN 13: 978-1-80407-355-1

See Black Library on the internet at

blacklibrary.com

Find out more about Games Workshop
and the worlds of Warhammer at

games-workshop.com

Printed and bound in the UK.

The Mortal Realms have been despoiled. Ravaged by the followers of the Chaos Gods, they stand on the brink of utter destruction.

The fortress-cities of Sigmar are islands of light in a sea of darkness. Constantly besieged, their walls are assailed by maniacal hordes and monstrous beasts. The bones of good men are littered thick outside the gates. These bulwarks of Order are embattled within as well as without, for the lure of Chaos beguiles the citizens with promises of power.

Still the champions of Order fight on. At the break of dawn, the Crusader's Bell rings and a new expedition departs. Storm-forged knights march shoulder to shoulder with resolute militia, stoic duardin and slender aelves. Bedecked in the splendour of war, the Dawnbringer Crusades venture out to found civilisations anew. These grim pioneers take with them the fires of hope. Yet they go forth into a hellish wasteland.

Out in the wilds, hardy colonists restore order to a crumbling world. Haunted eyes scan the horizon for tyrannical reavers as they build upon the bones of ancient empires, eking out a meagre existence from cursed soil and ice-cold seas. By their valour, the fate of the Mortal Realms will be decided.

The ravening terrors that prey upon these settlers take a thousand forms. Cannibal barbarians and deranged murderers crawl from hidden lairs. Martial hosts clad in black steel march from skull-strewn castles. The savage hordes of Destruction batter the frontier towns until no stone stands atop another. In the dead of night come howling throngs of the undead, hungry to feast upon the living.

Against such foes, courage is the truest defence and the most effective weapon. It is something that Sigmar's chosen do not lack. But they are not always strong enough to prevail, and even in victory, each new battle saps their souls a little more.

This is the time of turmoil. This is the era of war.

This is the Age of Sigmar.

PROLOGUE

Dead trees trembled in the wind. Their black branches reached towards the twilit sky as trails of grey cloud slithered across the face of the moon. Here and there pools of deep water were wrinkled in the breeze. The night-blooming flowers of devil's tooth and blood-root began to breathe their cold fragrance into the air. The wind rushed and moaned over the mire, and the trees clattered their branches together like praying hands.

A moth, like a scrap of tattered lace, skipped over the stalks of grass. Its wings were as wide as a lady's fan, and emblazoned on each was the suggestion of a staring eye. The wind buffeted and threw the creature, a trail of shimmering silver dust cast off by its wings. Still it kept its course, on, ever on, skimming the mire and the deep pools, threading its way through the branches of the trees until it came to a scattering of black stone that might once have been a castle.

A spire jutted at a drunken angle from the fenland, like a beck-oning finger. Beneath it was a wide sweep of crumbling wall, the remains of an old courtyard, the ruins of battlement and barbican. Moss and vine had colonised the stone, and drifts of dead autumn leaves crackled in the wind as it shuddered through the ancient square. The moth flew on, fluttering madly through the breeze, the trail of silver dust like a comet's tail strung out behind it. From somewhere deep inside the tower came a scream – the howl of someone past all hope, who yearns for death only as a last relief from endless torment.

The moth floated up the flank of the tower and gained the lip of an arrow-slit window. Beyond, there was nothing but a rich and oppressive darkness: shadows like living things, cold and vindictive, and the sense beyond them of a prowling, malign intelligence. The moth felt no fear or uneasiness, though. The feathers of its antennae quivered on the edge of the darkness, and after a moment it lifted from the stone and passed through the window, fluttering into the black. All that was visible in that impenetrable gloom was the faint trail of silver dust that fell from its wings.

'You return...' a voice whispered. It was a voice as dry as the dead leaves in the courtyard, as lifeless as the trees that shivered in the mire. It was a voice that was ancient and without pity, and for which mercy was a long-forgotten thing. 'Come, my child... Tell me all... Tell me what the night has seen in Kranzinnport.'

Another muffled scream rose and fell from deep within the spire, from dungeons far beneath the earth, along corridors of crumbling stone. The moth drifted through the shadows. Quick as lightning, a grey claw whipped from the darkness and gathered it close.

Outside, the clouds unfurled across the dusk. The moon throbbed with a sallow light and the fenlands trembled beneath it. The spire rose amongst the dead trees and the dry grass, a black column where no lamp shone. And then slowly, unfurling across the night, came the sound of dread laughter.

PART ONE

PART ONE

CHAPTER ONE

THE CITY OF KRANZINNPORT

Morning broke cold and clear; the sky was cloudless, and it promised to be another fine day in Kranzinnport. Odger woke early, as he always did, slipping from the bed where his wife Melita still slept. She could sleep through an ice-squall, one of those mad and blustering storms that came haring in from off the sea in midwinter, but Odger slept lightly. Dreams were all well and good, but real life happened when you were awake.

He leaned over and kissed Melita on the cheek. She drew the sheets up over her head. All he could see was the spray of her blonde hair across the pillow.

'You're up already?' she groaned. 'It's the middle of the night – market doesn't open till six.'

'It's dawn,' he said, smiling. 'I'll put some tea on. And the market can't open unless I'm there to see the stalls are all set up in the right place.'

She dragged the sheets up even further over her head. Her voice emerged from under them, muffled and complaining.

'Most important man in Kranzinnport, aren't you? Surprised the council even opens its meetings without checking with you first.'

'And just think how wise their decisions would be if they did,' he said, with mock solemnity.

'Odger Pellin, the saviour of his city...'

'And don't you forget it,' he laughed.

As he pottered about the house brewing Xintilian flower tea and getting his son's breakfast ready, Odger allowed himself to wonder what being on the council would be like. Kranzinnport always needed good folk to guide its decisions and he couldn't think of any better training for the ruthlessness of city politics than being the head steward in the market. The stallholders and traders were always at each other's throats. Barely a market day went by without someone arguing over who had the better patch, or who owed whom on goods promised and received, or who exactly was busy undercutting prices on the legal fixtures... Sigmar's blood, but it went on and on some days. You might look at a seamstress like Merosis and see only a pleasant, hardworking young woman, content at her tailor's stall with her displays of fine Verdian silks, but behind her eyes was the cold calculation of a seasoned warrior. After that, the debating chambers of the city council would seem like a playground.

Odger smiled to himself as he poured the boiling water into the pot. It was a dream, nothing more, and like he always said, dreams were no substitute for reality. He was no leader of men.

The smell of the tea quickly filled the kitchen and suffused the house. Odger opened the door onto the backyard, a little square of well-tended grass and conch shells arranged by Melita, and looked out across the silent grey streets as they dropped down towards the cliffs on the far side of the city. He let his eyes wander over the domes and the tall, twisted spires, the towers shaped like the coiled shells of molluscs, the walls encrusted with salt spray. He looked on the cobbled precincts and noted the glint here and there, in rooftop and pavement, of nacreous pearl. It was a dark town of twisting streets and alleyways, of high grim walls and houses as tough and well defended as the iron-hard shells of the deep-sea creatures they relied on so much, but to Odger it was a beautiful city too. Hunkered here on the edge of the Rocanian Coast, clutching itself to the lip of the cliffs, it was sea and land both, and all the better for it.

No one was up yet, as far as he could see. Even the traders would still be enjoying another hour's sleep before they started getting their wares ready. The fishermen would be waking soon, dragging their aching bodies from bed, gathering their gear with rough, salt-blistered hands as they hobbled down to the harbour. The caravan guards – tough, hard-faced men with missing eyes and missing fingers – would soon be rolling from the taverns and sharpening their blades before the first traders' convoys set off for the wider realms. Drunks would still be passed out in the gutters, and a few corpses would be waiting with all the patience of the dead for the city guard to collect them once the sun was up. The night watch from the Kranzinnport Sabres, the city's Freeguild regiment, would be changing shift on the walls. Odger loved this time of the morning. Everything silent and still, clean almost, the squabbling, rambunctious cut and thrust of city life still a few moments away. He thought of Melita drowsing in bed upstairs, a woman he had been married to for ten years now. He thought of his son, Clovis, whom he could just hear thumping down the stairs for his breakfast. He could count on the fingers of one hand the number of times a hard word had been spoken in this house over the last decade.

It's a tough, hard-bitten place, Odger thought as he sipped his tea, *but Sigmar has blessed it all the same.* There had not been a single raid from orruk warbands in nearly two years, and he couldn't remember the last time there had been a serious riot. He warmed his hands on the mug. *Truly, I am the luckiest man alive.*

Despite all his fears, it was a quiet enough day in the market. Merosis didn't threaten anyone with her pinking shears, Old Tamser actually used the proper weights on his scales for once, and the long-standing and pitiless rivalry between Krennin Brisker, the city's oldest purveyor of pies, pastries and baked goods, and Dravett Pynn, importer of the finest buns, rolls and bread loafs in Kranzinnport, seemed to have settled into an uneasy truce. Izuvell the Astromancer cast his horoscopes, claiming this new conjunction of the moons wouldn't be seen again for another thousand years; it was the most propitious occasion to tell your future. No one minded his nonsense today though. No one was stabbed. No one was bludgeoned over an argument about change, and no drunken scuffle turned into anything more serious than a cracked skull and a night in the town gaol. The sun shone high and clear, and the sharp bite of the sea wind put a spring in everyone's step. The aqualith sparkled in the centre of the square, brimming with water.

Everyone had a good word for him as Odger walked between the stalls, the change purse on his hip. Melita was always on at him to carry a weapon in case someone tried to make off with the market takings, but Odger thought the idea was ludicrous. He was no fighter, and anyway – this was the Kranzinnport market, about as close as you get to a truce day in the whole city. Who would ever steal from him?

As he walked round, Odger made sure everyone was satisfied with their position, and that they had no complaints for him to take forward to the next meeting of the Commerce Committee. More than once a choice cut of meat was pressed into his hands, nestled between two sheets of grease paper, or a bottle of fine vintage was handed over with a nod and a wink, but Odger always made sure he paid the market price. Everyone knew that with Odger Perrin you got fair dealing: nothing more, nothing less.

When the sun was past midday, he paused by the shrine to Sigmar on the east side of the market square. He lit a candle, paused for a while to read the prayers that were pinned to the spikes of Sigmar's heraldic crown. The god stood there as a golden statue three feet high, his hammer raised and the seaweed of his hair streaming down his back. His armour was of gilded seashells and starfish clung to his beard. The whole statue was covered in a light dusting of dried salt. Odger gave silent thanks for all that he had, and for all that the city had, too.

Melita and Clovis came over in the afternoon, holding a basket between them. Odger could smell one of Pynn's Living City loafs, and it looked like there was half a bottle of Thyrian fruit wine tucked under the checked cloth as well.

'Mum's got four of Brisker's jadespice buns,' Clovis said, 'but she says you're getting fat in your old age and you can only have one of them.'

'Is that right?' Odger said, eyes wide. 'I'll show you fat!' He roared and threw Clovis up onto his shoulders, the boy crying out with laughter.

'A late lunch,' Melita said, taking his arm. 'As a reward for all your hard work. I thought we could take it down to the bluff and look over the bay.'

'Sounds good to me.'

They strolled on to the plaza as the breeze picked up, coming out on the other side of the city into a wide, triangular space on the very edge of the cliffs. The marble flagstones underfoot were scuffed and dirty from all the passing feet, and the whole plaza was surrounded by a long balustrade of blue coral, the bars sculpted into the shapes of eels and fish. In the centre of the plaza was a square entranceway surrounded by a tarnished brass rail, which opened onto a flight of iron stairs. Folk were bringing up goods from the clanking cage lifts that led down to the harbour, far below at the base of the cliffs. Odger let himself be overwhelmed by the view, as he always was. It was breathtaking, the entire horizon from east to west filled with the majesty of the ocean, the Tendril Sea in all its muscular rise and fall. Seabirds cried and scattered above the waves, following the trails of the fishing boats as they sailed out from the harbour, their coloured sails stark against the gunmetal blue.

Far, far out to sea, forty miles or more, could be seen the airy puff of leviathans broaching the surface of the waves. Beyond that, so it was claimed, and so far that there wasn't a single sailor in Kranzinnport who'd ever attempted the voyage, the edge of the realm curved round in a glister of magic, so wild and dangerous that it would burn the flesh from your bones if you got within even a hundred miles of it.

They sat on a bench near the edge of the prow, eating and drinking while the afternoon drifted away. After much earnest negotiation, Odger agreed to split the last jadespice bun with Clovis, and the lad hared off with it towards the other side of the plaza to stare down at the western reaches of the ocean where the Rocanian Coast curved away towards Yska. He was a fine boy – eight years old, curious and adventurous all at once. Odger watched him run across the flagstones, his mop of black hair streaming in the breeze. He never did anything at half measures. Why should he? He ran at life full tilt, like any lad his age.

'I wonder what he'll grow up to be?' Melita said softly, resting her head on his shoulder. 'A market trader? An official in the council? Maybe a soldier on the city guard?'

Odger laughed. 'Any of that would make me proud,' he said. He stared out to sea, where the wash of blue was beginning to stain at the edges with dark clouds. The sea looked choppy now, the slow waves beginning to crest into whitecaps. He frowned. 'As long as he doesn't become a fisherman,' he said softly. 'Sigmar knows we value them here, but it's a hard and dangerous life…'

The clouds were thickening. From east and west they seemed to gather, rolling like banks of fog over the agitated water. The breeze quickened. There was something feverish in it, and the waves were rising higher, as if lashed to some strange purpose. The fishing boats were turning back to harbour, pitching and swaying in the tide.

Odger stood slowly from the bench and leaned against the rail of the balustrade. It was getting dark. He stared out at the ocean. There, to the south, something was stirring. It was like the sea was boiling, twenty miles out. He could hear the hiss of it from here, like a pot clattering on a stove, the liquid furiously bubbling. A lance of cloud seemed to pierce down from the heavens above it, black as pitch. There was a thick, cloying fog creeping over the waters, pale and billowing, like breath exhaled on a cold day.

Melita joined him at the rail, her brows furrowed. She placed her hand on his. They could hear the cries of the fishermen now, seven hundred feet down as they guided their boats back into Kranzinnport harbour at the foot of the cliffs.

'What is that?' she said. 'The water there, it's… Is it a leviathan? I never heard of one breaching so close to shore.'

Odger shook his head. 'I don't think so…' He looked to the other side of the plaza. 'Where's Clovis? I think we should head back to the market.'

But it was as if the market had come to the plaza instead. More and more people were strolling to the balustrade, leaning against the rail, pointing and arguing while they looked out to sea.

'Ain't no leviathan,' one old timer said. He tipped his straw hat back on his head. 'Damned kraken, that's what that be.'

'Kraken?' someone else replied. 'Have you been at the seaweed ale again, there ain't no such thing.'

'Is too. I done saw it when I was a lad, out there on the water like. Big as the cliffs here, with tentacles as long as Kranzinnport's tallest tower, and eyes wider than the moon.'

There was much laughter at this and the old man grumbled into his beard.

'It's no kraken,' Odger said confidently.

He shaded his eyes with his hand as the fog rolled in, as the banks of cloud rippled and contracted above the water. Soon they were spreading their turbulent vapour above the bay, and with them came a clammy sense of cold. He was aware of everyone nearby looking at him, deferring to him as one who never played anyone false. If Odger Pellin was saying it, so they seemed to think, then it was worth listening to. Odger cleared his throat and looked again.

'It's no leviathan either,' he said. 'Looks like… Looks like a damned *island* rising up out of the water.'

There was nothing else it could be, and soon enough everyone could see the same. Through the haze of fog, Odger could see the low-slung black shape frothing with water, the foam dripping back into the sea from crags and rocks and headlands. It was like a rugged disc of stone, shining black, twenty miles out and no more than five miles by five, if that. Rumbling across the water came a rolling boom, as if the very sea bed were protesting. Waves shook and thundered around it, surging back to strike the cliffs in long and angry breakers.

A pall seemed to settle over everyone. It was more than the clouds streaming in above the city, and it was more than the fog that crept ever closer across the bay. Something new had come into the world, unannounced and unexpected, and there wasn't a single person in Kranzinnport who knew what to say about it.

Odger rubbed at the bristles on his chin. He looked for Clovis in the crowds, saw the boy pressing through to get back to his mother.

'Did you see it, dad?' he said. 'Came straight out of the water, I ain't never seen the like! What is it?'

'I don't know, son,' he said quietly. 'I wish I did.'

He turned to go, taking Melita's arm and reaching for Clovis. He wanted to get back to the market, make sure everything was all right. More than that, he wanted to get home. He couldn't say why, but he just wanted to shut the doors and light the fire, and sit with his family. That's all he wanted.

The rain began to fall. The dark clouds broke, and the oily drizzle spattered on the flagstones. There was a smell in the air suddenly that made him wrinkle his nose. A smell of rot, and decay. All the bells from the Freeguild barracks started ringing then, mustering the garrison. The city was nowhere near large enough to support a Stormcast Eternals contingent, but it would be well defended all the same if danger approached. Odger was sure of it. This was a hard town carved out of the cliffs on a hard coast. He wasn't worried. Not really.

A shame, he thought as he hurried on. And it had seemed such a beautiful day that morning.

CHAPTER TWO

A VOICE IN THE WILDERNESS

The city was called Xil'anthos, and it was slumped in a fold of ground two miles distant. The shape of it seemed scattered and warped in the heat haze that lifted up from the green, abundant land.

Amara Fidellus peered at it, shielding her face from the sun with the flat of her palm. She could see the high walls curving around to hug the ground where it rose in the north, the roofs of houses and tenements just visible over the battlements. Further in there were tall black spires clustered in the centre of the city, like reed stems in the middle of a lake. As with most settlements in the Everspring Swathe, whoever had founded the city had first turned to the realm's bounty for their materials. The walls looked as if they were made from the dried stalks of the towering megalanthos flowers, which grew far to the north-west in the verdant forests of Yska. The spires of those buildings in the centre could well be the hollowed-out trunks of Yskian blackwood trees, some of which reached more than three hundred feet into the air.

It was hard to tell, though. The rising sun had beaten a hot mist out of the grass and it made everything seem smeared and indistinct. Amara could see the gates open wide in the flank of the city walls, the weather-beaten guardian idols standing on either side like sentinels. She could see drifts of smoke rising up from chimneys and cook fires. There was a road threading its way across the grain of the land, sweeping out towards the range of low hills that brooded in the west, slumped and wary under a cap of fume. Above the city the shattering blue skies of Ghyran were streaked with purple and red, and the clouds were like airy cathedrals raised in the midst of a crystalline sea.

Xil'anthos, she thought. She hitched her tattered robes around her, robes that had once proclaimed her a warrior priest of Sigmar's temple. *A city ripe to hear the truth.*

She had never been to this place before, but she knew perfectly well what to expect. It would be one of those ramshackle, backwater settlements that had grown up over time, hacked out of the wilderness by hard folk, supplied with agonising slowness by armoured merchant caravans, half of which went missing in the wilds instead of reaching their destination. Then, day by day, defended by spear and blade and crossbow, the village would become a town, and the town would become a city, slowly accruing new quarters and districts, the walls extended foot by foot into the wilderness, the ground cleared around it, the military patrols extended, fresh citizens drawn in for its burgeoning industries. Farmers, tough and hardy, would toil in the outlying land. Artisans would arrive to craft the luxuries a growing merchant class demanded. And before long a settlement built with blood and sweat had broken its original bounds and found itself more of a permanent fixture than had ever really been intended. Most of these places vanished in the wilds and were never heard of again, sacked by passing raiders and ravaged by warbands, their citizens murdered or enslaved. Some of them lasted, though, and they were the hardest places of all.

She smiled grimly to herself. If there was one thing she couldn't stand, it was folk with pretensions above their station.

Amara's dark skin was blistered by the sun. Her once-shaved hair had now grown back to a faint dusting of copper across her scalp. She was a young woman, but she was thin with the rigours of the wild and her face was as hard as carved wood. She had fought packs of flesh-wyrms and had run from the beastmen raiders who preyed on anyone foolish enough to wander alone. A scar cut diagonally across her lip and made her mouth seem like it was sneering. There was a bruise beginning to fade against her cheekbone, a souvenir she had picked up when she passed through Tillistyne further east on the Rocanian Coast two weeks earlier where the locals had taken exception to her message. Although her piercing grey eyes were as hard as flint, there was sadness in them too. For a moment she leaned her weight against the staff she had cut from a branch of ironoak, both hands gripping the leather wrist strap.

She may have worn the robes of a warrior priest, but Amara had left that life behind her many months ago now. The armour had been discarded along the way, the warhammer thrown into the bogs where the crusade had made its last stand. The priest had died there in the wilderness. In the valleys of Thyria, she had watched the Hedonites came down from the fold, wave after wave of them, screaming their lavish war cries, lashing their bodies with barb and whip. When the Dawnbringers tried to rally around their wagons, the priest had fought with Sigmar's strength until she was overwhelmed, and when she awoke there was only Amara left in her.

Sigmar had gone. Sigmar had abandoned them all.

She gasped against the pain of those memories, her grey eyes squeezed shut. She clutched the wrist strap until the leather cut into her hands – and then she tightened her belt against her dusty robes and strode off across the plains towards Xil'anthos.

She joined the road where it curved in from the eastern hills and swept across the grasslands. She passed a handful of farmers who were bringing in baskets of fruit from the orchards that were strewn in mellow groves to the south of the city, some of them with their baskets hoisted high up on their backs, others with carts and barrows pulled by long-horned kyne and oxen. They were hard-looking folk, some with deep scars on their faces, a few with missing hands or fingers. All of them were armed, and Amara saw cruel-looking sickles and barbed swords on their hips. They gave her a close look as she strode by, shielding their eyes from the sun or peering from underneath their wide-brimmed straw hats. They said nothing, made no challenge, just watched her with the wary suspicion of any country folk whenever a newcomer came into their midst. Amara said nothing in return. One man paused and made the sign of the comet against his chest, seeing the robes and the stern look in her eye, and coming to the obvious conclusion. She would disabuse him of that before the day was out.

The road was little more than packed earth underneath Amara's boots. No one came to visit places like Xil'anthos; these were outposts, flags planted in the wilderness. The walls loomed high above her as she got closer; twenty feet of khaki fibre from the stems of the megalanthos flower, as she had suspected. They were lashed together and reinforced with bracers of ironoak, but Amara knew no walls could keep out the dangers of the outside world for long. They were a necessary illusion so the folk here could sleep at night, that's all. She grimaced as she joined the crowd, pushing through the stinking peasants and the farmers bringing their goods to market, slipping by the guards who stood on either side of the gates with their billhooks and black steel helmets.

The gatehouse opened onto a wide avenue that was bordered by stands of swaying sourbark trees. Beyond was a square of dusty flagstones. She could see those tall black spires over the roofs of the houses on the far side of the square, the hollowed trunks of Yskian blackwoods, as she had guessed. She knew what type would live in those towers. High priests and councillors. Mayors, captains of the guard, rich merchants. Everyone else had to make do with the streets.

There were awnings stretched over the shops and taverns on either side of the square, protecting them from the sun that boiled in the blue skies above. Stone benches were laid out here and there, where all the citizens of Xil'anthos could take the weight off their feet and exchange the day's gossip. She saw street traders bearing trays of sweetmeats, beggars holding out their bowls, tea sellers threading their way through the crowds with brass urns on their backs and racks of clay cups in their arms. There were lantern lighters, their wide-brimmed brass hats decorated with burning candles; lay preachers in soiled loincloths, with heavy leather-bound copies of holy books chained to their necks; ratcatchers with capes of woven rat skins and ragged little terriers at their heels. A couple of aelven trackers sat under the shade of an awning over on her left, sipping glasses of tawny wine while they watched the crowds. There was a travelling illusionist standing under the shade of a coppiced tree on her right, his blue silk robes gleaming with embroidered silver moons. As Amara watched he tossed handfuls of red powder into the air, soaking up the applause as each handful transformed into a flock of tiny, flittering crimson birds. All in the square was bustle and haste, a flurry of folk buying and selling and laughing, or just passing across the wide and airy precinct as they headed deeper into the city on their own private business.

A comfortable place, Amara thought to herself, striding on across the flagstones. Comfortable, and no more prosperous than they need to be, and with no idea of what the world outside is really like, no interest in how others have suffered. As she had suffered.

A hand, reaching for her from the safety of the tent. A voice crying out in the wilderness. Red blades, red murder, and the end of all her strength.

There was a temple to Sigmar on the far side of the square: a tall, flat-fronted structure of white marble, with two wide pillars holding up a gleaming lintel of polished gold. Beyond, in the centre of the temple complex, Amara could see a cool portico and a statue of the God-King himself, standing on a marble dais with hammer raised to the heavens and a look on his sculpted face of infinite, stern compassion. The town's Banner Heraldor hung limp before the statue, the heraldry of whatever crusade had established this settlement faded with age. A short perron of marble stairs led up to the front of the temple, where priests and votaries sat and discussed theology, arguing the finer points of the *Intimations of the Comet,* some of them exhorting their fellow citizens to pray and worship to the greater glory of he who guards and protects them all.

'Come, my friends!' one white-bearded priest called to the crowds in the square. He was dressed in the red, ankle-length robes of a lector, the lapels embroidered with golden trim, and with a white cotton sash around his waist. A heavy golden sigil was strung round his neck, the sign of Sigmar's hammer, and Sigmar's comet was tattooed in blue and gold in the centre of his forehead. His beard was streaked with ashes and his face glistened with ritual scarring. He stood on the perron and raised his arms as if to gather them all in. 'Raise your voices in worship of the Most High! Gift your prayers to he who oversees us, stern in judgement, fair in all things!'

Amara felt the blood thrum in her veins. On instinct she reached for the loops in her belt which had once held a warrior priest's hammer and a copy of the *Intimations*, but those loops were empty now. The hammer she had cast into the bogs of Thyria. The book she had torn to shreds while she screamed in the wilderness, her hands red with the blood of those she had buried. She had burned those pages in a fury that she did not think would ever slacken.

The scar on her lip throbbed. The pain of old wounds bloomed anew. She pushed her way onwards, until the stairs stretched up beyond her, and the look she gave the white-bearded priest curdled the voice in his throat.

'Ah…' he stammered, at last. He reached out as if to usher her into the temple. 'One of Sigmar's brave priests, giving voice to the God-King in the wilderness! See, my friends!' he called out. 'Let us follow this young woman's example and take up arms in praise and worship of the Heldenhammer!'

She looked through the portico, where Sigmar stood in all his glory. Sigmar, in whose name they had marched from Dagoleth – civilians and soldiers alike, priests and prophets and penitents – with hymns of praise on their lips, forging into the wilds to found new settlements and civilisations. The metaliths had floated high above them, dragged on their chains of thrice-blessed brass and iron, bearing all the supplies they would need as they built their new homes from scratch and cleared the ground to plant their crops. She remembered it all, months ago now. Leaving Dagoleth with such a fierce determination, such a sense that they were doing his work. Trusting that she would keep them safe.

Amara turned and faced the crowd. Most of them still went about their business, strolling through the market stalls, lounging on the stone benches, but a few had turned to watch the priest as he praised her example. She wondered what they saw in her now.

How could they look on this scarred and stony face and see anything other than the pain she had suffered?

'People of Xil'anthos!' she cried, raising the staff above her head. Her voice was harsh, as dry as the dust that scattered across the flagstones. She had not spoken to anyone for nearly two weeks. 'Do not listen to these false priests, who spin lies only for their own enrichment! Sigmar cares not for your craven prayers or your servile worship, for Sigmar has abandoned us! The God-King has turned his face from humanity in all his arrogance and deceit, and cares not whether you live or die! Aye, you could crawl on your bellies before his altars all the days of your lives, and wet the stone with endless tears of contrition, but it would be no more than the morning dew to him, quick to burn into a fleeting mist!'

She felt a hand grip her wrist, turned to see the white-bearded lector gazing at her with incredulity. His scars were white on his face.

'In the name of all that is holy,' he croaked, trembling. 'What are you doing? What do you mean by these horrid blasphemies!'

'I mean to give them the truth,' Amara snarled. She snatched her hand free. 'I have seen Sigmar in the wilderness, old man, and he is no more than a shadow flitting across the empty sky, indifferent to our pain. Place your trust in him if you will, but I will do so no longer. He has taken from me all that I had.'

She saw again the column marching from Dagoleth, the red banners on the walls of her city snapping in the breeze. And she saw the bodies falling by the wayside as they crossed the coruscating plains of Thyria, the people who succumbed to disease or exhaustion, who fell to injury or fatigue and were left there dying in the dirt as the crusade forged on. And then, when they had been whittled down by the elements, and when all their food and water was exhausted, she remembered the Slaaneshi warriors' ululating call as they skimmed across the plains on their lithe steeds, their barbed arrows flicking through the press and snatching lives away to left and right. The Dawnbringers had given their lives for their god, and the Slaaneshi cultists had taken lives for theirs – and in the end what was it all worth, but a patch of worthless land in the middle of nowhere, stained with blood? What use was their devotion when it was not repaid in their hour of need?

Amara turned again to face the square, but the crowd was getting restless. The old priest scuttled back up the stairs to the safety of the temple. Something came sailing out and struck her on the shoulder, falling to the marble stair with a wet thump – a piece of fruit from the marketplace. Another came flying towards her and she flicked her head to avoid it. Jeering followed it, dismissive calls shouted out across the sunstruck afternoon.

It's just like Tillistyne all over again. Truly, there are none so deaf as those who will not hear.

'Listen!' she shouted. 'Listen to the truth of what I have to say, and live in darkness no more! I have been a voice lost in the wilderness, all my comrades dead at my feet, and Sigmar gave no answer to my prayers! We marched into the wilds to found a new settlement in his name, and when we were attacked he did not protect us. We stood shoulder to shoulder against the fury of the Hedonites and fought until we could fight no more, and though our prayers burned like fire on the land, Sigmar did not deliver us from the horrors we faced. He left us to die! Save yourselves, and do not wait for the gods to help you, for you will be waiting in vain all the days of your lives.'

More voices raised against her, obscene gestures, faces drawn and deformed by anger. Fists were shaken as the citizens of Xil'anthos realised what this young warrior priest was really saying. Amara held up her staff for silence, but then a stone came flying from the crowd and struck her on the side of the head. She stumbled, her vision black, the pain stabbing through her. Blood pattered onto the marble. Another stone cracked against her knuckles and made her drop the staff – and then she was tumbling down the stairs, pummelled and beaten as the crowd surged towards her.

'Hang the witch!' someone cried. A fist came thudding into her back, sending her sprawling as she tried to stand.

'She denies Sigmar! She denies the gods!'

A heavy boot slammed into her stomach, forcing the breath from her.

'This is Xil'anthos, blasphemer! We worship the God-King here, now take your filth away with you!'

Amara rolled across the flagstones, blood in her mouth, trying to wrap her arms around her head. Someone dashed the dregs of a cup of ale in her face, and then there were strong arms hauling her to her feet. She squinted against the sun, tasted the harsh copper tang of blood, groaned as another fist came swinging in to strike her across the jaw. Despite it all, she would not fight back. All these months wandering the wilds, telling the hard truths ordinary folk were too cowed or stupid to hear, and she had not once lifted her hand against them. She had walked from towns and villages under a rain of abuse more times than she could recall now, and each time with her head held high. She would spill no more blood in the name of the gods.

Dazed and battered, Amara hung limp in the hands of her tormentors. Two porters from one of the taverns held her up, their fingers like steel bands around her arms. Someone grabbed at her throat and tried to choke her; another tore the faded comet from her robes. She was crowded by angry faces, jabbing fingers, the stink of ale-drenched breath – the whole mad cacophony of it shouting and screaming at her. It was a sound like a river in flood, utterly relentless, without pity.

A tough, tousled-haired man with a wiry black beard filled her vision, his hand lashing out to grip her jaw. He wore a scratched leather waistcoat, his sleeves rolled up over his beefy arms, and there was a dishcloth over his shoulder. The tavern keeper, Amara assumed. His eyes were blazing, his lips flecked with spittle. Whoever would have thought that a tavern keeper would be so pious?

'What say you against Sigmar now, witch? Eh? What say you now? Choose your words carefully, for they may be your last!'

Amara, through cracked and bleeding lips, smiled at him. She felt the blood dribbling down her chin, the darkness swimming on the edges of her sight.

'Sigmar cares for you as much as the plough cares for the worm beneath it,' she said. 'No more, no less.'

Snarling with outrage, he drew his fist back and punched her square in the face.

'Sigmar rewards only the virtuous!' he screamed. 'He is mighty in the sight of all, not to be gainsaid!'

'Enough!'

A ripple of obedience swept through the crowd. The black-bearded man stepped back, rubbing his knuckles, wiping the spit from his lip with his dishcloth. As the crowd drew aside Amara saw the old priest approach across the square. He was holding her staff and his face was as cold as the white marble of the temple behind him.

'She denies Sigmar though her very life is at stake, lector!' the black-bearded man cried. 'She has no fear of the gods, none!'

'Hush, Danyel,' the priest said. 'You have done Sigmar's work in apprehending her.' The priest patted him on the shoulder and then turned to Amara. 'You have made yourself quite clear,' he said. His voice trembled, as if it were taking all of his self-control not to scream his words at her. He peered into her grey eyes. 'I do not know what foul taint of Chaos might have made you turn so viciously from your calling, if warrior priest you once were. But we will show you what we do to those who deny the gods in

Xil'anthos. Build a pyre!' he called. 'We will burn the blasphemy from her.'

CHAPTER THREE

THE WAGES OF SIN

She must have passed out for a moment. When she came to, Amara was lying on the flagstones with her hands tightly bound behind her. She could feel the hard swelling of a bruise against her face, a loose feeling in her jaw where a tooth had been rattled.

The sun had crept across the sky and the shadows were falling slantwise on the square. The tall ironoak spires in the centre of the city threw down their shadows like spears against the stone. As the afternoon crept on, the marble of the temple's great arched frontage seemed cool and was stained with a faint touch of pink. They were lighting the lamps outside the taverns, she saw. From inside them came great roars of laughter and merriment, folk knocking back tankards of ale and goblets of wine.

Amara rolled onto her back, wincing against the pain in her bound hands. She saw the pyre they had built behind her, here in the very centre of the square, where everyone would have the best view possible.

Nothing could have made her firmer in her judgement than

the sight of that pyre. Chairs and benches, doors and window frames, even a bundle of wooden spoons tied with a jaunty red ribbon, had been thrown into the mix. The folk of Xil'anthos were smashing up whatever came to hand in their haste to get the burning underway.

Truly, she thought, *fear of the gods makes men mad.*

People were clashing tankards outside the tavern, laughing and joking, looking over the pyre with all the quiet pride of craftsmen well satisfied with their work. It was no more than five feet high, but it would be more than enough to burn her, she was quite sure. Other folk had claimed ringside seats on the stone benches that lined the square, delighted at the prospect of this rare diversion, and the pastry sellers and costermongers were doing a roaring trade as they flitted through the crowds. Some were selling woven talismans that they claimed were unerring protection against the foul blasphemies this woman had brought into Xil'anthos. A street busker was drawing a catgut bow across his fiddle, playing a tune so screeching and discordant that Amara felt death by burning would be a mercy. Ossuary men, their faces covered by black leather masks and with round caps of yellowed bone, stood by with their carts, waiting to gather up the scorched remains when the fire had burned out; it would make good fertiliser for the fields, and was worth good money if any of their farmers cared to pay. The old priest stood there before the pyre, leaning on the staff that had once been Amara's, a pompous look on his face.

'You will get no confession from me,' she mumbled at him through her bruised lips. 'No frantic begging for mercy, no regrets. I'm sorry to disappoint you.'

She tried to get up onto her knees, but a foot in the small of her back sent her crashing face forward onto the flagstones again.

'Alas, it is too late for that, my child,' the priest said. 'Far, far too late.'

He nodded, and those strong hands gripped her arms again and dragged her up towards the pyre. A great cheer arose from the crowd when they saw. Tankards were raised, and the fiddler's screeching tune skipped and danced across the mellow air of the late afternoon.

So this is how I die, she thought as they hauled her to the pyre. *It could have been in that valley with a weapon in my hand, in the ruins of all that I loved. But no, instead it's this. An evening's entertainment for the credulous and the weak.*

A wooden chair had been brought from the tavern and planted at the top of the pyre, and they tied her to it with thick bands of rope. As he knotted the final tie, the one the lector had called Danyel laughed and spoke quietly in her ear. His breath stank of sour beer and as he leaned close Amara could see the long scar that cut down across his sightless left eye.

'They say it's the smoke that kills you when the flames begin to rise,' he said. 'But don't worry – this wood is bone dry and shouldn't smoke a bit.'

They brought the flame on a burning brand, lit from the lamps outside the tavern. The old priest took it and moved solemnly towards the base of the pyre, and when he set the flame to the wood the crowd roared its approval. She could see the lust in their eyes, the common cruelty of common folk.

Amara gazed up into the empty sky. The streaks of purple and red had faded now, the blue deepening to a smooth cerulean. She saw the black specks of birds wheeling slowly in the deep of it, could almost see the first faint glitter of the realmspheres as the afternoon faded into dusk. She could smell the sweat of the crowd, the sour reek of spilled ale – and beyond that, the warm scent of Xintilian flowers in the planters around the square; the fresh, unruly fragrance of Ghyran beyond the city walls, in all its fecund glory. She closed her eyes as the flames took hold, tried to quieten the fear as it flared up in her stomach.

The paint on the stacked window frames and the door panels blistered in the heat. The wood cracked like a black-powder gunshot. Amara relaxed against the ropes that held her. She could try to detach her mind from what was happening, send her thoughts soaring up into the blue as the fire crisped against her skin. She could let herself go, and the pain would be no more than a brief, eclipsing moment before her body slackened its grip on her soul. She could let herself die here. She could be free – of the sorrow, of the memories, of all that she had suffered. Wouldn't that be mercy, of a kind?

The fiddle skirled. The good folk of Xil'anthos laughed and danced in the light of the flames. The old priest raised his eyes to the heavens and intoned a prayer.

Amara smiled to herself. She could do all of those things. But why, in the name of a god she no longer believed in, would she give these morons the satisfaction?

The ropes were tight around her chest, but she could feel that the tavern chair she was strapped to was an old and rickety thing. As she threw her weight down and kicked out with her heels, the right rear leg snapped and sent her tumbling backwards. There was a spray of sparks, the flames hissing around her like a nest of vipers. She felt the heat scorching her face, the flames licking up the sides of her tattered robes, but as she crashed down the slope of the pyre and struck the hard flagstones, the back of the chair splintered and the ropes hung slack.

She heard the roar of the crowd, laughing, protesting. In a moment Amara had managed to stagger to her feet and shrug out of her bonds. Her hands were still tied behind her, but through the crowd she could see the long avenue that led to the town gates. She could run, burst through them, take advantage of the dusk and hide herself in the scrub outside the city. She could even head for those hills off to the west – a terrible danger by any stretch of the imagination, but surely no more dangerous than staying here? There was at least the chance that time and distance would cool the pious bloodlust of these people and they wouldn't come after her.

She winced at the pain in her head, the throbbing bruise against her jaw, her split and bleeding lip. They could count themselves lucky they had not met her when she bore a warrior priest's hammer…

The flames spat and crackled behind her as she circled around the pyre, looking for a break in the crowd, a gap she could run through. She saw the old priest, his white beard pale yellow in the light of the flames. He shook his head, and the tight smile on his face carried all the miserable self-satisfaction that Amara had come to hate from those who claimed to follow the gods. He was enjoying this, she knew. She had given them a moment's sport by trying to escape, but that was all. There was no way out.

'A brave effort, blasphemer,' the priest chuckled. 'But let us see you try the same trick twice, once we have broken your arms and legs.'

There was a ripple of laughter, a clink of pewter, and then a quick flurry of notes as the fiddler plucked out a jaunty pizzicato tune. The priest signalled for her to be held again, and Danyel, the one-eyed tavern keeper, stepped forward with a length of wood in his hand, slapping it confidently into his palm. His beard was split by a red grin.

The voice that boomed out then across the square was so ear-splittingly loud that people flinched away from it. It was like an avalanche, like a storm cloud cracking open in the sky.

'I'm only going to say this once, you bastards,' it cried. 'But if you don't keep the bloody noise down you'll be having your little party in the underworlds, or wherever it is you damned people think you go when you die! Can't a dwarf sleep off a hangover in peace, without all this capering?'

Slowly the crowd parted. Amara squinted against the light of the flames and the rising smoke.

Standing there in the middle of the square was the largest and most brutal looking duardin she had ever seen. He was as wide as he was tall, his arms and shoulders bulging with slabs of thick muscle, his massive chest bare beneath the plaited ropes of his orange beard. There were indigo tattoos curling across his shaved scalp, on either side of a soaring, fat-stiffened orange mohawk. A golden chain snaked from his nose to his earlobe, and he squinted at them out of one coal black, red-rimmed eye, the other little more than a scarred fold of puckered skin. He had a lion-faced pauldron of black steel on his left shoulder, and he was leaning his weight against what looked to Amara like a Fyreslayer's rune-axe – a huge, double-bladed weapon with a brazier in the centre of the haft that smouldered with a wicked red flame. In his other hand he held a gallon jug of foaming ale, and it took Amara only a moment to realise that he was equally adept with the jug as he was with the axe.

Nobody spoke. There was a wave of such threat and barely contained violence coming off him – not to mention the stench of sweat and stale beer – that not one person in the mob dared open their mouth.

In the silence the duardin drank off the jug of ale, sinking it in one long pull. His throat gulped and the beer spilled in glistening rivulets down his beard. He gave a titanic, rippling belch and then, slowly and with immense concentration, he scanned the crowd that had parted before him until his blazing eye came to rest on the fiddler. When he grinned, a terrible gap-toothed snarling grimace, Amara heard someone in the crowd actually sob with fear. Everyone took half a step back. The fiddler cringed, drawing his instrument up before his chest like a shield.

'And *you*,' the duardin rumbled, casting the empty jug over his shoulder. It shattered against the flagstones. He pointed a stubby finger as thick as a spear shaft. The two men on either side of the fiddler shuffled uneasily away from him. 'If I hear another bloody note out of that sodding thing, I'm going to ram it so far up your arse you'll have to pluck your tonsils to play it… Now,' he barked, wiping his mouth with the back of his hand. He glared at the crowd and swung his axe up onto his shoulder. 'Anyone mind telling me exactly what you buggers think you're doing?'

CHAPTER FOUR

THE BETTER PART
OF VALOUR

The old priest rallied first. The lector puffed out his narrow chest and drew himself up tall, the staff held out before him. He hooked his hand to the lapel of his red lector's robes, his wispy white beard quivering on his chin.

'What is the meaning of this?' he demanded. His voice quavered with nerves, but with effort he managed to keep it under control. A lifetime telling folk what to think, Amara knew, could stand you in good stead when it came to confrontation. 'Danyel,' he called to the black-bearded man. 'Who is this… this *duardin*?'

Danyel, who was a big man no doubt well used to getting his own way, and who was at least a head and a half taller than the mohawked duardin, looked almost comically puny beside him. Amara watched him shuffle over towards the lector, still gripping his wooden club.

'Turned up from the Living City, not three days past,' he said.

Danyel gave the duardin a nervous glance. 'Claimed he'd been in Chamon, of all places, rambling about some axe or another that he'd lost. He's done naught but drink the Cracked Flagon dry ever since, and he's been under a table since yesterday evening sleeping it off. I half hoped he'd died, Sigmar forgive me – he don't look like he's got more than two coins to rub together, and I didn't fancy asking him to pay his bill, if you know what I mean…'

'If you're going to talk about me, boy,' the duardin snarled, 'then do it to my face.' He slung his axe onto his back and turned to the lector. 'And you, priest. You've the look of someone who likes to be in charge. What's this lass done that's so offended you a burning's going to be the result of it?'

The lector shook his head with a grim little smile and ran his fingers through his wispy white beard.

'I will have no outsider question the customs of Xil'anthos, and it is not your business, sir, how we deal with blasphemers here. Be on your way, duardin.'

'Gotrek Gurnisson goes on his way when he damned well pleases!' the duardin growled. 'Not a moment before, and it'll take more than a damned scarecrow in a fancy red dress to make him do it!'

As the duardin tugged at his beard, Amara could see the glint of gold on his chest: a rune of some kind, hammered into the skin. It was a Fyreslayer practice, she knew, to decorate the flesh with their sacred ur-gold, and yet this duardin was like no Fyreslayer she had ever seen. The way he spoke, the restless energy that crackled around him… that and the fact that he was wearing trousers.

'What about you, lass?' he said, pointing at her. 'You still got a tongue in your head? Blasphemy, this old goat says – that true? What did you do, puke on his pulpit?' He chuckled richly. 'Believe me, we've all done it.'

Amara looked cautiously at the lector. The flames cracked and snapped behind them, casting out their bleak red light into the square. Beyond, she could see folk gathered in their dozens, some of them armed with staves and cudgels, with butchers' knives and blunt cutlasses, even a long-barrelled, black-powder firearm that might have been Freeguild make. Half the population of Xil'anthos must have packed into the square. They had come to watch the burning, but the entertainment they were getting now was an unexpected bonus. She had thought to open their ears to the truth, about the gods and their cruel indifference, but it seemed she had stumbled into a different story altogether.

'I was only passing through,' she said. The mob hushed to hear her words, wondering how she was going to justify herself now that she had been given this wholly unexpected reprieve. She wiped the soot from her cheek, felt the sting of pain where the embers had burned against her skin. 'I sought to tell them about Sigmar, only it seems they are too stuck in the mire of their own ignorance to hear it.'

The duardin groaned and wiped a meaty palm down his face. 'Don't tell me, another bloody god-botherer… Grungni's beard, if there's one thing this place needs a damned sight fewer of, it's folk whining at the gods.'

'I do not bother the gods,' Amara said defiantly, raising her chin. 'The gods cannot be trusted, cannot be relied upon, and I would like nothing more than for every mortal race to live our lives under our own auspices, our own efforts. All of us – human, aelf, and duardin. The sooner we look to our own strengths to solve our problems, the better. Tear down that statue of Sigmar!' she cried. 'Turn that temple into something ordinary people can use. A barn, perhaps. A granary.' She gave Danyel a bitter glare. 'Or a latrine for the customers of your tavern.'

A hiss blistered through the crowds. She saw folk make the sign of the comet against their chests, outraged. The lector was choking on his rage.

'Give the word!' Danyel cried, brandishing his club. 'By the God-King, give the word and I'll strike her down, I swear it!'

Quicker than the eye could see, the duardin snatched the club from Danyel's hands and splintered it over his knee. He tossed the two broken pieces over his shoulder.

'There'll be none of that, lad,' he rumbled. 'Seems an odd way to spend your time, I have to admit,' he said to her. 'Happens I was only passing through myself, and if no one in this dump has any objections, then the lass and me will just be passing on through together.' He glared around at them all, gathered on the edge of the firelight. None could meet his eye. 'We wouldn't want anyone to get hurt now, would we?'

The duardin called Gotrek strode to where Amara stood by the edge of the pyre, the sweat trickling down her face from the heat of the flames. He motioned for her to turn around, and tore her bonds as easily as another man would tear a stem of grass. Amara rubbed her wrists as the rope fell to the flagstones. She looked warily at the mob as it jostled and shoved its way forward, all eyes now on the lector to see what he would do in response to this challenge. Gotrek stared them all down, the pommel of his axe planted on the ground and his massive arms crossed on the head of it.

'You have my thanks, duardin,' she said under her breath. 'I owe you a debt, but at this point discretion is the better part of valour, I fear. If I were you, I would leave before the crowd turns ugly.' She looked at them, the snarling faces, the brandished cudgels, the mutter and roar as they shouted insult and threat. 'Well... uglier.'

'Call me Gotrek,' he said. 'And I'm no damned duardin. I'm a dwarf, although that seems a concept too strange for the dullards in these Mortal Realms.' He glanced quickly up at her with beetled brows. 'And don't you be thinking I'm no Fyreslayer, either! I've known one or two worth sharing a pint or three with, I won't deny it, but taken in the round they're sorry excuses for dwarfs.'

None of what he said made any sense to her, but Amara did not question his words. The folk of Xil'anthos were muttering to themselves, exchanging uneasy looks, testing the weight of their weapons. She may have lain down her hammer along with her faith months ago, but she had spent years of her life fighting in Sigmar's name and she knew perfectly well when combat was near.

They turned to go, passing by the pyre as the flames licked up red as fury into the sky. Amara willed the crowd to part for them. She knew more about the folk of Xil'anthos than she'd ever wanted to, but despite the dark looks they threw at them, the snarls of rage and hatred, she hoped they weren't foolhardy enough to challenge them now. The duardin at her side, this Gotrek Gurnisson, was more than just a seasoned warrior, she could tell. There was anger in him, a coiled rage just waiting to be released. She could see it in his gnarled, unruly face, in the glint of that cunning black eye. It was like a wild boar's eye, she thought. Dark and forbidding, and without fear.

The lector screamed for them to stop. The crowd roared, and from the walls of the town Amara could see the city guard charging their weapons.

'Run!' Amara shouted.

'Run?' The duardin boomed with laughter. 'Not bloody likely.'

Two rangy young soldiers came charging forwards suddenly, their eyes wide, more raw courage than sense in them. More alcohol too. One of them swung a billhook at Gotrek's head while the other drew a short-bladed sword. Gotrek, without breaking stride, slammed a fist as big as a boiled ham into the first soldier's face, poleaxing him to the ground. The billhook went clattering off across the flagstones. The other man tried to stab in with his sword, but Gotrek caught the lad's fist in his own and crushed his hand as easily as if it were an apple. The boy's eyes popped wide and he sucked in a breath that came out as a lacerating, high-pitched scream.

More of the guard came charging up the avenue from the city gates. The crowd was surging forward, working itself up into a fury. Gotrek threw the young soldier aside and unslung his double-headed axe, and the coals in the brazier, as if they were sentient things sensing violence, began to fume with a raw, red flame. The duardin roared with delight and patted the haft.

'Come, Zangrom-Thaz! Let's introduce you to some new friends!'

'Don't kill them!' Amara shouted. She ducked a blow from a cudgel, got her shoulder into someone's stomach and pushed them backwards. 'I won't see any more blood spilled because of him! Because of Sigmar, or any damned god!'

Gotrek looked at her with amazement, his mouth slack. 'Are you cracked? Have you forgotten that they were about to burn you alive not ten minutes ago? Because I can tell you right now, *they* haven't!'

Amara gripped his shoulder. It was like pressing her fingers into solid stone.

'I don't know what fate brought you to Xil'anthos or Ghyran,' she said, 'and I thank you for my life, but I'm sure you didn't come here to trade blows with ignorant peasants who don't know any better than what lies their priests tell them. Leave them to their madness, duardin. They are not worth it.'

She looked up and saw Danyel charging across the flagstones towards her, the soldier's dropped billhook raised and a look on his face of absolute rage.

'Well,' she said. 'Not all of them, anyway.'

The pyre growled at her side, the unruly flames snaking and buckling in the breeze as evening fell on the town. A branch smouldered on the edge of the fire and Amara snatched it up quickly, sweeping it back and forth in a great streaming arc. Danyel threw his arm up in front of his face as he leapt at her, staggering backwards as the sparks alighted and giving Gotrek more than enough time to sink his fist deep into the man's gut. Doubled over, choking for breath, Danyel dropped to his knees and spewed onto the flagstones. Amara allowed herself a grin.

She used the burning branch to sweep their way clear of the press. Even though these were hard folk who had carved their settlement into the harsh and unforgiving landscape, Gotrek's murderous glare was enough to send most of them reeling back. When he brandished the gleaming blade of his axe it was all they could do to scramble out of his way. Anyone drunk or foolhardy enough to take a swing at him was soon sent sprawling to the ground with a broken nose or a shattered jaw.

The way from the town was clear as they reached the other side of the square, the long avenue with its flanks of sourbark trees stretching on towards the open gates. Smuts and ashes were rising from the pyre as it burned itself out, drifting down on the town like the black snows of Aqshy. The bruises on Amara's face throbbed, and there was a sharp pain high up on the side of her head where the first stone had struck her.

'Clear aside!' Gotrek snarled at them. A line of townsfolk bearing pitchforks and brickbats melted away, eyes downcast. Amara looked back and saw the lector fuming there beside the smouldering pyre, stamping his foot and shaking his staff.

'Stop them! Stop them, I say! Sigmar protect us from their lies and from their blasphemous outrages!'

Amara pivoted and threw her burning brand like a spear, laughing as the lector yelped and scrambled out of the way.

'Sigmar protect you from *that*!' she shouted.

The gates were still open and they strode out into the soft evening light. The wide plains of Thyria stretched away from them, rich and fragrant, but no less dangerous for it. The beaten earth crunched under their feet. All was wreathed in a velvet dusk, bracingly cool after the heat of the flames behind them.

Amara turned and saw Gotrek staring warily up at her.

'What?' she said.

'Aye…' he muttered. 'Cracked all right. You've got the robes of one of Sigmar's hammer-chuckers, and that same damned certain look in your eye, but you're as much a danger to yourself as to anyone else, I reckon.' He hitched the golden mask of his belt buckle and strode on, shaking his head.

Amara watched him stride on down the road into the evening. He started to hum some rambling tune to himself, muttering and grumbling after each few bars, the axe resting on his shoulder and the great orange mohawk quivering as he shook his head.

'*I'm* cracked?' she said. 'Speak for yourself…'

CHAPTER FIVE

THE STORM

They walked through the night, too wary to stop and risk sleeping, following the road as far as it took them. For Amara's part, she wanted to put as much distance between herself and that town as possible, but for Gotrek it was as if it never occurred to him to stop. Mile after mile, indefatigable, the duardin had stomped his way along the path with Amara trailing along behind, muttering and carrying on some furious argument with himself that she couldn't understand.

The duardin seemed uninterested in her now, and he certainly didn't ask any more questions about what she was doing in the wilds. Amara had told him her name and he had nodded as if he expected nothing less, but she couldn't tell if the words had sunk in. For great stretches of time she was sure that he had forgotten she was even there. The violent exhilaration in the square of Xil'anthos had faded from him, and as they trudged on, a gloominess seemed to settle on his broad shoulders. Hunched, his head down, he would grumble to himself or emit harsh, mocking laughs, following the trail of old memories. At one point he raised his axe and brandished it at a thread of cloud that was drifting across the sky over to the north, as if it had in some way offended him. It was more and more difficult to speak to him. One glance at his flushed and glowering face would be enough for the words to die in her mouth. The odd depression that had gripped him felt brittle and unstable, as if the wrong word could easily crack through it to whatever volcanic temper boiled beneath. Amara thought it best not to find out.

What was she doing? She sighed again, squeezed her eyes shut as the fatigue swept through her. Her legs were trembling and there was a sour taste in her mouth. She felt weak, utterly worn out. She owed Gotrek her life, but...

Amara allowed herself a cynical smile. She had almost thought, *Sigmar knows where he's going and why*, but she had checked herself at the last moment. How hard it was, even in extremity, to fall away from accustomed habits. Sigmar knew, of course he did. But she would be damned if she would ask him.

She looked out across the rolling downs as they descended to the edge of a swaying field of brush, a plain that was studded from end to end with diasporgum – huge round balls of dried-out weed, each one as big as a house. They tumbled plentifully through the grasslands of north Yska. They had no roots, but curled their dead branches up into ragged spheres and let the harsh winds that blew off the Tendril Sea carry them far up into the Thyrian steppes.

'What brings you to the wilds on your own anyway?' Gotrek called back over his shoulder. 'Tired of life, are you? You're lucky to have made it more than a day out here.'

Amara hurried to keep up with him. 'I was part of a Dawnbringer Crusade,' she said. 'Founding a new settlement, a new civilisation in the wilderness.'

Gotrek gave a derisive snort. He threw himself down on the grass.

'Aye, I've seen the like when I was in the Living City,' he said. 'All bells and whistles and incense, and always led by the same sort of dullards who think wars are going to be over by Keg End. They never bloody are.'

'We came from Dagoleth,' Amara said. Her eyes glazed over as she looked back across those blank, black months. 'Far to the north. Crossed the wilds on the cusp of Yska, found a valley sheltered from the Thyrian winds. It would have been perfect, it… But then the wilds are never empty places, are they? There are always things out there that want to cause you harm.'

'Say no more,' Gotrek said. He snatched up a handful of grass and tore it to pieces. 'I've barely gone a yard in this place without seeing cruelty and oppression and… aelves tearing the souls from folks' bodies, goblins and ghouls swarming the lands, and dwarf kingdoms fallen to ruins or fleeing into the sky in their metal ships. I thought I could fix it, that I could fix these damned realms from one end to the other, but…'

He shook his crested head, muttering to himself, his voice so furious and low that Amara could barely hear what he was saying.

'Stupid bloody aelf, what did she want to do that for, eh? Do you hear me now? Wherever you are? What was the point?' He stared up at the sky and roared suddenly. 'You threw it away! And I… It's my damned fault, every bit of it!'

'What is?' Amara asked him, her heart thumping. His mood had changed quicker than an Everspring wind. 'Gotrek, what–'

He turned on her, his face deformed with rage. Spit flew from his mouth and his good eye bulged in its socket. Amara scrabbled around in the grass for a stone, a stick, anything she could use to defend herself.

'Maleneth!' he cried. The crest of his mohawk bristled. 'Aye, she was a spy and a cheat and a killer, but…'

The breeze picked up and it seemed to distract him for a moment. He slumped back onto the grass. The only sound was the wind moaning softly through the dry spheres of the diasporgum ahead.

'Korgan told me Grungni had run off to Azyr,' he mumbled. 'Content to make toys for that hammer-fondling excuse for a god, Sigmar.' He glanced at Amara, who felt her breath come steady once more. 'You've got the right idea, lass, let me tell you. Gods!' he spat. 'A waste of bloody time. Never there when you need them, and they won't leave you alone when you don't.'

'I prayed harder than I have ever prayed for Sigmar to save us,' Amara said. 'When the bodies were piled high in the valley and the grass was drenched in blood, but he did not come. He had abandoned us, and we only ever marched in his name. What is the point of a name that when you call on it, it does not come?'

'Damn all of them!' Gotrek shouted to the sky. He patted his axe and gave a great roaring laugh. 'I learned that in Chamon, if nothing else. Trust in this and your right arm and you won't go wrong!'

'Where do you go now then?' she asked him. 'What brings you to the edge of Yska?'

'A different axe,' he muttered. 'One of the only things I have left to remind me of where I came from.' He glanced again at the sky, where the realmspheres were just faintly visible in the tempered blue. 'Aye, and which I will never look on again…'

'And this axe is to be found here?' Amara said. 'On the edge of Yska? In Thyria? Where, exactly?'

'How do I bloody know?' he snapped, scowling at her. 'If I knew where it was, I wouldn't have to go looking for it, would I?'

Amara took a moment to parse his logic, which, she had to admit, was sound enough.

'I just thought you might have been following a clue to it, that's all,' she said.

'I heard tell of it in Chamon,' he grumbled. 'There were rumours amongst the Fyreslayers that there were lodges in the Jade Kingdoms that might have word of it. The Mistral Peaks, they said, a range of mountains. Course,' he scoffed, 'it's never so simple as just following the damned road till you get to your destination in this place, is it? A lot of singing and dancing you have to go through first – realmgates, and whatnot.' He shuddered. 'It's taken me months! Waste of bloody time.'

'So it's a Fyreslayer axe? In Dagoleth we once hired mercenaries from the Kavgad Lodge when we went to war with the orruks of the Gelid Swamps. Hard fighters. They dyed their beards green, and threaded vines through the crests of their hair.'

Gotrek gave a hearty guffaw, throwing his head back and then slapping his thighs, his voice splitting the silence.

'Now that I'd pay to see! Gods above and below, is there nothing sensible in this place? Dwarfs with flowers in their hair!' He wiped his eye with the back of his hand. 'But it's no Fyreslayer axe, I can tell you that much, lass. Not like this toy I've got on my shoulder here.' He slapped the haft of it. 'Although truth be told, it's served me well so far.'

'What is it then?'

'It's Grimnir's axe,' he said. He struck the rune on his chest with the blade. 'As this bloody thing is Grimnir's rune, more or less. No, it's nothing those fire worshippers could conjure up themselves.'

'Grimnir?' She thought back to the Kavgad warriors that had marshalled in the square of Dagoleth, the runes glowing like coals in their skin. She glanced at what she could see of the rune on Gotrek's chest – dull and brassy, not a hint of flame to it. 'But he's their god, is he not? So it *is* a Fyreslayer axe then?'

'No, it damned well isn't!' he barked, his mood twisting suddenly. He grasped his own axe in both hands, and for a moment Amara thought he was going to swing it at her. His eye flared in its socket and his lips drew back in a bestial snarl. 'It's older. Far, far older, than... Why are you so interested anyway?' he said. 'Bloody annoying, having this many questions thrown at you. No wonder they wanted to set you on fire in Xil-whatever-it-was-called.'

'Because I owe you a debt, Gotrek,' she told him.

'A debt, eh?' His mood softened. She might almost have said he grew wistful, as if recalling something long in the past.

'I will go now where you go, until the debt is paid. You saved my life, and the people of Dagoleth pay their debts. What we owe to one person becomes part of a chain of obligation, and it cannot be broken. That...' She paused, swallowed. 'I don't expect you to understand, but that is why I can't return to my city. I was the last survivor of a crusade that left Dagoleth, and for me that chain is no more. The web has been torn asunder. To owe nothing to anyone is worse than death...'

She could feel the horror of it snaking up her spine, wrapping its coils around her throat. With an effort she squashed the feeling back down. She could never return to Dagoleth, never again.

Gotrek shook his head and raised his eyes to the heavens. 'You've got to be bloody joking,' he grumbled. 'Cracked. Utterly cracked.'

He threw himself up from the grass and stomped off towards the downs ahead of them. He didn't look back, calling over his shoulder, 'Well I'm going to the Mistral Peaks. You can do what you bloody like, priest, but don't think for a moment I'm going to stop to let you keep up.'

Amara girded herself and followed. Despite his stature, Gotrek could move fast when he wanted to and she found herself almost jogging to keep his pace. They soon passed through the swaying field of diasporgum, jostling through the hollow spheres that, despite their enormous size, were as light as bundles of sticks. Amara reached up and patted the dry bark, pushing one easily aside as Gotrek battered them out of the way with the head of his axe. As they trod the grass, a diaphanous layer of moths arose from the feathered stalks, fluttering madly out of the way. On the other side of the diasporgum there fell a long and weathered sward, descending to the first isolated pines of what Amara thought might be the Mistral Forest, about five miles distant.

'If you're looking for the Peaks,' she told him, 'this would be the quickest way. From what I can remember, the forest sweeps round unbroken to the west from here, and the mountains are on the other side. A week's journey, maybe more.'

'You've been here before?' Gotrek demanded.

'I passed this way...' Amara shook her head. 'At least, I think I did, a few months back. I remember skirting the trees, but... I'm sorry, I can't remember.' She couldn't meet his eye. 'I wasn't in my right mind then.'

'Huh,' Gotrek huffed. 'I'm shocked to hear it.'

She tried to recall those moments, in the long aftermath of the crusade's destruction – days of grief and rage when everything she looked upon seemed stained with blood. It was like a mist sat before her memory. Delirious with her own wounds, deranged with her experience, it was as if she had moved through the wilds with no more presence than a gheist.

The treeline was still a mile distant in front of them. The pines were vast things, hundreds of feet high, their soaring branches like the arms of emerald candelabras. She had heard that the pine needles which fell from those trees were as long and sharp as sword blades. Folk risked being stabbed clean through when they gathered them for firewood, skewered by a falling needle before they could leap out of the way. On the edge of the forest she could see a few stragglers, stunted trees in lonely copses, though they still dwarfed any she would have found in Dagoleth.

'Storm's coming,' Gotrek muttered, looking back.

He pointed a stubby finger to the east. The clouds were rucked and rumpled, and a black pillar of mist was curling off across the hills towards them. There were bigger, darker shapes beyond it – clouds drifting in from the south, flattened out so they looked almost like monstrous birds, their wings gliding on the quickened wind. Gliding, as Amara noticed, against the wind, and not with it.

The long black column of mist quivered and shook, and then trailed out into a groping tendril that sped across the land towards the forest.

'What's that bloody noise?' Gotrek said. He waggled a finger in his ear and inspected the tip before wiping it on his beard. 'Sounds like I've got a damned flea in my ear.'

The duardin must have had excellent hearing. Amara, who wouldn't have been surprised if Gotrek had several fleas about his person, could only hear it now herself – a whining, buzzing roar, thin and high-pitched, but getting louder and more insistent. A crackle of wind sped across the land ahead of it, smelling of sour dough and vinegar.

'By the name I will no longer speak,' she said. 'That's no storm!'

It was a carpet of insects, at least a mile wide and so thick that it blocked out the sun. There must have been billions of them, swarming and thronging and circling each other, wings whirring together to make an unearthly screeching hiss; and beyond this boiling shoal swam three enormous birds, each as large as the tendril whales that surfaced in the foaming wrack on the edge of the Rocanian Coast. They stretched their scimitar beaks wide as they plunged into the mass of insects, gorging themselves on millions of them at a single mouthful, their iridescent feathers flickering green and gold as they fed.

'Run!' Amara shouted. 'Run for the trees!'

Gotrek threw the axe onto his back and started sprinting, beating his way across the turf until he was soon outpacing Amara. She ran, head down, arms pumping, and moment by moment the screaming roar of the swarm got ever closer. She could hear the heavy beating of the birds' wings, their guttural barking as they swooped and plunged again and again into the tide of insects. Jade eagles, they must be, birds that Amara had only heard about in legend – creatures that rode the thermals far above the plains, that built their nests of precious minerals high on the Mistral Peaks.

'Stop dawdling, lass!' Gotrek shouted back at her. He paused, skidded on the grass, grabbed hold of her robes and pulled her with him. Amara stumbled – but then the shoal was on them, screaming in their ears so loud that she thought for a moment she had gone deaf.

The force of the blow picked her up off her feet and sent her flying to the ground. She could see nothing but a swirling black fog, a chittering mass that swept over her, boiling across her face, her hands, any small piece of exposed skin. Amara rolled on the grass and screamed, tried to get to her feet, felt herself knocked clean over again. They were biting and stinging her, and even the sheer force at which they flew was enough to draw blood from her face. Each one was no bigger than her fingernail, shards of chitin fired at them like darts.

She saw Gotrek standing there bellowing with anger, waving his axe fruitlessly into the cloud, his entire upper torso swarming with a carpet of insects. They straggled through his beard, caught themselves in the crest of his mohawk, sparked into flares of smoke on the brazier of his rune-axe. And still the jade eagles dived and swept through the swarm, so close to the ground that the speed of their passing lifted the creatures for a moment from Amara's skin, and shook the treeline that was so achingly close.

Gotrek had descended into a red and purposeless rage. He was shouting war cries in a language she didn't understand, heaving left and right with his axe, beating his chest with his fist. She could see the hard weals raised on his skin, but each bite and sting seemed only to goad him into greater fury.

'Gotrek!' Amara spat. 'Get moving!'

Staggering against the weight of the insects, hands clamped to her ears against their incessant, thunderous roar, she ran across grass that was littered with millions of the crawling creatures. The jade eagles sped like lightning bolts through the sky above them, skimming the grass with a great, flat boom of their wings, then soaring up at the last moment to clear the line of trees ahead.

Amara reached the duardin and grabbed his wrist, trying to wrench him around, but it was like trying to pull one of those pine trees up by the roots. Gotrek seemed planted on the grass, immovable, and when he turned on her with a bloodthirsty roar she was sure he was going to plunge his rune-axe into her skull. His whole head was hooded by the insects; all she could see was the red tunnel of his mouth, his broken teeth, the glaring pin-prick of his black eye.

He was lost, she knew; he had strayed into the battle madness that it is death to interrupt, and so she did the only thing she could think of. Drawing her hand back, trailing a string of buzzing, biting insects, she slapped Gotrek as hard as she could across the face.

Everything stopped. Even the swarm seemed to slacken its assault, as if terrified of what would happen next. Gotrek's single eye flared, bright as diamond. The rune on his chest flickered with a rush of oily light. She saw pure murder before her, unstoppable. Then the spark faded in his eye and he clamped his jaw, the creatures crawling over his lips. Amara nodded, slowly, not daring to speak.

The treeline was no more than a few hundred yards ahead of them now. Heads down, trying to cover their faces as best they could, they scrambled across the grass towards it. The pine needles were strewn about the ground beneath the trees, each as long as her arm, and Amara gave a wary glance above them as they dashed into the shadows. To escape death by the swarming multitude of those creatures only to be impaled by a plunging emerald blade would be insult heaped upon injury.

The jade eagles were sweeping round towards the north now, skirting the downs and climbing higher above the mat of the forest. Soon they were no more than black specks against the sky, wheeling and drifting off towards their distant mountain peaks and their precious, gem-like nests. The swarm of insects had plunged for safety into the trees as well, rushing through the forest like a hurricane. Some scattered themselves into the branches of the canopy, where they hung like strings of writhing, buzzing vines, but the rest tore on between the stately trunks with a sound like a million sheets of parchment being torn in two.

Amara's face and hands throbbed with bites and stings, every inch of them swollen with hard red weals. Gotrek's skin was as bright as his beard and mohawk. He looked like a toad from the Gelid Swamps, he was so smothered in lumps. She could see the volcanic rage still bubbling away beneath the surface. His eye glared like a diamond.

She plunged on into the undergrowth, but no matter how much she slapped the creatures from her face, more and more of them kept buzzing down from the branches above them. Amara stumbled against a root, throwing her hands out to break her fall. A moment later, a razor-sharp pine needle stabbed down into the undergrowth in front of her, blade quivering as it plunged a foot into the ground. She risked a glance up, saw the great clouds of insects blundering and swarming about the branches, dislodging more of the needles. Each one was like a spear thrown down from the canopy.

'Run for the trees, you said,' Gotrek complained, spitting out a mouthful of the creatures. He batted a needle aside with his axe, danced lightly out of the way of another.

Amara pointed deeper into the undergrowth. There, half-hidden in the shadows between the trees, she could see the rising flank of what she thought at first was a wall of rounded stone. Then, as she peered more closely at it, she could see dark, overlapping scales, a glossy brown sheen of something that looked almost like a pinecone – but one at least a hundred yards high. There was a path leading away from it, two tall iron sconces on either side, and even as she watched, the sconces sparked into an eldritch green flame. There was a harsh smell in the air then of mint and linseed, of the bitter vyridin leaves that grew around the borders of the Gelid Swamps, which wary travellers would rub against their skin to protect from insect bites.

A rectangle of light appeared in the vast pinecone, a doorway that swung open as two figures stepped quickly outside. They wore uniforms of bark and scale, their steel helmets fixed with a fine mask of interlaced leaf fibre. Frantically, they beckoned for Gotrek and Amara to follow them.

'For the sake of the goddess!' one of them cried. 'Get inside now, or the harrowbugs will strip you to the bone!'

CHAPTER SIX

DRUHIEL

'The Goddess of the Green protect you, travellers, but what madness made you cross the Cadmium Plain when the harrowbugs were swarming? You could have been killed.'

Amara collapsed to the ground the moment they were through the gate. It was a tall double door of brass or ironoak, reinforced with overlapping plates of a thick, bark-like material that looked exactly like the scales of a pinecone. The two guards, if that's what they were, heaved the doors closed again. The fumes that sputtered from the sconces outside the door seemed to have kept the worst of the insects away. The smell of resin was thick and heady, and even the scent of it seemed to draw some of the pain from Amara's bites.

The guard who had spoken took off his helmet and mask, and gazed at them with incredulity. He was young, although his face was hard and flecked with old scars, and his green eyes were quick and penetrating. His hand dropped to the hilt of his blade.

'Forgive my caution,' he said, tapping his sword. 'Druhiel of the

Pines gives refuge to any who hazard the plains when the harrow-bugs fly. We're a welcoming town for all who respect the Goddess Alarielle, but a duardin Fyreslayer and a Sigmarite priest are not visitors we often see. Especially not ones foolhardy enough to cross open ground when the jade eagles were feeding.' He laughed, but it was not with malice. 'The harrowbugs would have flayed you alive if you'd stayed out there much longer!'

'I bloody well feel I *have* been flayed alive, or near enough,' Gotrek snarled.

Amara picked herself off the ground, glancing cautiously at Gotrek's scowling face. She could barely make out his features under the swollen lumps of the insect bites, and she dreaded to imagine if she looked any worse than she felt.

'My name is Amara Fidellus,' she said. 'This is Gotrek Gurnisson, although I would caution you that despite my robes and despite the colour of his hair and beard, I am no priest and he is no Fyreslayer.'

'The tale grows more curious,' the young guard said. He inclined his head to Gotrek, who gave him a vicious sneer in return. 'I am Inat, captain of the guard in Druhiel. And what might be your business in the Mistral Forest?'

'My business is my own, lad,' Gotrek muttered. His voice was low and dangerous, his fingers drumming across the haft of his axe. Inat's mouth curled at the corner and he tapped his blade.

'Merely passing through,' Amara said quickly. 'Heading for the Mistral Peaks, and misjudging our road. We are in your debt for sheltering us.'

'Here we go,' Gotrek grumbled, rolling his eyes. 'Another sodding debt to be paid...'

Inat gave them both a hard look, his green eyes pausing on Gotrek's axe. After a moment, he removed his hand from the hilt of his blade and saluted laconically with his fist against his breastplate.

'Then you may go about your business, travellers. The harrow-bug swarm will clear by dusk, but until then you are perfectly safe in Druhiel. They cannot broach our walls.'

Inat glanced up at the roof high above them – a curved space like a cathedral dome, formed of massive, interlinked scales. Only now did Amara realise how enclosed this settlement was. A path of dried matting stretched away from the gates and the covered gatehouse beside it. A road cut across it a few yards further on, paved in wooden scales and bordered on the other side by small buildings of wood and dried thatch. Amara could see a butcher's shop, game birds culled from the forest hanging in the window; a chandler turning columns of dried sap into candles. There were carpenters and leatherworkers, resin merchants and armourers, and the folk of Druhiel bustled between them all in their green and amber robes. Some wore fringed headdresses tasselled with autumn leaves; others wore cloaks of emerald ivy, or tough jerkins woven from the same dried matting that covered the path. The walls of the town curved away from the gatehouse, the other side at least three hundred yards away. Amara could see other gateways leading deeper into new halls, other chambers carved from these hollow conifer cones. A nexus siphon was embedded in the walls, glittering with ancient energy. Curving around the interior of the dome, high above the streets and passageways of the central hall, were wooden walkways and arcades, linked by narrow flights of wooden stairs. Dotted around the streets were tall lampposts carved from young pine trees, with globes of aether-fire flickering from them like the heads of blooming flowers.

'I've never seen such a place,' Amara said, with wonder. 'It's beautiful.'

'It is that,' Inat said with pride. 'If you would take my advice, you should head to the Amber Sap as soon as you can. It's a tavern,' he said to Gotrek with a wink, 'that I can heartily recommend.

Straight ahead from here. Tell them Inat sent you, and I'm confident the resin ale will be to your taste, master duardin.' He pointed at their faces. 'And they should give you something for the bites as well.'

Amara thanked him and led Gotrek away, down the gatehouse path and into the street, where their feet rang against the wooden paving.

'Bloody odd place, if you ask me,' Gotrek said shiftily. The talk of ale had improved his mood, but he still peered up at the ceiling high above them as if suspicious to have a roof over his head. As he shouldered his way through the crowds, Amara tried to ignore the stares they were drawing. Whether it was because they were so deformed by insect bites or because the inhabitants had never seen a duardin quite as peculiar as Gotrek before, she couldn't say.

'Who in Grungni's name would ever want to live inside a damned pinecone?' he complained. 'I'll never understand humans. All these trees around you, and your first thought isn't to cut them down and make a decent wooden hut? Resin ale, though...' He tugged at his beard thoughtfully. 'Well, never let it be said that I'm a dwarf who shies away from unfamiliar brews.'

'You share the same gods as other duardin then?' Amara asked him. 'Grungni the Maker? And Grimnir?'

They passed through an open space between two streets. There were low wooden houses and shops spread out on either side, their peaked roofs thatched in dried grass and vine. In the middle of this paved square, enclosed by a fence constructed from the same pine needles that fell in the forest, was a withered, mis-shapen tree trunk perhaps ten feet in diameter. The trunk itself was no taller than Gotrek and the bark was an oily black. There were rough cankers and scabs pitted across it, and it dripped with a foul-smelling sap. Despite this apparent decay, Amara could see fresh green shoots sprouting from the bark. The fenced off area was surrounded by a crowd of worshippers, all of them dressed in green robes woven from dried leaves, wearing mitres and head-bands fashioned from twisted coils of bark and nut shell. They all bore smoking sticks of a fragrant incense and were processing around the trunk, raising their voices in song.

'They're not my gods, lass,' Gotrek said. 'Gods…' He looked at the crowd with distaste and hooked a thumb at the procession. 'There's where gods gets you – simpering around a dead tree waving a stick in the air.'

Amara watched them, tight-lipped. 'You'll get no argument from me,' she said. 'Followers of Alarielle, I suppose. It's rare to see humans worshipping the Everqueen, although I have heard of it. Here in the depths of the forest, perhaps it makes the most sense to them.'

They found the Amber Sap on the other side of the square. It was a tall, narrow-fronted tavern with brass shutters on its windows, a stoop of rough-carved pine, and swing doors that led into a dark, wood-panelled chamber with a low ceiling of polished swamp mahogany. A fire blazed in the hearth on the far side of the bar, which curved round in a horseshoe shape at the other end of the chamber.

The barkeep, a short, thickset old man with feathery grey side-boards, and who Amara thought might have been half-duardin himself, gave them a suspicious look as they came in. Without a word he reached under the bar and clunked a green ceramic jar onto the counter.

'Inat sent us,' Amara said as they approached. She tried to make herself look approachable, but she had forgotten how.

'You're the strangers I've heard tell about,' he said, narrowing his eyes.

'Word gets around fast,' Gotrek growled.

'By the state of you, don't reckon you could be anyone else.

Here.' Gruffly he pushed the jar towards them. 'Vyridin lotion,' he said. 'Should sort those bites out.' His eyes settled on Gotrek. 'Duardin, eh? Well, while you paint your faces, how about some resin ale to slake your thirsts?'

'Most sensible suggestion I've heard all day,' Gotrek said. Amara thought she could even see a smile form under the lumps and swellings.

Gotrek slapped two shards of Chamonite teakwood on the counter and rubbed his hands together as the barkeep filled the tankards. Amara prised the lid from the jar and sniffed at the ointment, an ashy grey paste that smelled powerfully of mint and swamp water. She dabbed a little on her finger and gingerly smeared it on her cheek.

The relief was immediate. She could feel the lumps shrinking, the burning itch fading to no more than a mild discomfort.

'Gotrek, this stuff is extraordinary!' she said. 'Here.' She reached out to dab some on his blistered red nose, but the duardin threw up an arm to ward her off.

'Get off!' he sputtered. 'It bloody stings!'

'Call yourself a warrior?' she said. She batted his hand away. 'Come on, it's for your own good.'

She scooped up another handful and, to Gotrek's rumbling disgust, spread it over his face and his inflamed shoulders until it had soaked into his skin. In moments the bites began to fade and reduce. He was still as red and weather-beaten as if he'd been boiled alive, but Amara reckoned that was about normal for him.

The barkeep clacked the tankards down on the countertop and Gotrek drank deep to drown his rage. He smacked his lips and peered thoughtfully into his tankard.

'Not bad,' he mused. 'Not bad... Only tastes about half as much like goat's piss as I expected.'

To Amara's surprise, the scowling barkeep actually laughed.

'It's an acquired taste,' he said. 'Brewed from the resins tapped out of the Mistral pines. A touch of honey from the amber bees, a scattering of green hops and you've a brew to die for. The goat's piss is the secret ingredient, of course...'

Amara leaned against the bar and glanced round at the other patrons. Two men dressed in faded green tunics with hatchets on their belts leaned against the countertop further down the bar, talking in low voices to each other. An old couple, sipping thoughtfully at goblets of wine, sat at a table beneath the rugged beams of the staircase that led up to the guest rooms.

'You came at a good time,' the barkeep told them. He wiped down the counter with a dirty cloth. 'Day of Fecundity is here. Comes round every month. By nightfall this place'll be three deep at the bar.'

Amara nodded towards the door. 'The dead tree in the square?' she said.

'Aye. I'll tell you, it was a dark day a few months back when the Tree of the Pines seemed to sicken and die, but the goddess has sent us a sign that Druhiel is under her special protection again.' He leaned closer across the bar, as if sharing a secret. 'Not a day after it had shrivelled away to a blackened stump, it started to regrow, and regrow bigger and more fruitful than ever it had before. Month after month, it decays and seems to die, and then regrows even more beautiful. It's a marvel to behold, truly it is.'

'I've about had my fill of marvels,' Gotrek said, with a grim laugh. 'Can't turn a corner here without one getting in your way.'

'Ignore my friend here,' Amara said lightly. 'The harrowbugs have made him a tad grumpy. Well... grumpier.'

'If you don't mind my asking,' the barkeep said, 'being as you're travellers in these parts, you don't happen to have come from Kranzinnport way have you?'

'On the Rocanian Coast?' Amara said. She sipped her ale. 'No, we've come from the east. By way of Xil'anthos.'

'And in no great hurry to go back,' Gotrek said. He drained his ale and signalled for another, almost snatching it out of the barkeep's hands. 'I think I'm on the way to acquiring this taste,' he muttered.

'Why do you ask?' Amara said.

'There's not been much in the way of visitors to Druhiel, us being tucked so out of the way. I thought you might have had word about what's been going on there. We're in the dark ourselves, and it's grim doings as far as we can work out.'

'Why? What's happened?' Amara asked him. The barkeep leaned against the counter again, his brow furrowed.

'Hard to say, it's all just rumour and second-hand news as far as we're concerned. They say the whole city has been… Well, that there isn't really much of a city left any more.'

'What's this?' Gotrek scorned. 'The whole bloody thing's just up and gone, has it?' He drained his tankard and wiped the back of his hand over his lips. 'Let me guess, the whole place walks around on chicken legs, or it was built on the back of a giant armadillo, or something equally daft. Huh, wouldn't surprise me.'

'It's not the city itself that's gone,' one of the young men further down the bar said, 'but the folk who live there.'

He looked like someone who worked in the forest, his green jerkin streaked with amber sap, his hands rough and well used to hard labour. Nevertheless, he looked nervous, although Amara thought that was probably a normal reaction in Gotrek's presence. The duardin eyed the lad suspiciously, as if the young forester were building up to an insult, and Gotrek was keen to get his blow in first.

'I'm Amara,' she said to him, hoping to put him at ease. 'This is Gotrek. What's your name?'

'Khrispin,' the lad said. He doffed his green cap. 'Me and Henrick here work the south-western reach of the forest, and the border there is not two miles from the coast, down where Kranzinnport sits on the bluff above the bay. We were down there five days ago and the goddess strike us down if we're lying, but there's dark doings there and no mistake!'

'What happened?' Amara said.

'It's a busy place, Kranzinnport,' Khrispin told her. He gulped his ale, signalled to the barkeep to refill his tankard. 'Good market there, so they say, what with the coast road running through it, the road wardens patrolling to keep it safe, and the harbour there for ships as come in from Aquia and the Naiads. Often it is that me and Henrick will take our midday meal sitting on the treeline, watching the ships crossing the sea on the other side of the downs, watching all the caravans going out towards the east. But when we was there last, there weren't nothing coming out and no ships in the sea, not at all!'

'So?' Gotrek interjected. 'Maybe it was a holiday and everyone took the day off. You've got enough damned festivals and feast days in these realms, haven't you? No doubt they were all prancing around a tree stump or whatever.'

A gloom seemed to have settled on him, and Amara hoped it was just the beer. His moods whipped across him more changeably than the weather. He slumped down at a table near the bar with a fresh tankard.

'Ain't no holiday that can stop trade that much,' Khrispin said. 'I tell you, the whole city was empty.'

Henrick nodded eagerly. 'Weren't a single caravan on the road, and there weren't a sail in the bay.' He glanced anxiously at the barkeep, whose frown deepened. 'Tell you what was in the bay though…'

'Go on then, lad,' Gotrek sighed. 'Enlighten me.'

'Wither Island,' the young forester said. 'That's what.'

'Goddess protect us,' Khrispin whispered, 'and the Green give succour.'

'And what's Wither Island?' Amara said. She could feel a tightness in her stomach that was more than just the resin ale. An old feeling, one that she had long ago learned to trust. Warrior priest's intuition, she called it – the sense of something dark and unnatural drawing slowly near.

But I am no longer the priest I was, and what good did my intuition do when the crusade marched into that valley?

The barkeep swept his cloth along the already immaculate mahogany counter. He gave the impression that he was choosing his words carefully.

'Now, the two of you seem to me like well-travelled folk,' he said slowly, 'with wide experience of the Jade Kingdoms at the very least, and I wouldn't want you to think that we're no more than credulous yokels here.'

Gotrek snorted into his beer. Amara ignored him and gestured for the barkeep to continue.

'I might not rightly know what Wither Island is, but I'll tell you what it ain't. It ain't natural, that's for damned sure.'

'How so?' Amara said. She found that she was reaching for a pendant around her neck that was no longer there, the sign of her old office, the sign of the comet.

'On account of that it was nowhere to be seen a few months back, and where it sits now was no more than the open sea!'

Amara looked at them both. She was puzzled. 'It just… appeared one day?'

'Came bubbling out of the depths of the sea,' Khrispin said. 'Rose up from the deeps, and Alarielle knows what strange forces might be lurking down there. Trees in the forest on the southern reach started to sicken and die, and then all the folk of Kranzinnport disappearing, and–'

'Now, now, Khrispin my lad,' the barkeep said reasonably. 'No point in getting yourself worked up. We've got the Tree of the

Pines here, don't we? The goddess will see us safe. Ain't nothing that can touch Druhiel as long as we keep faith with her.'

'Faith?' Amara said. The feeling in her stomach had coiled into a knot so tight she could barely swallow. She felt the zeal swelling in her, the disgust, the anger at the caprice of those gods who would taunt their worshippers with the prospect of deliverance when the torments they inflicted were no more than a divine game to them. 'I would put your trust in more than the gods, my friends.'

'Rose from the water, did it?'

Amara had placed her hands on the countertop of the bar, and when Gotrek spoke his voice rumbled with such fury that she could feel the vibrations through the wood. Khrispin and Henrick took a step back, hands straying to the hatchets on their belts. The barkeep's lip trembled. Slowly, his brow darker than a thunderstorm, Gotrek stood up from the table with his axe in hand.

'Now, we don't want no trouble here!' the barkeep said. 'If we've offended you in some way, master duardin, it's–'

'Islands from the deep,' Gotrek spat, barely able to contain his fury. 'Folk disappearing from the coast. Whole cities vanishing into the sea foam and the fog...'

'Gotrek, what is it?' Amara said. She had no weapon, but she would not let him kill these men; for in that moment it seemed as if the duardin would not be content until he had spent his anger on these innocents and hacked them to pieces in the very madness of his fury. By the name she would not speak, who was this duardin? 'Tell me, what do you know of this?'

'Deepkin!' he roared. He flung his axe up and brought it crashing down, and as the cries of fear faded in the tavern, Amara saw the table where Gotrek had been sitting was now just splintered firewood. He stabbed out a finger at Amara, his face flushed and twisted with rage, his muscles bulging as if his foe were trembling before him. 'I swore the next time they crossed my path I would have my revenge on them! I swore an oath on her name, and by the fires of Grimnir I'll see them all dead for what they did!'

'Whose name?' Amara demanded. 'Gotrek, speak to me. What's going on?'

'Maleneth,' he snarled. 'The aelf, damn her eyes!'

He gave a great, heaving sigh, tamping his anger down until it smouldered like burning coals; tempered, but no less deadly for it.

'And if you dare get in my way, lass,' he said, 'I'll see you suffer the same fate.'

CHAPTER SEVEN

A TOUCH OF EVIL

Gotrek charged out of the tavern, to the other patrons' palpable relief. Smashing the doors aside with one blow of his meaty fist, he stalked out into the square where the worshippers still sung their hymns and chanted their prayers around the fenced-off trunk of the dead tree.

As she followed, Amara saw that what the barkeep had said was true – even in the short time they had been in the Amber Sap, the tree had begun to regrow. Whether stimulated by its worshippers' devotions or due to the spring of some inner vitality, the stump had thickened and stretched, another ten feet higher at least. The dark, oily sap no longer wept from the cankered bark. The green shoots had sprung into surging branches that were thick with dark leaves. Ropes of ivy were coiled around the trunk now, almost pulsing with an inner life as the sap surged and quickened in them. There were fissures in the bark that glinted and glistened with fluid, and a fine dusty rain of pollen was falling from the livid cones that had sprouted on the branches.

The worshippers were raising their voices in praise, some of them weeping with the pious gratitude that Amara could no longer look upon without a sneer of contempt. Let them thank Alarielle for whatever they thought she had done for them. Amara knew better. The Everqueen was deaf to their entreaties. Like all the gods, she was as selfish and capricious as a child.

She saw the duardin stalking across the square from the tavern, his axe up on his shoulder.

'Gotrek, wait!' she cried. 'Where are you going?'

'Where do you think?' he shouted back at her. 'This Wither Island, or whatever the damned place is called! Treacherous aelf heads need to be separated from treacherous aelf shoulders before the day is out.'

Amara sprinted after him. She set her palm against his massive chest and tried to stop him, but he barrelled her aside with ease. It would have been easier to stop the tide from striking the shore.

'Do you even know how to get there?' she said, running after him. 'Think, Gotrek. You need a ship to get across to an island, unless you intend to swim.'

'Swim, or I could just wait for those slippery bastards to come and get me.' He gave a murderous leer and ran his thumb down the blade of his axe. 'Aye, for all their fog and flying sharks and whatnot, they'd have a damned nasty surprise waiting for them, wouldn't they?'

'Who? Gotrek, I don't understand, and I want to help–'

'Damn your help,' Gotrek grunted. He shrugged off the hand she placed on his shoulder. 'I never asked for it, and I don't need it.'

'Would you have taken Maleneth's help, if she were here to offer it?'

She stood in front of him again, and this time he stopped. There, flashing briefly in that black boar's eye, was the merest hint of regret. The deep gloom that seemed always just a hair's breadth away from him, vying with the rage that bubbled under the surface of his skin, swept lightly across his face.

He was old, Amara realised. Far older than she had understood. The duardin were a long-lived race, but there was something ancient in Gotrek's face that made her feel for a moment like a child in front of him. What must he have seen in his long and violent life? What must he have lost in his time?

'Maleneth,' he said softly. He hung his head and grumbled into his beard. 'That damned aelf died for me. Saved me from the Deepkin and their magics, that creature that would have sucked the very soul out of me for its own ends. Aye,' he chuckled softly, 'she hated my guts as I hated hers, but I owe her all the same. I can't let the debt go unpaid.'

'As I owe you, Gotrek Gurnisson,' Amara said sternly. 'And I would not have you take *my* debt away from me until it is paid, either. Give me that much, at least. I know the Rocanian Coast, I know where Kranzinnport is. I can guide you there. Let me help.'

She looked up at the carven ceiling high above them, the narrow mesh slits that served as windows admitting what faint light fell through the trees of the forest outside.

'Dusk will be on us soon,' she said. 'Inat said the harrowbugs will be gone by then, and it'll be safe to travel once more. We should gather supplies, make ready to leave with a bit more of a plan than just charging in before we know what we're doing.'

'Aye,' Gotrek reluctantly admitted. 'But sometimes charging in before we know what we're doing is half the fun.'

They had stopped before a row of narrow shopfronts, the little wooden markets that served Druhiel on either side of the square. Each shop had a strip of board in front of it, arranged on which was a selection of wares, from bags and belts woven out of bark string to nuts and berries gathered from the forest that were more prodigious than anything Amara had seen before. Ghyran was a realm of untold bounty, and the Mistral Forest clearly served its people well. Amara went between the shops quickly, picking out a water flask, a knapsack made from tough, leathery leaf fibre, and strips of dried fruit and dried meat.

'I hope you have funds to pay for this,' she said, 'because I have not a drop of Aqua Ghyranis to my name.' She glanced across the square at the Amber Sap, where the barkeep was glumly tossing out the broken fragments of his table. 'And I suppose we should offer something for that poor man's furniture…'

Gotrek rummaged the golden haft of an old dagger from his belt, a couple of tarnished jewels, a few silver coins that could be easily melted down. He handed them over to the shopkeepers and the barkeep. He seemed more put out by this than by Amara stopping him from charging off in the first place.

'If I'd known your help was going to cost me good money,' he grumbled, 'I never would have taken it!'

'Saving for your retirement are you?' Amara said as she gathered up her things. 'I'll pay you back, don't worry.'

'What with?' the duardin scoffed. 'Correct me if I'm wrong, but I'm assuming your congregation isn't exactly passing around the collection plate any more.'

Amara scowled at him. 'Considering they're all dead, no, I shouldn't think they are.'

Gotrek shook his head with scorn. 'And I see you haven't bothered arming yourself either. I'm not stretching to decent forged steel, lass.'

'I'm not going to kill anyone,' she told him sternly. 'I have to make that clear. I will help you as much as I can, and I'll defend myself when I have to, but I will not take a life if I can avoid it. I told you.'

'Grimnir's arse,' Gotrek sighed. 'I can see you're really going to earn your keep, aren't you? A priest who hates the gods, and a warrior who won't fight – I'm not sure which is worse.'

'The gods have had all the blood out of me they're going to get,' Amara muttered. 'Let them choke on it before I spill a drop more.'

They crossed over the square from the market, skirting the tree as it shivered and stretched, and as the worshippers continued their chanting. At a chandler's shop, Amara picked up a flint and tinderbox, a clasp knife, some bandages and medicines, and a jar of the ointment the barkeep had used against the harrowbug stings.

'Gods above and below,' Gotrek brooded, parsing the odd collection of coins and phials in his fist. He chewed his beard. 'You've practically cleaned me out! You spend like a drunkard on a spree.'

'And you fret about coin like an old woman,' Amara snapped.

'Dagoleth's such a rich city, is it, that you can throw money around without thinking about where it comes from?'

'Like many places, Dagoleth has no currency,' she admitted. 'Everything we buy and sell is bartered for, and every exchange is another link in the chain of obligation. It's taken a bit of getting used to, the value people believe these little shards and embers have.' She picked up a silver coin, much battered by its progress through whatever economies it had once come from. 'How can this,' she said, holding it up, 'be worth a good leather belt or a hot meal?'

'You can tell you're a bloody priest all right,' Gotrek raged. 'Never had to put a hand in your pocket as long as you've lived, I'll wager!'

Amara tried to steer him off the topic, seeing how worked up the duardin was getting. 'Tell me about these… What were they called?' she said. 'The creatures you think are on Wither Island.'

'I don't think, I *know*,' he said. 'And they'll not be *on* Wither Island, they'll be beneath it, under the waves. *Deepkin*, they call themselves. Stupid bloody name, but then what do you expect from aelves? They skulk about at the bottom of the ocean, the damned cowards. Spirit themselves up to the surface in clouds of mist and fog, riding their flying sharks and fish and whatnot.'

'Flying sharks,' Amara said. She peered more closely at him. Exactly how much *had* he drunk in the Amber Sap, she wondered? 'That they ride on. I see...'

'I've seen it with my own eyes!' Gotrek shouted. 'Don't ask me how it's supposed to work. Magic, no doubt, it's always bloody magic. They steal the very souls out of decent folk who live by the coast, leave them as little more than empty husks. Then, when they've had their fill, they spirit themselves back to the bottom of the sea. And the worst of it is, none of you buggers can ever remember them afterwards.'

Amara didn't know what to think. Aelves in the sea, flying sharks, magical banks of fog and mist... It all sounded like some drunken fantasy. Gotrek seemed utterly certain, but she suspected that was normal once he got an idea stuck in his head. Still, she couldn't doubt his sincerity as he planted himself there before her, his fingers twitching for his axe. He had a face like an anvil, a temper that ebbed and raged more changeably than the tides, but he was telling what he thought was the truth, of that she had no doubt. Gotrek's grief was certainly no delusion; she knew what grief looked like, and there was no mistaking the pain that the loss of this Maleneth had caused him.

'If these Deepkin take the souls and leave the bodies behind,' she said, the thought just occurring to her, 'then why has Kranzinnport been emptied of its people? Those lads in the tavern said the place was empty. Wouldn't the folk still be there? Just... without souls?'

'How do I know?' Gotrek said as he stomped off. 'They're aelves, aren't they? Always changing the rules, you can't even trust them to be evil in a sensible fashion.'

Amara hurried after him. 'And they said the trees were all

diseased at that end of the forest, that there was a sickness in the woods. Is that something to do with them too, these Deepkin?'

'It wouldn't surprise me,' Gotrek spat. He flicked a gaze up to the mesh windows high on the walls of Druhiel. The sun was fading now. The light was a pale yellow, and dusk was on its way. 'Those piddling little insects should be gone by now. Gather your things, lass, and we'll get going. Make for this Kranzinnport across country, kill whatever beasts or bandits get in our way, then we'll see what those watery buggers have to say for themselves when we get there.'

The thought seemed to cheer him up as he barrelled on through the crowd. There was a look of glee on his face at the prospect of violence, and although Amara knew they had a hard march ahead of them, filled with danger, she suspected that glee would power Gotrek every step of the way.

They passed back across the square, Amara stuffing the supplies into the knapsack she'd bought with Gotrek's money. A crowd had gathered to watch the tree now as it flexed and shivered behind its cage. Some folk had raised their hands in delight, while others covered their faces as if too piously moved to look on it any more. A pulse beat through the vines, and the worshippers groaned and clasped their hands together to see it. The leaves trembled and the branches shook.

It was extraordinary, but it must have grown at least another two or three feet just while Amara and Gotrek had been passing through the markets. The bark glistened and shone, a pale grey now instead of the necrotic black it had been before. The pollen from the flowers as they budded on its branches fell in a steady, sweet-scented rain. There was a rich smell in the air of the congregation's incense, fragrant as woodsmoke on an autumn evening. The green wisps of smoke from their censers curled up towards the town's high domed ceiling, and the scent brought Amara straight back to the temples she had known in her time as a priest. The stained glass, the worn wood of the altar, the heavy lectern with its leatherbound copy of the *Intimations*…

She shook her head clear. Those days were over now. She had given them up to spread the God-King's justice on the flat of her warhammer, and she had given that up to turn folk away from empty faith before it could snare them too deeply. She glanced at the worshippers as she pushed through the crowd, seeing in their ecstasy and grace a glimpse of what she had once known and would never know again.

There – just beneath the smell of the incense. Amara caught it at the back of her throat and gagged, whipping around as if the stench were something she could see before it flitted away. It was a smell of rot, and more than rot – a heady, cloying stink of corruption, just the faintest touch of it. She paused, looking at the worshippers. None of them seemed to have noticed – but then she saw one young woman, with vines of ivy entwined in her hair, wrinkle her brow. The woman coughed, retched suddenly, threw a hand up across her nose. Disgust rippled through the crowd. One frail old man, supporting himself on a gnarled walking stick, trembled and fell to the ground. He coughed once and then vomited up a stream of black liquid. Drawing his robes up across his face, another worshipper stumbled away and gagged against the stench that was now billowing through the square.

'What in the name of Grungni is that stink?' Gotrek said. 'Smells like a snotling privy.' He inhaled deeply, a quizzical look on his face. Amara was astonished that the smell didn't make him sick. 'Or a troll's loincloth.'

'Gotrek!' Amara cried, stifling a cough. 'Look!'

The tree in the centre of the square, having regrown so quickly from a shrunken stump, was now tall and dark and swollen. The bark looked like the skin of a rotten fruit, mottled and weeping, and the branches began to leak a syrupy yellow liquid. Scabs blossomed on the trunk in thick, dark crusts. Cankers popped from the bole with a sulphurous stink. Amara had seen people in the Healing Temples in Dagoleth when epidemics of dropsy and distemper had spread through the population, and the tree reminded her of them. It looked diseased. The vines that encircled it, ropes of ivy as thick as Gotrek's arms, were starting to quiver. Even as she watched, the vines began to slacken and detach from the trunk, whipping around and feeling their way through the bars of the fence.

The congregation reeled back in disgust, some raising their hands in supplication as they called on Alarielle to protect them. Others staggered away instead, choking, clawing at their throats and gasping for air.

'It is a sign from the goddess!' one man cried. His grey hair was dishevelled, his eyes wild and unseeing as he clawed at his face. 'We must turn away from the trappings of civilisation, lest we rot and decay as the tree decays!'

He gripped the lapels of Amara's robes. His face was threaded with purple veins, his eyes clogged with pus. Amara, sickened, shook him off and he stumbled on across the square, crying and waving his hands.

'What is this?' Amara said. 'Gotrek, what's happening?'

'Damned if I know,' Gotrek muttered. He had his axe up and had fallen into a wary crouch.

The vines that had snaked away from the trunk looked more like tentacles now, like hollow tubers reaching up from the earth. A great fissure had opened in the centre of the trunk, shivering as it gaped open. It was fringed with shards of white bark that looked almost like teeth – but then Amara realised that they *were* teeth, that the fissure had split into a vast, distended mouth, champing and gnashing and boiling with maggots. Even as she watched in horror it breathed out a charnel reek that made her turn and vomit onto the ground.

Ivory horns were slowly sprouting on the tree. There were nubs of calcified bark spiking out from the branches. Three huge buboes of clustered yellow cells had blossomed on the trunk, each drupelet quivering as it dribbled out a stream of rancid pus. Maggots writhed on the bark, dropping to the overlapping pine-cone scales that paved the square. White spots sprouted across the surface of the tree, emitting pale clouds of noxious gas.

People were screaming. Some threw themselves to their knees and wept, while others ran for shelter. The market shops had slammed their shutters, and in moments the whole of Druhiel was in uproar. Folk scattered across the square, sprinting to escape as the tree groaned and trembled, emitting a great roar. Its tentacles wavered in the air like the fronds of some disgusting deep-sea anemone.

Most of the worshippers who had led the procession were on their knees before it, their hands clasped in prayer, their censers raised as if the fragrant incense could in any way mask the grotesque stench of corruption and disease that poured off the tree – a disgusting odour of rotting teeth, decomposing corpses and excrement. The vines snaked and flickered at them, pushing through the bars of the fence and anointing them with smears of filth. Flies danced from the weeping sores on the bark and alighted on the worshippers' faces, burrowing into their eyes and ears, buzzing into their mouths as they screamed. In moments their skin was threaded with those same purple veins, and their noses ran with thick ropes of pus. Gargling and choking, their flesh erupting in foul buboes and cankers, the priests and congregants staggered to their feet and lurched across the square.

Amara backed away. Weeping claws snapped at her. The congregants' hands had fused into weird, bisected tentacles, pitted with sores. Putrid abscesses had opened on their skin, like ragged, screeching mouths. A man who had once been a priest groaned and gurgled at her, two oily yellow lumps bulging out of his skull, his hands raised as if to drag her into some corrupting embrace. Amara darted back out of his reach, just as Gotrek came leaping across the square with his axe raised above his head and a blood-curdling cry on his lips.

The blade carved the priest's head in two, burying itself deep into his chest. Gotrek shucked it free as the body flopped to the ground in a gout of blood. Snarling and laughing at the same time, he gave a roar as he charged into the rest of the diseased congregants.

'Gotrek!' Amara cried. 'Be careful!'

The axe blade whirred and flashed, flinging bodies to left and right. She knew it wasn't their fault. They were ordinary people turned into monsters by this rapacious infection, and although every part of her flinched to see them cut to pieces in Gotrek's assault, at this stage she knew that death would be a mercy to them. A tentacle whipped for Gotrek's head but he slashed it aside in a spray of bilious green fluid. One shuffling priest lurched across the flagstones like a crab, moaning, his face buried in a mound of swollen, suppurating flesh, his eyes bulging. Mucous dripped from his distended jaw – and then Gotrek had planted the axe in his face, ripping it aside with an awful wet crunch of bone.

Whatever foul disease had gripped the priests and the worshippers, it had soon spread across the square. Amara saw shopkeepers from the market stalls collapsing onto the wooden pavements, vomiting blood. A member of the city guard, a burly veteran with a bristling moustache, shrieked and wailed as his neck swelled like a balloon, his eyes near popping from his head as they fused together into one sickly, blood-streaked orb. Khrispin and Henrick stumbled from the doors of the Amber Sap, slack-jawed with horror. They looked on the thrashing branches of the diseased tree and wrung their hands in prayer.

'It's like the southern reaches of the forest!' Henrick cried to Amara. 'Faith and the goddess protect us if it's spread to Druhiel!'

The two young foresters' nerves failed them; they took one last look at the square and ran.

Everywhere, the infected turned on those who were not yet touched by sickness. Even the merest touch of a suppurating limb was enough to spread the disease, and as fast as Gotrek cut them down, more of Druhiel's wretched populace succumbed.

'Don't let them touch you,' he cried. 'Keep out of their bloody way, if you won't fight them!'

He hurtled off across the square, swinging his axe like he was clearing a path through an overgrown jungle. Blood sprayed across the flagstones. Limbs went sailing, but even above Gotrek's demented roar she could hear the groaning and the weird, chuckling laughter of the infected.

Inat and five of his guard came charging from the gates, their swords drawn. The guards looked across the scene with abject disgust, stumbling backwards as the tree flailed before them and the diseased people of Druhiel staggered into the streets.

A lurching hulk of a man shuffled towards Inat, giggling and dripping with pus, his tunic tattered from the quivering buboes that had burst out across his chest. The young captain retched and then parried the slopping swing of a tentacle before lunging to skewer the deformed creature through the throat. He kicked the rotting corpse aside with disgust.

'Is this your doing?' he barked at Amara. 'Do you bring plague to my city?'

He raised his blade, but Amara held out her empty hands.

'We had nothing to do with it,' she said. 'Ask your priests instead, perhaps your goddess has turned on you.' She pointed at the deformed tree, the great maw in its trunk biting and snapping as it spewed out another froth of maggots.

Amara held his eye. Inat gave her a dark look, and yet he did not strike.

'Plague? Ha!' Gotrek laughed as he jogged back to the edge of the square. 'Is that helmet too tight, boy? This is no natural illness.'

His axe blade was drenched in filth, his face streaked with blood. He looked utterly deranged, and the dull gold of the rune on his chest was flickering with an inner flame. Amara could see the trail of corpses he had left behind him. He barely looked out of breath.

'Seen this before,' he said. 'Same filth, same stench of corruption. Same folk staggering about like the leavings of a sanitorium.'

'What is it?' Amara demanded. 'If it's not plague, then–'

'The Grandfather,' Gotrek spat. 'Nurgle, and all his pestilential minions. Came across his followers before, and in this damned realm too. Can't have one without the other, it seems.' He fingered his axe with a greedy leer. 'Still, they go down to the edge of my blade easily enough, even if they do tend to burst a bit when you hit them.'

Inat blanched, his face white.

'The taint of Neiglen, here in Druhiel? Goddess protect us all!'

'You need to protect yourself, lad,' Gotrek said. 'Now get to it!'

Inat shuddered. He snapped the mesh faceplate to the front of his helmet. 'Masks!' he cried to his guards. 'For the sake of the Green and the city, with me! Keep them back! We must save the sacred tree, if we can!'

'Good luck with that,' Gotrek muttered.

'We need to help these people,' Amara said, as the city guards charged forward. She saw them sweep out their blades and carve their way through the infected mob. 'They're innocents, nothing more than pawns in yet another god's dark game.'

'It's too late for them, lass,' Gotrek said. 'I've seen it all before. I've fought these creatures in Ghyran, in the Old World, in the damned Realm of Chaos itself, and believe me, when the Grandfather's hooks are in your blood, it would take a miracle to cure you.'

She looked at the creeping, shuffling hordes as Inat's guards cut through them, as more guards came rushing in from the other side of the square and lent their weapons to the fight. The surface of the square was a quagmire of rotting guts, of blood and pus and all the filth vomited up by the afflicted.

'I don't believe in miracles any more.'

'Then what *do* you believe in?' Gotrek roared at her. 'The gods be damned, priest, but you can't live with nothing in your heart but despair!'

The force of his rage crashed over her, but when she met his glaring eye she saw something like regret there too.

'Take it from one who knows,' he said bitterly. 'Believe in yourself, if nothing else. Don't live as if the only thing you want to do is die.'

He hauled up his axe and a dark scowl fell across his face like a portcullis. Whatever that brief, unguarded moment had been, it was gone now. The careworn old duardin fell away, and in his place was nothing but the Slayer.

'Now,' Gotrek said, biting back his fury. 'Let's bloody end this.'

He sprinted across the square and bounded over the fence that caged the tree. The thick pine-needle bars had been no match for its thrashing tentacles, or for the swollen roots that bulged from the earth beneath it. The tree, as if sensing that danger was near, emitted a low, groaning hoot from deep within its chambers. Boots squelching through a carpet of maggots, ducking a tendril that came whipping towards his head and slashing the tip from another, Gotrek leapt and slammed the blade of his axe deep into its flank.

The yawning, serrated mouth screamed. A pulse of yellow slime dribbled from the cut as Gotrek tore his axe free, hacking in again and again with a bellowed duardin curse. Splinters of rotten bark flew up into his face. He batted away the branches that scrabbled to push him aside. The tree at its fullest extent must have been about ten feet wide, but in moments Gotrek had carved such a bloody tranche into its side that it began to sway and slowly topple, crumpling in on itself as the rotten sap bubbled from the wound. The pulsing, infected wood began to screech, the trunk twisting as it fell. Gotrek ducked a branch as it sailed by an inch from his head, and leapt out of the way as the tree crashed to the ground. The roots were torn from the earth, white and bloodless things that quivered in the air like worms. The stench that billowed up from the scar in the ground was unholy, a roiling miasma that stank of burnt offal and mouldering pus. The weird fissure of the tree's mouth gibbered and shrieked, screaming almost as if it could feel pain. As Amara staggered over, covering her mouth from the stench, the duardin laughed as he hacked in again and again, slicing off branches, shattering buboes, chopping the grotesque thing to pieces.

His face was red and sweating with the exertion, but there was such a wild joy in it that Amara baulked at the thought of trying to stop him. Each blow he hammered down onto the infected tree seemed thrown with the force of something supernatural, and in moments the strewn fragments of bark were like so many slabs of rotting meat. The awful groaning howl gurgled away into a death rattle. Gotrek, leaning on his axe amidst the wreckage as he gathered his breath, gave her a snarling, gap-toothed grin.

'There!' he shouted. 'Should have started with that really, would have saved a lot of bother.'

Inat and his remaining guards had managed to clear the square of the infected worshippers, cutting them down with tears in their eyes and starting the grisly task of gathering the bodies for burning or burial. Amara tried to help, grimacing as she looked at the scattered body parts from the mayhem Gotrek had unleashed. Inat strode over, his breastplate smeared with blood and ichor and his helmet askew. His sword was broken in his hand, but he still wielded the hilt and a few inches of jagged steel.

'We'll gather our own dead!' he cried, pushing her away from the corpses. 'Haven't you done enough? By all that's holy, leave this place now, and never come back.'

'Done enough?' Amara snapped. 'Damn you, if it weren't for Gotrek, what do you think would have happened to Druhiel?' She pointed at him as he clambered out of the debris. With his blood-stained beard and his ruddy, battered face, she had to admit that he didn't look like the most wholesome of saviours. 'This place would have been overrun in moments.'

'Save your breath,' Gotrek said to her grimly. 'Someone's got to take the blame now, and it may as well be us.'

Cautiously Inat looked at them both, his chest heaving. When he glanced at the ruins of the tree, Amara could see the pain in his face, the despair. No matter what it had done to the people who venerated it, Gotrek had literally cut the sacred heart out of the city. All that was left for Inat was to clean up the mess: the corpses of the infected dead, the filth that had somehow poisoned their community.

'I cannot say if you are truly to blame,' Inat said. He looked uneasily at them, and then at the mayhem in the square: the bodies, the blood, the flies that still coursed and flickered in the air, the people who knelt by the dead and wept. 'But there will be many who think you are. For your own sakes, you should go now. The people of Druhiel need to mourn, and plan our defences if such horrors should visit us again.'

Amara could see the survivors wandering dazed through the square, and the dark glances that they threw at Gotrek.

'Come on,' she said, drawing him aside. The fight over, the duardin seemed oddly subdued, although when she glanced at him she could see the calculation glittering in his good eye. She looked to the windows high on the walls of Druhiel and saw that night had fallen now. At least the harrowbugs would be gone. A small mercy.

Amara gathered up her knapsack from where she had dropped it, shrugging it on as they walked to the gates. She looked back at the wreckage they had left behind them.

'Diseased trees in the southern reaches,' she said quietly to Gotrek as he stroked his beard in thought. 'This monstrosity here. Do you still think these aelves have anything to do with what's going on at Kranzinnport?'

'Maybe,' he growled. 'Maybe not… But I say Wither Island is worth a visit all the same.'

They broached the doors, pushed out into the fragrant dark. The cool night breeze was a clean and welcome thing after the foetid horrors of Druhiel, the stench and the chaos. Ahead and through the trees, gleaming in the moonlight, Amara could see the level sward of the plains as they swept off towards the Rocanian Coast.

Three days should do it, she thought. She looked at Gotrek, his brooding menace stumping along the forest floor beside her.

And woe betide anyone who gets in his way.

CHAPTER EIGHT

WITHER ISLAND

The sea was curdled where it met the shore. Runnels of foam came spattering over the rocks, sloughing back into a crust of scum, and the rocks themselves were stained an oily green. The water stank of bile and sour milk. It was beginning to congeal where the long slope of the beach dropped down to the tideline, like a scab trying to cap an ulcer. Corruption gathered over the surface, festering and fretting against the stone and the sand. A hazy shimmer rose up from the scum, like sour breath.

Further out, the sea was still clear. The hard-packed waves chopped up against each other, dazzling in the sunlight, trimmed with spray. Wide breakers rolled in from the open ocean, shifting as they met the unexpected barrier of the island and smashing themselves against the rocks on the southern edge. To the north, the blunt prow of the island pointed towards the wavering line of the Rocanian Coast twenty miles away, a blustered landscape of towering grey cliffs, fringed with a carpet of emerald green. The ocean battered at the cliff face like a besieging army, the waves booming across the deeps. Sea birds lifted from the spray, spiralling off into the cloud-strewn sky. Here and there black shapes moved in the waters – flense fish on the prowl, hunting for the weak, scavenging for the dead. Rising from the mist above the cliffs were the round peaks and towers of Kranzinnport, spiralled and spired, fan-shaped, conical, like clustered seashells fashioned from grey stone. When the wind slackened in the bay, and when the afternoon fell for a while still and calm, the sound of screaming drifted hesitantly from the city to the shores of the island.

Bilgeous Pox, with an odd fastidiousness, drew up the hems of his robe as he picked along the foreshore. A low hood of mouldering grey cloth covered most of his face. Only his mouth was visible, twitching with amusement, the yellow teeth flashing sharp and feral as he gazed down into the wrack of foam. Scrolls and pouches dangled from the rope tied around his waist, and his chest and stomach were wrapped in folds of frayed brown leather. In one hand he held a tall staff of twisted black rotwood, a rusty bronze hook at the very top. Back and forth he walked along the tideline, peering down as the viscous, stinking water slithered up and sloshed into his sandals.

'Yes, indeed...' he muttered to himself. A black tongue darted out to lick a pale incisor. 'Quickening, *burgeoning*, and... The hours and the days advance... No more than eternity's yoke... But I have nearly done it. Yes, it is so close...'

The sorcerer stooped quickly, a shrivelled grey arm snatching out into the murky water. It felt as warm as blood. He hissed with satisfaction, his fingers groping through the submerged rocks. He felt it slithering through his fingers, squeezed, nails digging into the flesh.

'Here we are, at last, at *last*...'

The creature he pulled from the water had been birthed in no ocean of the Mortal Realms. On first inspection it might have seemed like some species of fish – it had the same pendulous, teardrop body of many types that were to be found in these waters, the same fringe of gills that palped and rippled in its side. But as Bilgeous Pox held it up to the light he saw those traces in its flesh that betrayed its origins as being altogether more exotic and unexpected. The globular eyes were flecked with amber. The skin rippled with a subcutaneous glow, like a corpse-flame burning on the other side of a darkened moor. The pupils of its eyes floated in a jelly that seemed as much congealed starlight as a loose form of sclera, and he knew that what pulsed through its veins was more magic than blood. The smell that rose from its mottled skin made him think of mulch and compost, and seemed to conjure a picture in his mind of fan-bladed ferns and jungle vines, all of them creeping and choking and rotting. He thought of glutinous slimes, the blackened fluids of a leaking canker, the moist fecundity of things growing and dying and growing once more.

Bilgeous closed his eyes and breathed it in, bringing the creature closer to his mouth. Like a worm nosing the soil and seeking the fresher air, the black tongue emerged from between his yellow fangs to brush its tip against the glorious unreal flesh. So cold and clammy, slathered in such rich decay…

It shuddered in his hand. Slowly, as though even this cool day were too hot for its form to suffer, the creature began to melt. The eyes evaporated into a sickly steam. The flesh dribbled from his palm, and what bones the thing may have had dissolved into a tacky paste. As Bilgeous watched it fade into the aether, he was soon left with no more than a palmful of slime that he flicked from his fingers onto the rocks. He gave a slow and only partially disappointed smile. It was only one amongst many after all, and the conjunction was almost upon them. As he gazed down into the cresting foam and the curdled sea, he knew that there would be many, many more to come.

* * *

The sorcerer walked around the coast of the island, to the headland of the north. The wind tugged at his robes. His staff clattered against the pebbled shore and his sandals slopped through the glutinous tide. The sand and the pebbles were strewn with ropes of rotting seaweed, fizzing in the sunlight as the tide withdrew, breaking down into an oily green slime. Liver ticks and flux beetles scurried on the stones, popping under his feet with a greasy crunch as he walked on, leaving behind them a rich scent of rancid fat. Bilgeous Pox did not need to eat to find sustenance, but he found the smell oddly satisfying all the same. It conjured up an old appetite he had abandoned many hundreds of years before.

Off to his right the beach sloped upwards in a gentle gradient towards a line of eager, unruly jungle. It was dark and rich and feculent, a knot of serrated leaves and tubers, of thick green shoots and swollen fronds. A shimmering green miasma hung over it like a bank of cloud, and it was flecked with the bumbling black shapes of insects. There were globular trees with hairy trunks bursting through the canopy, the pendulous blue sacs of their fruit dripping with ichor. Bloat Flies rose lazily from the creepers, dragging their distended abdomens through the heavy, succulent air. The drone of their wings was a constant chorus, and from deeper in the jungle Bilgeous could hear other murmurings and shrieks, the liquid babble of creatures so far unknown to him. Slowly, with infinite patience, they were building something new here, something that had never been seen before–

No, he checked himself. He permitted a ripple of laughter to escape him. Not something new in the slightest. No, something old, something very, very old indeed… For the foot of the Grandfather himself had once trod this world, so the legends said, in a time that was unimaginably distant.

Far over the canopy he could see the Rot Flies of Cholerax's Maggotkin troop sweeping low over the jungle, the Blightlords mounted on their high saddles scanning the borders of the island for trespassers. As if anyone would dare, Bilgeous chided them inwardly. He shook his head. Even before the raids had started, this channel of water carried a dark reputation to the mortal fisherfolk and seafarers who lived along the coast. Ever since the island had risen from the waves, even the most desperate oystermen would avoid trawling here. Here on the very fringes of the Jade Kingdoms, the usurper Alarielle and her lackey Sigmar seemed very far away. What the blank spaces of the map concealed for the ordinary, ignorant folk did not bear thinking about.

Still, Bilgeous thought with a sigh, Cholerax must have his martial routines to keep him occupied. A Lord of Afflictions was a proud warrior, commanding a combat elite; not for him was time best spent in silent devotion and humble prayer. Cholerax thrived on strife, and must be given his head. He was a powerful ally and a superlative warrior, dedicated to the Grandfather's beneficent cause. A prayer was never far from his ulcerated lips, but even so, he did not *feel* the Grandfather's presence as Bilgeous himself felt it.

But then, of course, Cholerax had never *been* there… Centuries ago, he had not waded for that brief moment through the slime and the rot of the Garden. He had not lived and fought amongst the Mulch of Ages, and he had not danced through the ecstasies of Rotwater Blight in the sacred presence of Bolathrax and his Rotguard, knowing that Nurgle himself was but a hair's breadth away.

Bilgeous watched the Rot Flies bank heavily away to the east, their spindly legs trailing above the leaves and their twin sets of tattered wings catching the light with an oily iridescence. The Blightlords atop them hefted their rust-stained scythes and drew the creatures down until they passed from his sight. Bilgeous sighed once more, and then breathed deeply of the green miasma that streamed from the jungle. The water belched and slapped at his feet. The crust of scum bubbled and the air was flecked with pestilent spores.

Soon, he told himself. Soon.

The discordant tootling of the Bilepiper caught his ear, a droning melody announcing the return of the reaver ships and their cargo. Bilgeous limped quickly up the shingle. He stepped through pools of mucous and crossed the runnels of waste that trickled out of the scrub. Before long he had come out onto the broad headland of the island, an elongated crescent of rock, notched and crumbling, that was split in the middle by the stony wings of a wide natural harbour. The waves crashed against the walls that had been reinforced and extended with much cheerful industry, but inside the ramshackle port the water was calm. Out at sea, planing smoothly through the choppy waters, two schooners of black ironoak approached. They had twin masts, their tattered black sails rigged on spars of leviathan bone. The hulls of the ships, streaming with water where they lifted out of the waves, were crusted with grey barnacles. Each bore a carved figurehead of loathsome horror: a glistering, tentacled face on one, a blunt-nosed half helm with a leering, unslung jaw on the other. The *Rust Scythe* and the *Diphthemious* – two of the most feared Maggotkin ships that plied the Tendril Seas, now dedicated to Bilgeous Pox's service.

No, he reminded himself. Now dedicated to *Nurgle's* service. Bilgeous was strict with his devotions; it would not do to get ideas above his station.

A scattered crew of mortals, cultists dedicated to the Grandfather and liberally rewarded with his gifts, were dotted around the flanks of the port. They had been hard at work for weeks now, extending the harbour walls and clearing new slipways so the ships could moor on the headland. As the schooners came in, the big ships blowing their ivory horns, the cultists shuffled and slouched to the slipways, readying themselves to tie the guide ropes to the hawsers. There was something mournful about the sound of the ships' horns, a cetaceous call that was redolent of deep and lonely seas, as if the schooners were great water beasts broaching old hunting grounds and finding them long abandoned.

Bilgeous limped onto the wharf, his staff clacking on the stone. He could see Lord Cholerax skimming in on his Rot Fly from the east, the droning creature trailing its gangly legs in the green water as it approached the harbour.

'This should do it,' Cholerax cried as he came near. The Rot Fly bucked across the wall, its tattered wings beating out a sweet stench of pestilent meat. Cholerax slipped from the saddle of his throne as the Rot Fly hovered slackly above the wharf, his black, rust-pitted iron boots crunching on the stone. 'This should be the last of them, Pox, if that damned pirate has done his job. And then it can begin, at last.' He pointed to where the city of Kranzinnport sat hunkered above the cliffs of the Rocanian Coast, little more than a drab grey line in the distance. 'I doubt there's a mortal left alive in that place now.'

He gave a snicker, high-pitched and strangely incongruous from one who presented such a martial appearance. Cholerax was liberally strapped with armour. There were interlocking plates across his pauldrons; his breastplate hung loose against a drooping goitre that flapped down from his neck. His right arm, sheathed in a rusty greave, was pink and inflamed, as if a deep infection brewed beneath the surface of his skin. His left arm was a coiled green tentacle studded with red boils – an early gift from the Grandfather in the days when Cholerax, so the rumours went, had been a general in the service of one of Sigmar's cities. His head was masked in a full-face great helm that was severely corroded. Three round holes had rusted through the iron, high on the left hand side – the three sacred buboes of the Grandfather. Through them Bilgeous could see the suggestion of a glistening compound eye. Beneath the sheets of his breastplate, Bilgeous was reasonably sure he could hear the gnashing of a secondary mouth, although for whatever strange reason of his own Cholerax liked to keep this a secret.

'Kranzinnport is a large enough city for this part of the coast, Lord Cholerax,' Bilgeous said. 'We have tapped most of its population,' he nodded, indicating the big ships as they berthed themselves by the slipways, 'but hopefully this last consignment will be enough for our purposes.'

With a last doleful blast of their horns, the schooners began to toss mouldering lengths of rope to the hawsers and drop their anchor. The crew started to furl their sails up like discarded shrouds. Bilgeous limped down the wharf towards the slipway, a stone ramp that was pitted with black puddles, the gaps between the flagstones choked with oily moss.

'Come, Lord Cholerax,' Bilgeous said. 'Can you not feel it? The ache in your pustules, the pain that threads through your guts? The time grows ever nearer. Here on this sacred land, by the Grandfather's gifts.'

'By the Grandfather's gifts indeed,' Cholerax said.

He strode purposefully, at least two heads higher than the hunched form of the sorcerer, but he kept his swaggering bulk always a respectful few feet behind. It always made Bilgeous feel mildly uncomfortable, this deference. He was the conduit for the Grandfather's will, it was true, but no more. This land underfoot, even the carved and orchestrated structures of the harbour, was the true repository of their devotion. He could smell the bacterial stench of it, could almost taste the rich encrustations.

By the slipways, the crews of the two great ships began to drag and beat their cargoes from the hold. Whimpered screams rose up into the air, cries of unutterable distress. Bilgeous grinned to hear them and Cholerax chuckled good-naturedly. Slowly, with much prodding and with liberal use of barbed whips, the captured men and women of Kranzinnport staggered in their chains down the gangplanks.

Hunched and trembling in abject terror, they rolled their eyes at the sight that greeted them. Bilgeous tried to imagine what it might look like to them, unaccustomed as they were to such wonders. The gathered cultists slopping over the berths, say, their faces distended with growths, or the droning Rot Flies quartering the jungle as they flew on tattered scraps of wings. Even the nightmarish miasma that made many of them vomit as they met the open air must have been a shock, although to Bilgeous it was perfume of the highest order.

Some of the prisoners had not survived their journey in the hold, short as it may have been from the city across the water, and their corpses were dragged behind the survivors as they were thrashed towards the wharf. The Blightkings who crewed the vessels, a motley company of pirates and cut-throats armed with scimitars and short-hafted axes, some of them with mouldering tricorn hats stuffed onto their heads, gurgled with laughter to see them off.

'Still more where that came from!' a hacking, mucoidal voice cried out. Bilgeous looked up to see Pertussis, the captain of the *Diphthemious* and the admiral of this small fleet, leaning over the gunwale of his ship with his rusting trident in hand. 'Plenty of them rats still scurrying about the streets and hiding in its sewers. Aye, we've set the beasts to them for now, and happen we'll have good sport of them later.'

Bilgeous quashed a feeling of irritation. 'My felicitations on the success of your venture, captain. Perhaps when your crew is sufficiently rested,' he said mildly, 'then the return voyage to collect the remainder would not be too arduous a task for you?

After all, as I have expressed on many an occasion, we need all that we can get if my ritual is to be completed. If there are rats left scurrying about in Kranzinnport's streets, then I suggest you go back and get them.'

Captain Pertussis waited a beat and then gave a lazy salute with his lobster-clawed hand, narrowing his single, bulbous eye. He had a fanged mouth in his gut, and a sinuous purple tongue emerged from it to lick the edge of the gunwale.

He didn't like being given orders, Bilgeous knew. All these pirates, they may have seen the truth of what the sorcerer was trying to do, but they were renegade spirits more than loyal disciples. They were used to the open seas, to plundering and pillaging on their own terms, and they chafed against the discipline necessary for this great venture. Rituals were nothing without a principle of order – something instinctively anathema to those who plied the reaver's trade.

'I don't like these plague-damned pirates,' Cholerax muttered. He hawked and spat behind his helmet, and a trickle of clotted vomit dribbled down his neck. 'Too free and easy with their service if you ask me. You can't trust they won't up-anchor and sail away on their own terms whenever they feel like it.'

His tentacle strayed to the hilt of the short sword on his hip, while he gripped the haft of his scythe with his swollen hand.

'You have ever been a stern and committed warrior, Lord Cholerax, and do not suppose for a moment that I am not grateful for it.' Bilgeous shuffled forward as the prisoners were brought up across the berth. 'But alas, needs must when the Grandfather calls. If we are to build again his Garden in the Mortal Realms, then we need the help of pirates and cut-throats, as much as we need loyal and devoted followers. Kranzinnport is the nearest habitation to our blessed isle, so recently raised from the sea, and alas, the sea is a road few of us can walk.' He smiled pettishly at Cholerax's Rot Fly. 'Or indeed fly, and still bring back as much as we need.'

Cholerax stayed him a moment with his tentacle. It left a smear of discoloured mucous on Bilgeous' robes.

'Is it true?' he said urgently. He turned to look over the broad and tangled sweep of the jungle behind them, the calcified headlands beyond the harbour that were crumbling in flakes of milky-white stone into the encrusted sea. Bilgeous could see the flicker of that compound eye through the trio of holes in his helmet. 'I *feel* it, I know I do, but... To think that this island is a shard of Nurgle himself? It's too much, it's far too much.'

'What does your heart tell you, my son?' Bilgeous asked him.

'My heart rotted from my chest many years ago,' Cholerax admitted.

'Then what is it that keeps you going? That has made your frame so powerful, and that has gifted you with so many wonderful growths?'

'*Faith,*' Cholerax whispered.

'Indeed. Faith. Faith in the God of Plagues, crowned with maggots. Faith in he who loves all his children, and who left this fragment of himself for us to find.' Bilgeous lifted up his staff. 'Yea, though the centuries and the millennia fell into the silence of ages past and the lands were swallowed in the deluge, still the toenail of the Grandfather was left on the bed of these seas for his followers to raise with their prayers and offerings. For his foot once walked this soil, did it not, in a time when the Mortal Realms were merely dust and magic coalescing in the maelstrom of the void? And as he walked, then so his Grandson's foot will follow in the path he took.'

Cholerax reverently bowed his head. Bilgeous tapped him lightly with the staff, the black wood ringing on the armour plate. He leered at the prisoners as they were beaten along the wharf. Men with crazed eyes, horror-stricken. Women tearing at their hair with their manacled hands. There were a hundred at least, which was more than he expected. After the thousands they had used so far, he was surprised there were still so many left. None of the prisoners could look at the two figures who stood there to greet them, and instead they drooled and muttered in their distress. No one begged for mercy, at least. That, Bilgeous knew, would come later.

'Now, my friend,' Bilgeous said, as the prisoners were led past him, 'if you will excuse me, I will show our new guests what need we have of them.'

No one spoke to the stranger when he arrived in Xil'anthos. That was just the way he liked it. If he wanted to talk, then he would ask questions, and if he asked questions then he would expect answers. Otherwise, there was no converse that was worth his time or his attention.

He took a room at the Cracked Flagon. The barkeep was a burly type, thick black beard, lots of front. No substance to him, though. The stranger sized him up the moment he was through the door, noted how he couldn't meet his eye. He'd start on him later, but for now he needed to rest, get some food into his belly, half a cup of whatever passed for wine in this place. Xil'anthos seemed no better or worse than most of the backwater towns in Thyria. Hadraeder, Piliscutt, Tillistyne, and any number of smoking ruins wiped off the map by orruk raids or beastmen stampedes – he'd been through them all the last few weeks. Now Xil'anthos, with its walls of cultivated vine, its little square, its homely little temple to Sigmar, which the locals probably thought was as good as Hammerhal's Great Cathedral.

He'd seen the scuff of soot and scorched stone in the middle of the square, figured they'd had themselves a burning the last few days. No charred corpse hanging from the lintel above the city gates, though. Maybe it hadn't gone to plan. He'd find out later. He always found out.

There was a desk in the room facing the narrow, shuttered window; a single cot with a thin straw-filled mattress; a washstand. Simple, functional, all that he needed. He sat for a while at the desk with the shutters open, watching the comings and goings of the good folk of Xil'anthos. Priests scurrying up the steps of the temple. Market traders setting up their wares along the flank of the square. Moneylenders exchanging Aqua Ghyranis for whatever currency you needed. All of the simple folk of Sigmar's dominion. Unthinking, uncomprehending, innocent. Cruel little folk, selfish and greedy, frightened, and nowhere close to understanding how frightened they should really be.

He read through his papers until the light began to dim, the dusk creeping fast over the plains. Descriptions, sightings, confessions. Somewhere, far from here, he could hear the whispering of the forests, the wind coursing thinly over the grasslands and the empty places, heading down towards the distant coast.

Where are you? he thought. Where have you gone? Where are you going?

He looked down at his papers again. The lamps were being lit in the streets outside. After a moment he shuffled the documents together and returned them to his saddlebag. His horse had died a month back, not ten miles outside the Living City. He'd pay a visit to the trader who sold him the mare when all this was done. Let him know the official penalty for cheating. Let him know the private penalty too, and give him the choice of which one he would prefer.

The stranger sat back in the chair and looked out at the streets. He took off his wide-brimmed hat and placed it on the desk, shrugged out of his duster, laid his pistols and his sword in the corner of the room. He'd rest for an hour or two, he figured, catch up on his sleep. Then he'd put on the hat and the duster again and go downstairs to the bar. He'd start asking questions, and he'd get answers to them. He always did.

PART TWO

PART TWO

CHAPTER NINE

THE RUINS OF KRANZINNPORT

The bluff was streaked with drizzle, a chill rain that flecked in from off the sea. Where it spattered against his skin, it smelled to Odger Pellin like spit or bile. There was a sour, doughy stink to it, and it made the flagstones underfoot slippery and treacherous. He remembered the day the rains had first come. The clouds across the city, the mist across the sea. A day he would never forget.

He glanced up at the flank of the old counting house by the corner of Anemone Avenue. The building's grey stone was pitted and chipped, and the windows were blown out from the fire that had briefly raged there before the rains had smothered it. Broken sea glass littered the steps. Inside, he knew, all was a blackened ruin. The cannons those monsters had fired from their ships down in the bay had only just reached the city, it was so high on the cliffs, but where the iron bombshells struck they had done appalling damage. There was barely a building left in the city that was untouched by fire or smoke.

Iron was one thing, but they had used worse than iron, too…

Odger shuddered, passed a hand through the beard that had grown in over the last few months. He remembered the hollow spheres that had fallen into the streets – ceramic balls that split apart when they hit the stone, releasing clouds of flies – and the disease that followed in their wake. Folk puking their guts up in the streets. Others so torn and deformed by mutation that they were barely recognisable. Not half a day later the raiders had returned, only this time they seized the harbour and made their way into the city, scouring the streets for survivors. Four times they had done this, sailing their deadly ships across the bay from where that hump of rock had appeared, their troops pouring into the harbour at the base of the cliffs and raising themselves in the cage lifts up to the city. Those who managed to hide lived for a little while longer. Those who tried to fight died where they stood, like the Kranzinnport Sabres who had mustered in the market square and were either cut down without mercy or succumbed to the even fouler brew of illness the raiders brought with them.

There had been weeks of this horror, more weeks than he could count, endless days of hiding in the ruins and creeping out at dusk to scavenge what food they could for the handful of survivors who had made it this far. As for the rest, their fate didn't bear thinking about. The lucky ones had been killed in the fighting. The unlucky ones had been snatched from the streets and dragged in chains back to those awful boats, lurking out there on the grey waters, blockading the harbour down at the base of the cliffs. Loaded onto those boats and then taken back to Wither Island, for Sigmar knew what.

The island lay out there like a black thumbprint pressed against the glass of the open sea. Odger spat on the pavement, tried to hold back the pain and the fear for another minute or two. That's all he could do now. Just make it through the day a minute at a time.

It was no good, though. Unbidden, breaking their way through the shield he had raised to protect his sanity, came the memories of Melita and Clovis, his wife and son. Odger swallowed, gripping his spear with white knuckles. He saw the chains around their hands, the terror on their faces, the laughter of the bloated freaks that had stolen them away with all the others. Their home burning behind him, the wreckage that he tried to free himself from as his family was taken. There was nothing he could have done, nothing. He was lucky to have survived the fire, and he would not let himself die now until he knew what had happened to his family. Only when he knew for certain that they had not survived would he embrace death with gladness and fervour, and he would kill as many of these monsters as he could before he did so.

'I will see you soon, my loves,' he whispered, stifling a sob. 'I know it. But not yet, not yet.'

If there was anyone left that Odger believed in, he prayed to them now to make sure his family was safely dead.

He had sent Merosis and Uffo down to keep watch at the corner of the street, while the others hunted through the warehouses on the eastern side, where the avenue spilled out into the open precinct. There, the statues of Kranzinnport's founders had been toppled from their plinths, and the stalls had been ripped apart and plundered weeks ago. Shops had been looted, homes had been ransacked. There was barely any food left in the whole city; what hadn't rotted away was corrupted by the same touch of disease that had killed so many good folk here. It was too dangerous to stay and too dangerous to leave. Every exit from Kranzinnport was well guarded. It was as if the raiders wanted to keep them bottled up in here, as if they were saving the survivors for later.

He well remembered Captain Ismeala's vain attempt to flee with the remnants of the city guard, hoping to get help from Druhiel or even the Living City in the north. The harbour had long been abandoned to those *things*, but the paved track that led down to the western road was no place to be caught in the open. They hadn't gone more than a few hundred yards when those flying monstrosities dropped out of the sky...

Odger gnawed his thumbnail. It was no use. They just had to stay, had to survive as long as they could. Help would come, he knew it. And if it didn't, they would all just have to find their own place to die.

Kranzinnport was a small city as these things went, narrow but tall, with all its homes and houses and public buildings clustered together on the bluff like barnacles clinging to a ship's keel. Odger, crouching at the side of the street, his knee crunching in the rubble, could see down the length of the avenue to where the street dipped away into the lower tiers. Far out there to the east was the coast road, a white ribbon wavering across the lip of the cliffs, and then the first green fringe of the Mistral Forest. If they could get out there somehow, maybe find cover under the trees. It might be possible...

He heard the clatter of broken glass, the sharp report of masonry falling from the walls. Baffin, somewhere in the depths of the building, hissed for silence, but it was more aggrieved than worried. Odger let his nerves relax slightly. If they could find a crumb of food it would be more than they'd rustled up for the past few days, and if they could do it without drawing the attention of whatever monsters remained in the city then so much the better. But it was getting harder, all of it. Their water barrels from the last clean rain were almost empty, and he didn't fancy drinking any of this rancid drizzle. Odger sighed, passed his hand once more through the knots of his beard and bit at his lip. He went back to scanning the eastern approach while Baffin and the others went on rummaging through the wreckage of the counting house.

And then he saw it – faint as you like, no more than two dots poked into the dun strip of the bluff as it ribboned up towards the city. Two miles away, perhaps, and still too far to be anything but a faint apprehension, but Odger would have bet what little he had left that there were two people now approaching Kranzinn-port along the coast road.

'Merosis!' he said in a harsh whisper.

She looked back from the other end of the street, where she leaned at the corner with her sword in hand and a buckler in her fist. He beckoned her to him, and the young woman jogged at a crouch after a last keen glance at the square.

'What's up?' she said. 'Trouble?'

Odger could smell the sweat coming off her, the tang of unwashed clothes. Her face was hard and thin, her lank black hair tied back. She had been a seamstress once. She looked like a soldier now. Gods, he had once been no more than a steward in the marketplace, and here he was leading a gang of scavengers and survivors, trying to make it through each day as it came.

He pointed down into the lower tiers of the city, to where the road ran out onto the bluff. 'Tell me what you make of that,' he said.

Merosis shielded her brow and peered down into the east. The sun was still high, blurred out by the drizzling cloud, but columns of light broke through where those two black dots walked. Odger watched a frown form on her face.

'Looks like… Two of them, far as I can tell,' she said. She looked at him, her mouth turned down at the corners. 'Is it… *them*? They don't normally come by the coast road.'

'I don't think so. They look like people, I'd say. Real people.'

'Then what in Sigmar's name do they think they're doing? They won't last five minutes if they're coming to the gates.'

'Maybe they don't know,' Odger ventured. 'Maybe they're traders. Do you even get folk mad enough to travel on their own?'

Merosis gnawed at a fingernail. She looked troubled. She tested the blade of the sword.

'Kranzinnport's cursed,' she said. 'Everyone knows that. There ain't none that would come here to trade. Sigmar help them if they're coming from the coast road,' she murmured. 'I only hope it's quick for them.'

'Get the others,' Odger told her. He picked up his spear. 'And find somewhere to hide.' His mouth was a grim line. 'If they get through the gates, then we need to know who they are and why they're coming to this forsaken place. We've survived far too much to take any chances.'

The coast road was a paved track ten feet wide, with runnels cut into it over the years by the passage of cart and wagon wheels. How many centuries must it have taken for those wheels to mark the flagstones, Amara wondered. She could imagine caravanserais coming in from the Living City in the north, bringing all the bounty of that fertile city, or strings of traders' wagons hacking in from the rougher country in the south-east of Yska. Silks and jewels, Aqua Ghyranis, bottled zephyrwine. Trappers and farmers and dealers, all bringing their wares to be loaded onto the ships in Kranzinnport's harbour at the base of the cliffs. Looming there above them on the bluff, the round grey domes and curlicued spires were silent, and the gates into the city, still a few miles distant, looked smashed and broken. According to the folk in the Amber Sap, Kranzinnport had a dark reputation now, and it seemed that no one came near it these days.

'I've seen more life in a cemetery,' Gotrek said warily. He had his axe in hand, gripping the haft, the brazier sputtering at his knuckles.

There was a short strip of feathered grass on Amara's left, on the other side of the track, and then the bluff fell away down to the churning sea. The cliffs were high, at least seven hundred feet, and the ocean as it spread out towards the rim of the realm, an unimaginable number of miles away, was like a sheet of dented steel. Whitecaps tumbled, the waves slopping and crashing, but it was all as far and distant as a dream. The sea was covered in a gauze of mist and the wind cracked and buffeted around them.

'Look,' Amara said. 'Can you see that?' She pointed into the wrack of spray. Out there, very faintly, she could see a smudge of darkness rising out of the waters, perhaps twenty miles distant. She felt a chill on her heart. 'Wither Island, I presume.'

'Aye,' Gotrek said. He gave the shape a dark stare. 'Looks like ships in the harbour there as well. Twin-masters, maybe two of them.'

The duardin's eyes were far sharper than her own, Amara realised. Gotrek gave the gates of the city a wary glance; they still had some distance to cover.

It had taken them three days to cross the rough country from Druhiel. Following the line of the forest, keeping an eye out for clouds of harrowbugs or for herds of the great horned yethars that would stampede and trample anyone foolhardy enough to cross their territory, they had hiked on until the forest drifted away to the north and the coast road had unravelled on the strip of bluff ahead of them. Each night they had stopped for a few hours of rest, but Amara knew the duardin could have just carried on by himself, as indefatigable as ever. She was supposed to be helping him, paying him back for saving her life, but more than once she had wondered if it was Gotrek who was helping her instead.

Take it from one who knows, he had told her. *Don't live as if the only thing you want to do is die.*

Did he see something in her, she wondered, something that

reflected what he saw inside himself? And did she truly want to die? Why else did she stride so confidently into every town and settlement she passed, insulting what people held most dear? It was as if only by suffering their violence could she expose their hypocrisy. But to what end? And when the men of Xil'anthos had dragged her to the pyre, how much of what she felt had been relief? Perhaps she had died in that valley after all, and everything that followed was just an echo of the life she had lost. Everything, until she had met Gotrek...

They hurried on to where the coast road merged into the avenue that led up into the city. The buildings were all clustered together, some of them hanging off the crags and outcrops of the cliffs, others stacked on top of each other in disjointed tiers. The broad frontages of the buildings were segmented like seashells, some of them looking more like the accretions of a coral reef. Wherever she looked, the windows of those buildings were dark and empty, the glass broken. The sun was still high, hidden behind its blanket of cloud, but no lamps were lit on the avenue and no streetlights seemed to flare in the streets beyond its calcified, overarching walls. There were smears of black soot against the grey stone, and here and there the battlements were shattered.

Amara kept a keen eye on the spread of forest a few miles to the north-east, and the long swathe of level ground between them. There were gatehouses on the sward, half a mile away, along with smallholdings and farms, simple cottages and crofts. No smoke billowed up from their chimneys and there was no sign of any workers in the fields, no cattle or flocks. The roofs of the houses looked like they had collapsed. There was a faint smell in the air, she realised, like a sickroom once the patient has succumbed and been carried away. A smell of emptied bowels, of old blood and vomit.

'You smell that?' Gotrek said. 'Reminds me of that bloody great tree in Druhiel.' He gave a great, lung-filling inhalation. 'Not quite the same fragrant bouquet, but near enough.' He looked at her and shook his head, disgust etched all over his battered face. 'Anytime you want to arm yourself, priest, you just let me know.'

'I'm no priest,' she said through gritted teeth. 'And I told you already – I will help, but I will not kill.'

'There's a comfort for a dwarf in his old age,' he grumbled.

The avenue that sloped on a steep gradient up to the broken gates of Kranzinnport was bordered on each side by a low balustrade of white marble. The stone was weathered by long years of exposure, but here and there Amara saw the stark white scars of recent damage. There were bloated vines coiling around the balusters, thick ropes of pale yellow ivy that looked like nothing so much as intestines. She didn't dare touch them. There were dead leaves and chips of stone underfoot, and scattered on the slope as they climbed she saw rusted military helmets and dribbles of dried slime. There were human bones as well, some of them still ruddy with dried blood, tossed heedlessly about the marble as if cast aside by some feeding beast.

'You still think those sea aelves have anything to do with this?' she said. She looked again out at the sea, but the two ships had slipped beneath the line of the cliffs. 'I thought you said they had flying sharks, not twin-masted schooners.' She kicked one of the bones and sent it skittering across the marble. 'And you never mentioned anything about eating human flesh.'

'For Maleneth's sake, I hope they've got something to do with it,' Gotrek glowered. The brazier of his axe seemed to flare up, casting a dangerous red glow across his face. His good eye went dark. Amara flinched at the sudden burn of anger in him. It was almost as though he was glad this Maleneth had been killed trying to save him. It gave him an endless source of rage, and Gotrek never seemed happier than at the prospect of turning that rage into violence. 'But even if not, I can promise a damned good thrashing to whoever's responsible for all this.'

They were halfway up the slope, the broken gates ahead of them yawning wide into the darkened depths of the city, when Amara heard the droning sound. At first she thought it was the harrowbugs again, but when she looked to the sky it was empty. No dark clouds were sweeping in from the forest, no swarms cutting in across the fields. She glanced at the farmland to the north, where the abandoned cottages and gatehouses lay isolated in their meagre fields, lonely wreckage huddled under an overbearing sky.

There, where the roofs had crumpled in, something began to stir. Amara saw a hump of green flesh swelling between the broken roof beams of a farmstead not fifty yards away. Plaster and masonry tumbled from the unsupported walls and then, with a dull, monotonous whine, hovering up from where they had been nesting, four Rot Flies stretched their oily, diaphanous wings and took to the sky.

They were bloated creatures, each as big as a horse, with a chitinous carapace and a vicious underslung stinger. Their bulbous eyes were flat and black, their long, spindly limbs trailing in the grass as they quickly covered the ground from the farmland to the avenue. Each was spotted with buboes and angry red boils. Rancid pus dripped from the cankers in their greasy abdomens. The stench of them billowed across the field as they swarmed near, a stomach-churning stink of rotten ordure and sour sweat.

'Run for the gates!' Amara cried. She grabbed Gotrek's shoulder but the duardin was immovable. He chuckled richly to himself, his feet planted on either side of the avenue while he hefted his rune-axe. There was a demented look on his face, leering and ecstatic all at once.

'Gotrek, what are you doing? We need to get under cover – now!'

'Come to me, my beauties,' he snarled. 'Doom awaits you, or my name's not Gotrek Gurnisson!'

The Rot Flies swept in, plump and sickly, three darting down with their stingers extended like swords, while the other droned towards the gates of the city to block their escape. The blurring beat of their wings wafted the stench down to the road. Amara felt the vomit surge in her throat. Gotrek seemed utterly unaffected. Roaring with laughter, he jumped up onto the edge of the balustrade and leapt, his rune-axe thrown back behind his head. His beard bristled like fire; his mohawk caught the sunlight like a crest of flame.

The blow nearly split the first Rot Fly in half. With a bellowed oath, Gotrek swept the blade clean through the bulbous sac of its head, chopping down until it had spewed its guts onto the marble of the avenue. Drenched in filth, he rolled across the ground as another fly came surging in, sweeping aside the stinger as it jabbed at him and then whipping round to hack the organ clean off. As the axe sheared away a chunk of the fly's belly, its heavy drone stuttered into a grinding shriek and it rose off into the sky. There was a coiled loop of guts hanging out of its abdomen, dribbling slime. Amara saw the monster crash into the fields beyond the edge of the city as it tried to haul itself back to its nest.

She ducked as another one of the flies bobbed above her. The flabby tube of its proboscis huffed out a blast of sour breath, while its dangling legs twitched above the balustrade. The wings were a blur of motion, like a streak of green flame. Its single black eye quivered in its socket like jelly and its leathery face was studded with wiry brown hairs. Retching at the stink, Amara snatched up a stone from the ground and pitched it as hard as she could. The shard of marble pierced the creature's eye, a stream of black ichor seeping out onto the ground. The fly reeled back for a moment, hissing, but then launched itself forwards as its proboscis, a foul, segmented pipe that dripped with slime, came slithering towards her.

Amara, not daring to take her eyes off the thing, fumbled on the ground beside her for another stone. She had vowed not to spill blood in Sigmar's name, but she would be damned if she'd let her life be snatched away by this disgusting monster. Humanity still had a chance to turn its back on the gods, but this foul creature was merely a deity's plaything, a toy of Nurgle sent down to torment the living for nothing more than dark amusement. She grabbed hold of a length of bone and swung it like a club, trying to force the monstrous fly back.

'Move yourself, lass!' Gotrek roared. Amara didn't think, just rolled out of the way instinctively. She saw a flash of red, a trail of fire from the brazier of the rune-axe. Gotrek sprinted along the edge of the balustrade and launched himself at the Rot Fly, swinging in mid-leap and hacking the tattered sheet of its wing clean off. Fatally unbalanced, the Rot Fly crashed to the ground, fizzing in anger, the awful proboscis slapping on the marble as Gotrek hit the ground and got to his feet. Grinning savagely, he stalked towards it as it quivered there, its torn eye rolling in its socket, blind and weeping.

'I grew out of swatting flies when I was a beardling,' he said. 'But there's nothing wrong with revisiting childish pleasures.'

A few blows from his axe and the thing was dead, the chitinous carapace hacked aside, the head smashed to pieces on the stone.

Amara hauled herself up and looked wildly to the gates at the other end of the avenue, where the last surviving Rot Fly had hunkered down to stop them escaping.

'The other one's coming in!' she cried. 'Gotrek, move!'

'No, damn it!' Gotrek snarled suddenly. He doubled over as if struck, one hand up to massage his chest. 'Not now, damn you to the hells, I won't...'

He screamed, but she could see it was not pain he felt; it was pure, unadulterated rage. His eye blazed with fire, and the rune hammered into his chest sparked with a low, rich flame.

'I'll carve you from my flesh myself, do you hear me!' he shouted. 'Damn you, Blackhammer, I'll hack this free and cast it into the deeps if it… If it *dares*…!'

Gotrek buckled over, bent double. The Rot Fly shivered and bumbled closer, the stinger in its abdomen flexing and dripping foul poisons. Amara, without thinking, leapt forwards and threw herself in front of Gotrek, swinging the bone she had snatched from the ground. She felt it connect against the creature's leathery hide, striking with a sound like a butcher chopping meat. The vibration shuddered up her arm and the bone split apart, leaving her with a shard in her hand as sharp as any blade. Amara stabbed and cut, slicing into the monster's flesh until it was dripping green slime onto the flagstones.

'Gotrek!'

Whatever force or pressure had gripped the duardin started to slacken. He had turned his indomitable will against it and taken control of himself again, and the rage burned more cleanly in his glittering eye. Then, as if responding to some distant call, the wounded Rot Fly raised its cankered head and gazed off towards the cliffs. Chattering and droning to itself, banking quickly to avoid Amara's strike, even as Gotrek pounded ahead with his axe, the Rot Fly rose up from the ground with a buffeting stench and withdrew.

'It's drawing off,' Amara said. Still holding her shard of splintered bone, she watched the creature bob across the edge of the cliff and head slowly over the sea. 'It's flying to Wither Island.' She looked at the carnage around them, the smeared guts and organs, the smashed corpses, Gotrek slathered head to foot in black ichor and green slime. He looked utterly demented. 'I don't blame it.'

Amara glanced up at the gates at the end of the avenue. 'Come on,' she said. 'We need to get inside the city in case that thing comes back with some friends. And we need to get you cleaned off, I dread to think what foul illnesses might be brewing inside those monsters.'

Gotrek nodded, wiping off his axe on the edge of the balustrade. He ran his palm across his face and flicked the slime onto the ground, and then followed Amara as she cautiously jogged up the slope towards the gates. Amara glanced at the rune in his chest, as dull as brass. For a moment there she had thought he was going to rip it from his body, even if it killed him.

'That rune,' she said. 'It's more than just a Fyreslayer rune, isn't it? I've known Fyreslayers, but I've never seen anything like it before.'

Gotrek grunted, and for a moment he said nothing. He seemed to be struggling with something, a decision he didn't want to make, but then he said, 'Aye, it's more than the daft trinkets those fire dwarfs hammer into themselves. Krag Blackhammer's master rune,' he grumbled, tapping it with the edge of his axe. 'Bloody thing. Can't get it out of me now. Not even sure if I want to, or if...'

'What?'

Gotrek scowled. 'You can turn your back on the gods,' he said, 'but they're jealous bastards, all of them. Turns out they can't leave any of us alone. But I'll be damned if I'll let this thing take me over again, I swear it!'

The anger flared up in him again; he bared his teeth in a snarl, his massive shoulders flexing as he gripped his axe.

'Everything always pushing me in the same direction,' he said, looking up at the grey walls of the city. There was pain in his voice, Amara heard. Pain and regret. 'The gods, the past. Even people, ordinary people. Doing what they can, striving, surviving, but always expecting someone to save them – Sigmar, or Alarielle, or even Grimnir. But no one's coming to save us, no one at all. Got to do it yourself. That's all there is to it.'

His voice drifted off into a grumbling mutter. Amara could see that he wasn't talking to her any more. Whomever or whatever he was arguing with, it was deep inside him, lost in the mists of his past, in the trials that had led to Maleneth's death, or that had caused him to have this rune struck into his body in the first place. She didn't understand any of it, but she knew that whatever he was saying, Gotrek would not turn aside from anyone who needed help. He had saved her life when she was nothing to him, and he was ready to charge out of Druhiel with no more notion of what he was facing other than it might get him revenge for a friend who had died.

'You're a riddle, Gotrek Gurnisson,' she said. 'I don't think I've ever met someone as reckless with their life as you, but who seems to resent being asked to risk it all the same.'

Gotrek grinned savagely at her, his mood swept away once more.

'It's the asking I resent, lass,' he chuckled. 'Never the risking.'

They reached the gates, the black ironoak smashed aside, each door leaning drunkenly against the jamb. Amara peered into the street beyond. It was an empty avenue flanked by tall, flat-fronted buildings, the facades tiled with pale shells. There was an abandoned guardhouse just inside the gates, a crust of blood on the floor. The street as it stretched away from them was littered with dust and shards of stone, rusting weapons and scraps of cloth.

'Looks like an army's been through here,' Gotrek said. His voice boomed through the canyon of the street. He strode on purposefully, not in the least bit cautious. He stooped to pick up a notched sword. 'Someone put up a fight at least, but I don't see any bodies.'

'Gotrek!' Amara hissed. Carefully she scanned the higher floors of the buildings that loomed above them. 'Keep your voice down, you sound like a bullgor roaring in the charge.' She sighed. He was like a child in many ways, scornful and impulsive, and it was almost impossible to tell him what to do regardless of whether it was for his own good or not.

She still had the splintered human bone in her hand, she realised. With a grimace she leaned it up against the guardhouse, careful not to make any sound. Every crunch of their footsteps scraped around the walls of the street, and even their very breath seemed to echo uncomfortably. Pressed against the wall, Amara slipped forwards while Gotrek strode determinedly down the middle of the road.

It was true what he had said – it did look as if an army had swept through Kranzinnport. There was rubble in the street, broken doors and windows, discarded weapons and armour. There had been hard fighting at the gates, it was clear, but even the upper floors of the tenements and the high, spiralling towers were blown out and blackened. Signs of war, and signs of something else as well – a thick, slimy moss growing between the flagstones, ropes of diseased ivy clambering up the walls. Wherever she turned there was a stink of rot and excrement, the high, sweet scent of corrupted flesh. But no matter where she looked, Amara could see no bodies. Someone, the survivors of Kranzinnport perhaps, must have buried or burned them. *Or,* she thought with a grim shudder, *someone has taken them away for another purpose entirely.*

'There's not a soul here,' Gotrek said.

'And I doubt many could have escaped with those creatures guarding the entrance at the coast road,' Amara agreed. 'Remember what the barkeep said in Druhiel, they haven't had word out of Kranzinnport for some time.'

Gotrek tugged his beard and frowned. 'Then where is everybody? It pains me to confess it, lass, but I think you're right – those damned sea aelves aren't the culprits here.' He ran his thumb down the blade of his axe. 'More's the bloody pity.'

The avenue stretched on towards an open space ahead, a market-place similarly littered with the wreckage of defeat. The remains of a barricade blocked the entrance to the square from the street, a feeble barrier of broken barrels, planks of wood, chairs and tables from some tavern or another. It reminded Amara of the pyre they had built for her in Xil'anthos. For a moment she felt the heat of the flames again, the stench of smoke, and the sweat came easily to her brow. She wiped her forehead. The barrier here had been smashed aside and was no more than splintered wreckage now, crusted with blood and dried slime. As she stopped to examine it, a feathered moth as big as her fist lifted up from a length of wood and sailed lightly into the air, scattering off like a rag caught in the breeze as it headed to the north.

There was a crunch of stone and the sharp scrape of steel being drawn from a scabbard. Amara whipped round and saw an arrow pointing at her from an upstairs window. Two more joined it, bows wielded by women with angry, reckless eyes, their lank hair tied back from their faces. Slowly Amara pivoted to look at the other side of the street, where three men had slipped from the broken windows with swords and axes in their hands. Two of them were older, hard-faced and grim; the other was a younger man barely old enough to shave. Their faces were smeared with dirt, their clothes torn and dusty, and it didn't look as if they had eaten in some time. Gotrek stood there with a supercilious look on his face, leaning casually on his axe as if none of this both-ered him in the slightest.

'We don't mean any harm,' Amara said. She held her hands up.

A door swung open on a shattered hinge and a man with a patchy beard and a spear in his hand emerged from the shadows. Amara recognised the look on his face. There was anger there, but it was outweighed by his grief. She had the feeling that if she looked in a mirror she would see the same thing.

The man stepped down into the street, the blade of his weapon pointed directly at her.

'We're allies,' Amara said again, as she looked him in the eye. 'I swear it.'

'I'll be the judge of that,' the man said. 'And I'll cut you both down where you stand if I think otherwise.'

CHAPTER TEN

THE REMNANTS

They took Gotrek and Amara deeper into the streets, moving quickly and silently, their weapons raised. They passed from the gatehouse to a narrow alleyway that ran along the side of the city walls, and every step of the way Amara could feel the spear point resting lightly in the small of her back. She glanced up as they moved. The battlements above her were shattered in places, the crenellations like broken teeth. Dried slime was thick on the cobblestones. She risked a glance over her shoulder at the bearded man but she couldn't read his intentions at all. He looked like someone who had only made it this far by killing first and questioning himself after. The others held their swords and bows at the ready, two of them scouting in front, always scouring the rooftops for danger.

Amara looked at Gotrek, but the duardin still seemed unconcerned. These might be desperate people pushed to the limits of their endurance, but they were still civilians as far as she could see, and she doubted Gotrek saw them as any kind of threat. If he went with them as they hustled their prisoners further into the city, then it was only out of some mild curiosity to see where it would all end. He was an enigma, she thought. You couldn't predict from one moment to the next what he was going to do or how he would react, to anything.

They came to the edge of an open square. One of the women with a bow, lean and with limp black hair, her face so drawn that it looked chiselled out of stone, carefully scouted around the corner. The square was deserted, littered here and there with overturned crates, broken barrels, scraps of dirty cloth. The aqualith in the centre was dry and clogged with weeds. Further on to their left was a broken doorway that opened onto a flight of stairs leading down into what must have been a storeroom or cellar. The man with the spear jerked his head towards the door.

'Down here,' he said. He glanced quickly at the empty square and then hustled them down the stairs.

The cellar was dark and grimy, the rough stone floor covered in patches of oil, and the only light came from a barred window high up in the wall. There was a smell in the air of stale beer and spilled wine; a tavern's storeroom, Amara thought.

'Up against the wall,' the man muttered. He gave a quick thrust with his spear.

Amara did as he said, and with maddening nonchalance Gotrek did the same. The man stepped back slightly, spear at the ready, his comrade with a drawn sword standing at his side. Amara was acutely aware of the two women holding their bows ready, the strings still loose so they didn't lose any tension and the arrows nocked.

'What brings you here?' he demanded. 'Who sent you? Them? Speak, or I swear we'll cut you down where you stand.'

'We're here to help,' Amara said. She spread her hands. 'We were in Druhiel not three days past and have seen some of what ails you here.'

'What do you mean?' the man demanded. He darted a look at Gotrek, who stood there still covered in slime. 'What do you know of what ails us in Kranzinnport?'

'Terrible diseases,' Amara said. 'People mutated by hideous infections, driven mad until they're more monsters than men. We've seen ordinary folk corrupted in moments to become mindless killers, intent only on spreading their infection to everyone they can reach.'

One of the women lowered her bow very slightly. She glanced at the man with the spear, a troubled look on her face. Amara hurried on.

'They worship Alarielle there,' Amara said. 'Their sacred tree sickened, became diseased or mutated in some way. Whatever it was, the tree attacked people, began to spread some awful distemper. We heard tell of a similar disease afflicting the forests out this way. Some folk we met in Druhiel said that Kranzinnport itself had been abandoned.'

'It's not abandoned!' the other woman cried. Her arrow was taut against the string and it was pointed straight at Gotrek. 'We're still here, aren't we? Sigmar knows, we're still here!'

'You might not be for much longer,' Gotrek rumbled, 'if you keep pointing that bloody arrow at me.'

'It's only a matter of time, Odger!' the woman shouted. 'Look at him, he's been exposed. He'll turn, like Farroway turned, and then it'll be too late. Kill him now!'

'Hold, Merosis,' the man she had called Odger said. 'We don't know if it's like Farroway, not yet.'

'What happened to Farroway?' Amara said quickly. Anything to distract them a moment longer.

Odger lowered his spear an inch. A spasm of pain passed across his face. He ran his fingers through his beard and his eyes were distant, as if looking once more onto a scene too grim for him to bear.

'Let me guess,' Gotrek said. The roughness was gone from his voice. Amara might almost have said he spoke kindly. 'He caught whatever this infection was and you had to deal with him.'

'The man was a friend of mine,' Odger said distantly. 'Known him all my life. And I had to do that to him...'

'Kill them,' the woman called Merosis said. She drew back her bowstring. 'Kill them, Odger, we can't take the chance. Look at the state of the duardin, he's covered in that filth.'

'I can vouch for him,' Amara said. She held her hands out, a cold feeling deep in her stomach. 'You know duardin have far hardier constitutions than humans, and believe me, it would take a lot more than this to bring him down.'

'Odger, we've made it this far,' Merosis growled. 'Sigmar knows we've had to do terrible things to stay alive, and we can't risk letting them live. They could be spies for all we know.'

'Do we look like bloody spies?' Gotrek laughed. 'Even I can admit that we don't exactly blend in now, lass, do we?'

'Let's everyone just calm down,' Amara said. 'You're scared, it's understandable, but we're not spies and Gotrek's not infected. We only want to know what's happened here.'

'Gotrek, that your name?' Odger lowered his spear another inch.

'Aye. Gotrek Gurnisson, although it's a damned cheek to ask a dwarf's name at arrow point, if you ask me.' He looked around the cramped, stinking cellar, at the hard faces that were arrayed against him. He shrugged. 'Although given what you've gone through, I'd be willing to let it pass. I can't say fairer than that.'

'I'm Amara Fidellus,' Amara said, still with her hands spread wide. 'I'm unarmed.' She ignored Gotrek's derisive snort. 'You can see that we mean no harm.'

'Odger, I swear...' Merosis said. Amara could hear the creak of her bowstring.

The other woman slowly stepped forward. She was younger

than Merosis, her dirty blonde hair cut raggedly about her face. 'Sigmar,' she whispered. She reached out for Amara's hand. Amara felt Gotrek tense beside her. 'Look, all of you.'

She took Amara's hand in her own and gently drew back the sleeve of the tattered robe. The tattoo on the inside of Amara's wrist was revealed: the sign of Ghal Maraz, the hammer of Sigmar. The sign of the warrior priest.

'See,' the woman said. She looked into Amara's eyes and smiled. 'They're telling the truth. I know it.' She turned to Odger. 'Sigmar has sent them. They're on our side.'

'Baffin…' Odger began, but after a moment of tense silence the grief and anger in his eyes faded to a dull resignation.

'Lower your weapons,' he said wearily.

Merosis, wrestling with her anger, lowered her bow.

'My name's Odger Pellin,' the man said. He gave a bitter laugh as he rested on his spear. 'And I suppose I should welcome you to Kranzinnport, or what's left of it.'

'What happened to this place?' Amara asked him.

Odger shook his head. 'Not here,' he said. He beckoned to Merosis. 'Scout ahead, see there's nothing waiting for us on the other side of the square.' He glanced at Amara and Gotrek one last time, as if he was still weighing up the decision. 'We'll get somewhere safer first. You don't want to get caught out in the open if those monsters are still around.'

They left the cellar and the survivors led them around the edge of the square, careful not to walk across open ground. Deep into the streets they jogged, scouting ahead at corners, ducking through smashed buildings, always scanning the rooftops and the alleyways that stretched away on either side. Wherever she looked, Amara could see the evidence of taint in the rubble. There were drifts of rotting leaves piled against the walls, sprays of pus-yellow ferns erupting from the cracked flagstones, a pervasive ammonia stink threading through the avenues. Plump green Bloat Flies lumbered through the air at head height. Dark shapes that she hoped were just rats skittered away into the drains. There were glutinous smears of dirt on the ground, which all of the survivors were careful to avoid. Amara ran where they ran, trying to memorise the route back to the gates so she could retrace it if need be. She might have made them trust her and Gotrek, but she wouldn't entirely trust them herself until she knew what was going on here.

They reached what must have once been a governor's mansion or council building on the other side of a flagstone precinct. It was a wide residence with high windows and gabled arches, and a tall double door standing open at the top of a low flight of stairs. There were statues on either side of the door holding up the entablature, caryatids of blank-faced female warriors with tridents and nets. The stairs were cratered and broken, and Amara could see that the windows had all been smashed.

'In here,' Odger said. He stood at the door, scanning the street while the rest of them slipped inside.

The hall was covered in wreckage. There were toppled statues, clumps of plaster that had fallen from the ceiling, broken boxes and baskets. They passed on deeper into the building, heading up a spiral staircase to an upper floor. They came out into a long corridor that was barricaded at the far end, with another set of doors beyond it. Two young men crouched at the barricade, spears in their hands, their eyes wide when they saw the new arrivals. They were little more than children, Amara realised.

'Watkyn,' Odger said. 'Tell Aybel we're back. And tell him we've got some new friends with us.'

The room beyond these doors looked like it had once been a council debating chamber or a meeting room. A long table of polished swamp mahogany had been pushed to one side and was covered in what few supplies the survivors had managed to gather. A low fire crackled in the grate on the far side, providing only a little heat. There were buckets of water against the other wall and a ladder leading up to a hole that had been cut in the ceiling. A handful of other men and women crouched by the broken windows, keeping watch on the square. Some of them seemed young and eager; others were older, middle-aged, weary with the rigours of survival in a city that was already dead.

'This is where the Commerce Committee met,' Odger told her. 'I can't tell you the number of times I've sat through meetings in this room, nodding off I was so bored. Now look at it...' He turned to Gotrek. 'You can clean up over there,' he said, pointing to a corner of the room. There was a tin bathtub, a few buckets of water and a rough sheet for privacy, but Gotrek had no need of it. He stood in the corner and slathered the slime from his skin, grunting and huffing at the cold water, combing his beard and his mohawk with his stubby fingers.

The rest of them huddled around the fire. When Amara shared what remained of the dried food she'd bought in Druhiel, they fell on it ravenously.

'Is this all that's left of you?' she said, glancing around at the scattered survivors. 'Isn't there anyone else remaining in the city?'

'There are more,' Odger said, when he'd checked on the sentries at the windows. 'Can't say how many exactly, but we try not to gather in large groups. Easier to stay safe if you can't be detected.'

'There's Brisker's group over in the Warrens,' Merosis said. 'Kelter and some of the reservists from the guard were in the tanning yards over on the northern side.' She shook her head and her hair fell over her face. 'Although I haven't heard from them in some time.'

'Brisker,' Odger said, with a faint laugh. 'Takes more than the end of the world to get rid of that old sod. He's tougher than those rock cakes he used to bake.'

'What happened here?' Amara asked him.

'It started… I don't know how long ago now.' Odger slumped down beside the fire. He looked exhausted. 'One afternoon, late in the day, the whole coast was covered by this bank of dark cloud. More than a storm cloud, if you can imagine it – something dark and unearthly, rolling across the waters, sparking with green lightning. We all saw it rising up from the sea, far out over the water there. Thought it was a kraken at first, though they're just legends, so they say. Took a while before people realised it was an island, a spur of land twenty miles out. It was covered in this layer of mist, so you couldn't rightly see it, but you could tell it was there. No one had a good feeling about it. Then the rain began to fall. It wasn't natural either. It stank like swamp water, and where it touched the grass or the trees they began to die. Everyone knew, somehow we *knew*, that it was an ill omen, all of it. Gods…' He stared into the low flames in the fireplace. 'If only we'd known how ill that omen truly was. This town has survived orruk raids and bandit slavers attacking our walls. We've weathered everything that's ever been thrown at us. This, though…'

'Did anyone try sailing over to this island, exploring, see what was there?' Gotrek said. He wiped his face on a dirty cloth as he came over to the fireplace. Odger made space for him and Gotrek squatted on the ground, warming his palms. As they sat side by side, Amara couldn't help but note the contrast between the wiry, underfed humans and the brooding, bull-necked duardin. He might have only come up to their chests, but she was sure he could tear them all in half without breaking a sweat.

'Some did,' Odger continued. 'A few fishermen took their boats out to investigate. But they didn't come back.'

'Folk started getting sick,' Baffin said. 'Same as the trees and the grass, they started withering away – I suppose that's why it's called Wither Island. It seemed to bring nothing but distemper to the city.'

'Started with a cough,' Odger added. 'Mild at first, then getting worse and worse over the course of the day. Got so bad that folk afflicted by it were hacking their lungs up by the evening. We tried to quarantine them, but then with all the plants and the crops in the fields starting to rot, we got all these flies appearing, and the flies seemed to spread the disease even further. People found maggots bursting from their skin, and they coughed up this green slime that… Well, whatever plague it was, it ripped right through Kranzinnport. Didn't even kill everyone, not exactly. Some started to… They started to *change*.'

'Aye,' Gotrek growled. 'And I can imagine what into.'

Amara leaned forwards. 'We saw something similar in Druhiel,' she said. 'Those infected by the tree, they started to mutate.'

'Neiglen's Gift, that's what it is,' Merosis cut in. 'The growths, the boils and cankers, and everything with it. Gods,' she spat, turning to Odger. 'If Druhiel's infected now, then what's left? Xil'anthos? The whole coast's drowning in it, and how much longer before the Living City's in the path of this plague? We've got no chance, none! We're just waiting to die here!'

Despite her hard young face, Amara could see the tears brimming in her eyes. She was on the edge of despair, and there was no more dangerous place to be in a situation like this.

'What about the people?' Amara said. 'What happened to them?'

'The ships came,' Odger said. He picked a thread from his filthy tunic and tossed it into the fire. 'Fired on the city with their cannons, smashed up most of the buildings. There were *things* in the cannon-balls as well. Flies, specks of disease floating thick in the air, ticks that burrowed under your skin. People were losing their minds, there was panic everywhere. Some folk tried to run, but the coast road was blocked by those monsters you saw. They'd fly down and pluck folk off the path, and then take them away to their nests. Sigmar knows what happened to them after that.'

'Hosts for their eggs, I'd imagine,' Gotrek said flatly. 'Not the most pleasant way to die.'

Amara gave him a scathing glance. The duardin gave an innocent shrug. Odger blanched and looked sick, but he rallied himself. He was utterly worn out by the stresses of surviving, but there was still a solid core there that kept him going. Rage, hatred, a bloody-minded will to continue – whatever it was, he wasn't ready to give up yet.

'Once the ships took the harbour, then the raiders came. Pirates, reavers, utterly ruthless, all of them touched by Neiglen's Gift as well. More than touched. If they were men once, I don't know what they are now. Monsters, I call them – huge, lumbering things armed to the teeth. They have no pity in them, none, and they *laughed* as they cut us down.'

'They wanted us alive,' Merosis said. She clawed back her hair from her forehead. Her cheeks were hollow, her eyes ringed by dark circles. 'Saw my mother and father snatched by them, hauled to the ground in nets, chained up and dragged off to their ships.' She grimaced, and drew a thumbnail down the length of her dagger.

'My wife,' Odger said. 'My son…' He looked around, but he couldn't meet the others' eyes. 'All of us have a story like that, of those who have been taken from us. There was a raid not half a day before you came, but we hid from it and they didn't find us. Don't know about anyone else though. Maybe that's what happened to Kelter's lot.'

'Why didn't you try to sail out through the harbour to escape?' Gotrek asked. 'Place like this, must have had a fair few boats going spare.'

'The harbour was blocked by those ships to start with,' Baffin said. She wiped her eyes with the back of her hand. 'Some tried, but it's a long way down to the harbour. The cage lifts made too much noise, and if you took the tunnels...'

'There are things in the tunnels,' Odger told them. 'Beasts of some kind, things out of nightmare. We're trapped in here. Waiting, just waiting for the raiders to come back and round up the rest of us. But for what reason, only Sigmar knows.'

'And if he knows,' Amara muttered, 'then he is not telling.' She looked at Gotrek, saw the glint in his eye, the set of his massive jaw beneath the blood-red beard. 'These are the games of the gods,' she said to Odger. 'And it is Kranzinnport's misfortune to be caught up in them.'

'You're a priest of Sigmar,' Baffin said. She reached out and touched Amara's wrist, looked again on the hammer tattoo there with something like reverence. 'Haven't you come here to help us, to bring Sigmar's grace to the city? For we're pious folk here in Kranzinnport, I swear! We worship Sigmar in all things!' She turned to Odger, almost pleading. 'Tell them, we do!'

Amara pulled her wrist away. 'I am no priest,' she said angrily. She sighed and ran a palm over her close-cropped hair. 'And I do not know what fate brought us here, but I owe this duardin a debt. I will be with him until it is paid, and unless I mistake him entirely, I would say that Gotrek will not let you down. We'll help any way we can, even if that means heading out to Wither Island. As for myself, I will not sit by and see ordinary folk tormented by the whims of the divine.'

Gotrek scowled and turned to face the fire. Amara could see the flames reflected in the rune on his chest, in the black eye that squinted into the flickering light. He said nothing, despite all the eyes that were turned on him, and the hope that shone so clearly in them.

'Regardless,' Odger said. 'We can do nothing for the moment.

Dusk is on us now, and it's always more dangerous after dark. We need to rest.' He gave a weary smile. 'The food you have brought, and the sense that we are not entirely alone, has been more of a gift than you know. At dawn we can show you the entrance to the harbour tunnels and the cage lifts, although, I must tell you, you would be taking your lives in your hands.'

'We'll judge it in the morning,' Amara said. She stood up from the fire and sought a corner where she could lie down to sleep. Stepping past Gotrek she gave him a wary look, but the duardin was silent, lost still in the flames as they flickered and died.

It took her hours to fall asleep, wrapped in her robes with her head resting on the bare floorboards. She felt she had transgressed somehow by offering their help in Gotrek's name. How well did she know this half-mad duardin anyway? What was this certainty she had, that he would help these people without question? Amara had expected him to erupt with anger when he heard these folks' stories, but the tales seemed to have done nothing but plunge him into a deep depression instead. For the bare week she had spent in his company, Gotrek seemed to her capricious, unpredictable and wholly erratic. He was gripped by moods so violent that they threatened to undo his very sanity, but then just as quickly they could fade away and send him blundering off on another avenue entirely. And yet, whatever force was in him, she knew it was guided towards good and not evil. Gotrek was no one's idea of a perfect champion – he looked like a hog, and he certainly stank like one; he drank heavily and he was capable of the most astonishing violence. But things like this, where ordinary people were caught in a dark web not of their own making, seemed to provoke him like no other. Was it just his disappointment that these sea aelves were clearly not involved? Had he hoped to slaughter them in revenge for Maleneth's death, and then–

No, Amara suddenly realised. She rolled onto her side and saw

Gotrek sitting slumped in a corner of the room, his good eye closed and his axe resting across his knees. It was not just that he wanted to drown his pain in violence against those who had killed his friend. It was that he wanted the chance to die fighting them, and it was as though she had taken that chance away from him.

CHAPTER ELEVEN

THE RITE

Night was falling over the island. The sky that lowered on its valleys and ranges, that settled like a blanket on its putrid spread of jungle, was livid as a bruise. This was always the time when the Grandfather was closest to those who loved him, Bilgeous knew. This was a holy moment, that cusp of the day when it decayed into evening, when the rot of night enveloped the dusk only to brighten to a new and abiding dawn once more. It was Nurgle's holy cycle written in the very stars, in the passage of the realm-spheres as they brought light and shade to all the living things beneath them. And all things that live must die, and rot, and be reborn anew, again and again, for time without end.

The prisoners they had taken from Kranzinnport lumbered along the muddy track from the harbour, following its trail through the thickset trees. Strange creatures, studded with boils, slipped uneasily through the upper branches. Bloat Flies rose from the night-blooming flowers, trailing a stink of vomit. Rot Flies, their larger brethren, hovered noisily above the canopy. Here and there, lamps of a green luminescence had been hung from the branches, and they cast down an eerie glow onto the scene.

The prisoners shrieked and sobbed with terror as they were thrashed along the path. Some of them darted frightened glances at the Maggotkin cultists who guarded their flanks with whip and trident, desperately searching for a hint of human feeling to spare them this agony. Some of the prisoners only wept sadly to themselves, resigned to whatever dark fate they imagined awaited them. Bilgeous, following behind, wanted to reassure them – it was only as dark as their fear made it. In truth, if they would only see, it was a wonderful thing they were doing here. They should be rejoicing as they threaded their way through the jungle. They should be dancing and singing hymns of praise, laughing and joking amongst themselves, eager to reach their destination in the sure knowledge that they were all joined together in the midst of a joyous venture.

Alas, Bilgeous thought to himself with a sigh. *There are none so blind as those who will not see.*

The track opened out after half a mile into a wide clearing, perhaps fifty yards across. The trees and the scrub that encircled it rustled with motion, with night-seeing eyes eager to watch the festivities. The lamps hanging from tall poles of twisted rotwood made the clearing near as bright as day, and so it was with much agonised distress that the prisoners looked onto what was laid out before them.

'No! For Sigmar's sake, please!' one of them cried, a rangy old man who surely was too close to a natural death to deny himself this opportunity. He struggled against his chains, tried to drag himself away, until a loping cultist cuffed him savagely on the temple. The old man sagged against his bindings, crying miserably to himself.

Come, come, Bilgeous wanted to say to them, but he was ever conscious of his station. *Is this any way to behave? Show some dignity, my friends!*

Before them, and almost as large as the clearing itself, was an open pit that simmered and seethed with thousands of rotting corpses. Limbs poked from the tumbled mass. Hands reached out in agonised claws, their fingernails black. Slumped bodies heaved and flopped with all the pressures of decay. Rising from deep beneath the surface, bubbles of ichor popped with a deathly stench.

On the other side of the pit, a dozen plump creatures, like wingless Rot Flies, slobbered to the edge. Their bulbous eyes were glazed with slime, and instead of a proboscis, each had a blubbery sac for a mouth, the lips peppered with warts. One by one they coughed and retched over the pit, and then spewed out a jet of foaming green liquor that splattered onto the corpses. Where the liquid touched the dead flesh, it began to smoke and dissolve. The stench was overwhelming: the reek of unwashed feet, digestive acids and diarrhoea.

Screams cut across the night. The prisoners writhed against their bonds and cried out for mercy, but there would be no mercy for them now. They were too important. Didn't they see? They were essential to this holy venture. They were doing Nurgle's work in the Mortal Realms.

Bilgeous clambered up onto a low, rocky platform on the other side of the pit and allowed himself a moment to breathe it all in. Behind the shroud of his mouldering hood, he closed his eyes and fell into reminiscence. Once more he was striding in the vanguard of Nurgle's legions, following the march of Bolathrax all those centuries ago as the spreading miasma colonised the feeble greenery of Alarielle's realm.

He saw again the Great Unclean One's mighty antlers dripping with filth, proud against the darkening sky. Once more he felt the pestilential rains spattering onto his skin. They had been so close back then, *so close*… But as life itself surges and decays and falls to ruin, so must the hopes and efforts of all who serve the Grandfather. It was the way of things, not to be denied, though every seeming defeat was only a moment of abeyance in the grand scheme of the cycle. As the wheel turns, what was beneath rises up to the top once more.

Bilgeous had spent many a century since their defeat in the Everspring Swathe hiding in the swamps of Thyria, planning and plotting and waiting for the opportune moment to strike back. Not for personal glory, or even for the chance of victory against the Grandfather's misguided enemies, but only so that he could praise him in the most exalted way possible. In a simple hut he had built from swamp root and brush, he had sat and pondered the higher mysteries. Long had he brooded on the nature of change and decay, thinking deeply about the myths and legends that had accrued to the Grandfather in the ages before the Mortal Realms had fully come to be. Alone, communing with the King of All Flies, taking care of the humble creatures he sent to comfort him, Bilgeous waited until his god showed him a sign. And then at last, after centuries of waiting and praying, the vision came to him one night while he lay on his simple cot. He saw the seas boiling, and an island rising that had long been lost in the deeps – an island that was itself a shard of Papa Nurgle, cratered with rot and as fecund as the Garden itself. As the Grandfather's foot had once walked on these realms, so a fragment of his toenail had been left behind, and from that fragment something wonderful could emerge.

Bilgeous saw a frenzy of decay spilling out from that island across the seas. He saw the Rocanian Coast, and Yska, and then the whole of Thyria, succumbing to that tide. He saw the Garden regrown in the lands of Ghyran, and new armies rising that would sweep all before them, and at their head an aspect of the Grand-father himself to lead them all… At last, Bilgeous had known what he must do. He had wandered in the wilds of Ghyran for an age, spreading his message, scattering his disease, until he had gathered his disciples to help him bring his vision to fruition.

He had tasted the Garden once, and now all would taste the Garden in turn.

Bilgeous drew himself back to the present moment. The screams of the prisoners intruded into his mind once more as he shifted his weight against his staff. The scrolls rustled on his belt and the pouches slapped their wet leather against his thigh. He smiled benignly on the gathered prisoners as they looked with horror at the pit. No doubt some of them saw the faces of friends and family in that green stew, which certainly explained their distress, but Bilgeous now had little time to waste. Like a cook tending his pot, he knew the recipe required constant attention if the meal was not to be spoiled, and what he was cooking here was infinitely more important than any mere repast. In fact, he mused, realising there was a more apt metaphor, he was more midwife than cook here, and the confinement was reaching its most crucial moment. He had not a moment to lose.

He closed his eyes, reached out with his mind to gather in and weave the threads of magic that were so strong here they almost overwhelmed him. They felt like ropes of spiderweb, like cords of sinew and muscle slippery with rot. He could almost taste them on his tongue.

'Now,' he commanded, his voice strident across the clearing, cutting over even the desperate cries of the captives. 'Let us join ourselves together and bring forth new life from old decay.'

The cultists slumped forwards, roughly pushing the prisoners to the edge of the pit, thrashing them with their whips or beating them with their cudgels. The men and women of Kranzinnport cried out and begged for their lives, some falling to their knees and praying to a god who could no longer hear them. Not here, Bilgeous thought. Not as we gather on this shard of the Grandfather's limitless, cheerful grace.

The knives came out. Throats were cut, skulls were beaten in, and bodies tumbled one by one into the soup. The screams rose above the canopy of the jungle, exciting the Rot Flies as they danced and swooped through the humid night air. At the side of the pit the flabby creatures puked their slime onto the corpses, and as the flesh began to melt into a rich, pullulating mass, Bilgeous Pox wove his spells in holy ecstasy. Piece by piece, he framed the architecture of the rite. Invisible to all who might have chanced to look upon it, but as dazzling as the stars to Bilgeous himself, he stretched the ladder of his prayer up into the void and down into the deeps, linking each with each, and giving the Grandson the handholds to haul himself out of the aether.

The soup in the pit gurgled and belched. The shimmering mass of corpses rose and fell like an ebbing tide. The surface bulged like a great eye, the sclera shot through with streaks of red and green – but then, as Bilgeous harnessed the magics that flickered through the air, the bubble slackened and fell back, and the surface simmered once more like a pot on a low boil. Maggots writhed through the fester, feeding on the dead. Blood steamed in the warmth of the night, and the flies fizzed across the lens of slime.

It was not enough.

Bilgeous felt the rage kindle in the shrivelled purse of his belly. Every prisoner they had taken from Kranzinnport, every throat they had slit and every corpse they had tossed into the mire, and it still wasn't enough! The caul had caught around the Grandson's face and held him fast, and no matter how fierce the ritual he weaved, it would take even more of this holy mulch to free him.

That imbecile Pertussis! Bilgeous raged inwardly, feeling the invisible patterns of the rite blend back into the muggy air. He could imagine the captain and his pirate Blightkings bumbling through the ruins of Kranzinnport, pillaging and destroying, drinking and sporting rather than getting on with what they had been commanded to do. How many people remained in that unhappy city, who should by rights be mouldering in this pit? Cholerax was right, these pirates couldn't be trusted. Where was the discipline, the urgency! If it weren't for Pertussis' ships and the warriors he brought, Bilgeous would have sent him packing weeks ago.

He sighed richly, took a deep breath of the stench that rose up from the rotting corpses. True, he admitted, the rite had been more difficult than he had assumed. However many bodies they tossed into the pit, it always seemed to demand more. It was a work the likes of which he had never attempted before, and it had drawn on every aspect of his sorcerous abilities, but then why should he have expected anything less? He had been gifted an extraordinary honour here, and he would not waste it.

The cultists rattled the chains they had taken off the prisoners and milled about the clearing, awaiting instruction. He would have to send the pirates back immediately to complete the task they had been given, and hopefully this time the last of the survivors would be rounded up more efficiently. The spheres had held in perfect conjunction for days now, but soon they would wing their way across the cosmos and the moment would be lost. A hundred years would pass before they fell into the same essential pattern, strengthening the dark magics he drew upon, and Bilgeous could not wait that long. Not after the centuries he had already spent in hopeful prayer, hiding in the swamps, begging Nurgle to show him a sign. The Grandson would be born into the Mortal Realms, and the Mortal Realms would suffer torments unparalleled. He swore it.

There was a crash of broken undergrowth along the path back to the harbour. Bilgeous dismissed the cultists as Lord Cholerax flew hastily into the clearing, mounted on his Rot Fly and with his scythe across his knees. The lazy beat of the fly's wings sent up a scattering of dead leaves, the glistening hook of its stinger scratching across the dirt.

'You seem agitated, Lord Cholerax,' Bilgeous said. He clambered down from the platform with the help of his staff. 'Is anything the matter?'

'That remains to be seen,' Cholerax said. The flesh of his calves bulged over his rusted greaves as he slipped down from the saddle. His goitre quivered as he waddled over towards the sorcerer, and the mouth he kept secret behind his breastplate gave a soft chitter that Cholerax silenced with a slap of his tentacle. 'A Rot Fly has returned from the gates of Kranzinnport.'

'Your beast has abandoned its post? Most unusual,' Bilgeous said with a frown.

'If so, it is only out of self-preservation. Alas, for all my affection for the blessed creatures, the flies are too low a thing for us to fully understand. But from what I can gather, there may have been a rebellion or an attack on Kranzinnport. Three of the flies have been killed, and only the fourth has escaped to warn us.'

Bilgeous halted on the path. He tried to collect his thoughts.

'Is this true? What force would be capable, so near? I can think only of Druhiel, but they should be busy with their own concerns by now. Disease spreads even to the eaves and bowers of their forest.'

'I know not,' Cholerax admitted. 'And from the fly's garbled mewlings it seems the force is no more than a patrol in strength, but even so…'

'Even so,' Bilgeous agreed. 'We are at a critical juncture. The first fronds of the Garden are growing under our very feet. We must not let them be stamped out, Lord Cholerax. Do you hear? We must not!'

He tapped the butt of his staff on the ground while he thought. They had forces enough gathered on the island to hold off an attack in strength from anyone foolish enough to cross the bay and attempt it, but the real risk was the time it would waste before the ritual could be completed. They must not be distracted, not now.

'Tell Captain Pertussis to sail with his ships back to Kranzinn-port, the very moment dawn breaks,' he said. 'Round up those left in the city, without exception, and defeat this force, whoever they are. Go with him, Lord Cholerax. I would have someone on whom I can rely oversee this, rather than trust to those drunken dolts.'

Cholerax drew his scimitar and saluted. For a moment, Bilgeous could see the mortal general behind the gifts he had been given – a martial human warrior, keen for battle and quick to defend his honour.

'It shall be done,' Cholerax said. 'I will cut these fools down who think they can delay the great work, may the Grandfather witness my oath!'

'Be careful, though,' Bilgeous warned. 'I would not trust all to the warnings of a Rot Fly, no matter how well intentioned. Do not risk yourself unduly, if this force is more substantial than expected. Do you understand? The ritual must not be disturbed, not for a moment.'

'I understand. The Grandson must rise.'

Bilgeous gave a jovial smile. He was not worried, not really. He had faith in everything they were doing. He tapped his staff once more on the ground and glanced back at the pit.

'The Grandson must rise,' he said.

CHAPTER TWELVE

DEBT OF HONOUR

Sunlight trembled through the broken windows, watery and weak. Odger had been awake for hours. He couldn't sleep these days, wouldn't give himself the luxury. Sleep only led to dreams, and he could not bear his dreams now. Better the nightmare of waking, where things were exactly as bad as you knew they were. Dreams only led to hope, and hope was worthless against the horrors he knew were lurking in the streets of Kranzinnport.

He had relieved Aybel from his sentry duty at the window past midnight. He had sat there watching the square, scanning the entrance to the avenues on the eastern and the southern sides, but the city had been quiet. Quiet, that is, apart from the ever-present drone of Bloat Flies, the gurgling rustle of vines creeping tighter around the pillars and porticoes of the buildings, the slopping sound of things quietly rotting in the alleyways. Kranzinnport was never really quiet. In better times, you could always hear the broad and booming call of the sea down at the base of the cliffs. That sound used to comfort him at night when he was a boy, but it tormented him now. The sea used to be the source of the city's bounty. Now it was nothing but the hard road that led to ruin, the path the raiders had taken when they came to tear apart his home. It was from the sea that Kranzinnport's misery had risen.

When the light was clearer, he brewed some seaweed tea and chewed on a crust of bread while he waited for the others to wake. The duardin, Gotrek, hadn't slept either, as far as he could tell. He just sat there slumped in a corner of the room, his black eye glittering in the darkness, his axe across his knees. It was incredible, but his bath in those Rot Fly guts didn't seem to have affected him in the least. Anyone else would have been sporting a dozen buboes by this point, their skin green and scrofulous, but if anything had even mildly infected him then the duardin had just shrugged it off.

Gods, but he was an absolute beast. Odger didn't think he'd ever seen a mortal thing as powerfully built. His arms were like sides of beef, his great rolling shoulders like rocks, and he looked like he'd spent a lifetime opening doors with his face. His mohawk was stiff with animal fat and the shaved sides of his head were decorated with curling tattoos. Even with the mohawk he didn't come up much further than Odger's chest, but he'd made damn short work of those Rot Flies outside the city gates, creatures which had killed a score of good men and women not two weeks past. If he could cut down those monsters without stretching himself, then what could he do against the raiders and the pirates who'd set themselves up on Wither Island?

He looked at the axe across Gotrek's knees. It was a vicious-looking weapon, with a wicked edge to its blade, but it was still as beautiful and ornate as only the duardin could craft. He wondered how many heads Gotrek had carved open with that thing. How many battles had he been in, how many tavern brawls and savage skirmishes? Odger dreaded to think. It was hard to imagine

Gotrek had ever come off the worst in any of them. How many monsters had he dug out of their dens in his time, he wondered.

It was the strangest thing, but when he looked at Gotrek he no longer felt quite so afraid.

He turned away with a shake of his head. He scanned the street outside again while he sipped his tea, and chided himself for allowing a grain of hope to colour the sky. The hell with hope. If Sigmar had sent these two, then he had picked damned strange champions to save Kranzinnport. No, he would not put his faith in Gotrek, or in this angry, hard-faced priest who claimed to hate the gods. If they wanted to see the tunnels down to the harbour then he would show them, but otherwise he had to think about the remaining survivors. The flies were gone from the coast road – for now. Better to get folk out while they could, try to run for the forest. Hope to Sigmar that the harrowbugs weren't swarming this time of year, that there were no beastmen herds stampeding through the moors, and that the woods themselves were free of grots and feral dryads. He could try to save a life or two, but there was no hope for Kranzinnport now. There was no hope for Melita, for Clovis.

He tossed back the dregs of his tea, felt the bitter taste sharp against his tongue. He squeezed the bridge of his nose against the tears that threatened to fall from his eyes.

There was no hope for any of them.

But Sigmar help him, he still had to *know*.

Some of them had injuries they'd sustained just in the course of staying alive: cuts and scrapes and sprains, or a broken bone badly set. Amara went between the dozen or so survivors with the bandages and medicines she'd bought in Druhiel, helping where she could. One young lad, Watkyn his name was, had a nasty gash on the side of his neck which fortunately hadn't become infected.

Amara boiled some water on the stove that had been dragged into the chamber and cleaned the wound.

'Are you here on your own?' she asked the boy. He winced against the pain as she drew the wet cloth across his injury. The dried blood was crusted and black, but he was lucky the wound was healing cleanly. 'Do you know where your parents are?'

'Gone, miss,' he said. 'I haven't seen them for weeks.' His voice cracked slightly, but his pale blue eyes were as hard as stone and his face was as stern as any veteran's. He'd done all the crying he was ever going to do, she knew. She pressed a fresh dressing to the cut.

'I'm sorry,' she said. 'Truly, I wish more than I can say that this had never happened to you. To any of you.'

He gave an uneasy glance towards Odger, who was still standing by the window clutching his spear and staring out at the street. 'What do you think happens to them on the island?' he whispered. 'Do you think there's a chance they...' He shook his head. 'Odger's not been right since. I were friends with Clovis, we went fishing and hunting together every week's end. He's a good lad, tough as his dad, but decent and honest, and now this... It don't seem fair. If it were me,' he said with a sudden snarl, 'I'd fight! I'd fight till they killed me for it.'

'I don't know what's happened to them,' Amara told him. How much to varnish the truth here; how much to give the boy the undoubted facts? She was sure none of those taken from the city were still alive, but then the followers of the Plague God were strange and unpredictable, as sinister as they were curiously merry, no matter how dark their works. Who knew what they were really doing with all these people? She held his shoulder, looked him in the eyes, tried to let him feel the sincerity in her voice. 'But I will find out, I swear it.'

Watkyn nodded his head and his eyes glazed over as all his

attention slipped back towards the horrors inside him. He picked up his spear and took his place over at the windows again.

'Made that decision for us then, have you?' Gotrek rumbled at Amara's side. 'I never said I was going to take a swim over to Wither Island, not for these folk anyway.'

Amara packed away her medicines and slung her knapsack over her shoulder. She stood up and looked down into Gotrek's scowling good eye.

'Of course you are,' she said.

'Is that right?' He leaned on his axe, his feet planted on either side as if he were daring her to try to move him. 'And what makes you so damned sure?'

'Why else are we here?'

'I told you,' he growled. 'It was those sea aelves I wanted to kill, the Deepkin. This is no fight of mine. The Mistral Peaks are far to the north of here, and I've got an axe to find.'

Amara shook her head. 'I don't believe that for a minute.'

Gotrek held her eyes then, his lip curled into a brutal sneer. He was testing her, she realised. Pushing her, seeing how far her offer of help really went, and how much it was worth – if anything. If he did decide to head off to the Mistral Peaks, then would she follow him as long as her debt still had to be paid? Or would she stay here and help these people, take a stand, risk everything for what was right, and damn the gods either way? What was her sense of debt really worth?

'You were never looking for that axe,' she said. 'You might have believed you were, but it was only ever an excuse.'

'Know me that well, do you, lass?'

'The axe of Grimnir?' she said. 'If it even exists, it would be an artefact of extraordinary power, a relic of a lost age–'

'A relic of a lost world,' Gotrek said gruffly.

'Is that really what you came to Ghyran to find? You were

wandering the wilds on the off chance it might turn up, hoping vague hints about Fyreslayer lodges in the Mistral Peaks would lead you there? It's the weapon of a god, it would be like me hunting for Ghal Maraz and getting distracted by any and everything I found on the way. It doesn't make any sense. I don't accept for a moment that you would really let yourself be sidetracked from finding something so important by the lust for revenge against these Deepkin. Or the lust for death.'

Gotrek's brow darkened. His voice, when he spoke, was like the rumble of distant thunder.

'What do you know about revenge, girl? Or death?'

'*Everything*,' Amara spat. She jabbed a finger at him, her voice choked with anger. 'And I know that if the axe of Grimnir isn't what truly motivates you, then neither does vengeance. There's enough of the priest left in me to see through to your soul, Gotrek Gurnisson, and you have been searching for a way to die for years. I can see it. But you still care about more than that, much more. Innocent people are still suffering, still dying, still being used as the playthings of forces they can barely understand. And that's something you can never turn away from. I see it in you, Gotrek. You're a warrior, but you've never fought just for yourself. If you once just fought to find an honourable death, then those days are long behind you now.'

'And what about you then, priest?' he snarled. 'You say the gods have abandoned god-fearing folk, so you're going to stand up for them yourself are you? You? Who won't even pick up a weapon to defend yourself, let alone anyone else?'

'Something like that.' She looked at Watkyn, the dressing she had placed against his wound, and the others she had tended with bandage and ointment. She gave a fierce nod of her head. 'Yes, why not? If the innocent suffer, then the strong must do what they can to help. And help can take many forms.'

A long moment passed as Gotrek glared at her. Despite the fury in his eye, Amara held her ground. It had been months, she realised, since she had felt so certain of what she was doing. She was aware of the silence in the chamber, the tension as the survivors waited to see what would happen. If they were naturally frightened of Gotrek, then they had a new fear of her too, for who would dare talk like that to someone like Gotrek if they weren't prepared to back up their words with action? Slowly though, the duardin smiled.

'Well,' he shrugged. 'I suppose it beats telling the innocent that they're nothing but a bunch of morons for everything they believe in.' He threw his head back and gave a cackling laugh. 'There it is,' he said. 'There's the fire I always knew was there. You still want to pay off that debt of yours?'

'Yes,' she said. 'There is no freedom for a Dagolethi who owes an obligation to another. I would see the debt discharged.'

Gotrek turned to Odger, who stood on the other side of the room with his spear in his hand and a nervous expression on his face.

'Come on then. If you don't have anything stronger than that seaweed tea, let's cut this breakfast short and get on the move. Take us down to this harbour of yours.' He slammed the pommel of his axe on the ground, so suddenly that everyone jumped, and gave a manic grin. 'This city's suffered enough.'

CHAPTER THIRTEEN

THE CALL OF FAITH

They cut across the precinct in groups of two and three. Odger and Baffin were in front while Merosis held up a hand to hold Gotrek and Amara back. Hunkering down in the lee of the tall double doors, Merosis watched Odger reach the other side and scan the street that led south towards the prow of the city, and the sea beyond it. After a moment, he looked back and beckoned them on.

'Let's go,' Merosis said. 'And keep your heads down. You never know what might be watching.'

Amara shifted the clasp of the armour Odger had given her, a tarnished silver breastplate from the city's Freeguild regiment. Merosis clutched her sword and checked her shield on her back, and then led the others across the flagstones at a fast crouch. Amara followed her movements, dashing as fast as she could to the shelter of a broken fountain halfway across, but Gotrek was content just to trundle behind with his axe up on his shoulder. It was as if he'd spent the day chopping wood in a forest and was merrily making his way home.

'Gotrek!' she snapped. 'Take cover, damn it.'

'From what?' Gotrek boomed. 'These streets are empty, take my word for it. And if they aren't...'

He patted his axe. Amara shook her head and looked back to Merosis, who was sprinting to the shelter of a cloister on the other side of the precinct. It was becoming more and more obvious that Gotrek simply wanted his enemies to find him. There was no nihilism in this, no despairing desire to get the fight over and done with, but something like a brute pragmatism instead. Why waste time scurrying through the streets like this, when you could stand in the middle of the square and roar your challenge unafraid? He had not the slightest fear that he would ever lose.

Odger led them through the southern quarter of the city with some skill, taking an indirect route that skirted the residential areas and threaded through back alleys and passageways where they were less likely to be seen. The ground beneath their feet was awash in dark green slime, and the flanks of the buildings they passed were pitted with blossoms of a suppurating purple lichen. Amara caught up with Odger and Baffin as they crouched behind a shattered length of wall. Odger peered over the crumbled top at the street ahead, which opened out at the other end into a wide plaza overlooking the very edge of the cliffs. Amara could hear the sea beyond it, sloughing and rolling, the breakers coming in to shatter themselves against the rocks a few hundred feet below.

'You've had military training?' she asked him, keeping her voice low. 'You move like you know what you're doing, and you read the ground well.'

Odger shook his head. He didn't take his eyes off the street in front of them as he replied.

'I was a steward in the market here,' he said. 'Told the fishermen where to set up their wares, made sure none of the stalls tried to take another's patch, kept order if any fights broke out. I reckon for all our faults, Kranzinnport was as safe and orderly as you can get in Yska, and any trouble was never more than I could handle. I barely had to raise my voice most days.'

'It will be a safe city again,' Amara told him. She laid her hand on his arm and felt his muscles tense. 'You just need to fight for it. You need to have faith in yourselves and you can build anew.'

'Is that from your scriptures?' he said. There was an edge of anger in his voice, the touch of resentment. He shook his arm free. 'Don't your sort usually tell us to put our faith in Sigmar? Well, I've had enough of Sigmar's word,' he said. 'Meaning no offence, but it's never brought us any help.'

'It brought us these two,' Baffin said. Her green eyes, dark as the deep sea, glittered. 'Didn't it? That's something, ain't it? Got to be, if you ask me.' She smiled, almost abashed.

'The provenance of the words doesn't matter,' Amara told them, 'as long as the sentiment is true.'

Odger laughed lightly, but it was a cynical sound in that dead air. There was no real mirth in it.

'You can tell you're a priest,' he said. 'Always got an answer for everything.'

'And you can tell you're a steward,' Amara rejoined. 'Always doing your best to keep order, and to keep people safe.'

Odger looked at her for the first time since they had set out. The pain she could see in his eyes was unbearable. He looked like a man who had stared into the abyss for too long and was just waiting for it all to be over.

'Not all of them,' he said bitterly. 'Not those who looked to me for protection, more than anyone else.'

Baffin squeezed his shoulder. She reached into the front of her tunic and took out a pendant on a long gold chain. A hammer, Amara saw. The sign of Sigmar.

'I believe, miss,' she whispered. She kissed the pendant and tucked it away again. 'I always have, and I always will. Sigmar has sent you and the duardin, I know it. For all prayers are answered in time, ain't they? Even though you may not recognise the answer when it comes.'

Amara gritted her teeth and looked away. She said nothing. What would be the point? Why disabuse someone of their faith here, in the midst of such utter ruin, if it was all they had left? If the hope in Sigmar got Baffin through another day, then...

She sighed. Let her keep her faith, and clutch to it like a drowning woman clutching at a spar. If it kept her afloat, then what was the harm. But the gods had a strange way of helping if Amara and Gotrek were the answer to her prayers.

The dawn was not long past, but the day was already sultry. Amara felt a trickle of sweat creep down from her scalp as they cut down the street into the plaza. It was an unnatural warmth. Kranzinnport was a city right on the very edge of the coast and it should have been blistered day and night by the bracing sea winds, but instead it laboured under this sweltering jungle heat.

The plaza opened up before them. It was a long, triangular-shaped space that pointed to the very lip of the cliffs, with a balustrade of sculpted blue coral around the edge. The view was astonishing, the entirety of the Tendril Sea laid out across the horizon – a shuddering wrack of steel blue, flecked with white-caps and scored with long black breakers that pitched from one end of the ocean to the other. Farther than she could rightly see, Amara caught the glimpse of the realm's edge in the unimaginable distance – a glimmering sheen of emerald and jet, sparkling like fresh-mined crystal.

But for all its breathtaking beauty and grandeur, there was darkness on the water. There across the misty reach sat Wither Island. It was a low, hunkered oval, flattened against the shield of the sea. A sultry haze rose up from it, poisoning the air and masking much of it from sight. Even at this distance she fancied she could smell the rot streaming off it, the cloying vapour of decay. She shivered as the breeze picked up, although the wind was still warm. Could they really get over there by themselves, just her and Gotrek? And what could they possibly do when they did?

'You see that?' Gotrek said. He shielded his eyes and pointed out to sea. Amara followed his direction. There, perhaps a league out from the island, came those two twin-masted ships. Their sails were tattered black things that caught at the breeze, full-bellied. Long white wakes crested out behind the ships, streamers of disturbed water. They were moving fast.

'The raiders,' Odger said. His voice trembled. 'They're coming back. They were just here yesterday, they don't normally return so quick.'

'Then that's their hard luck,' Gotrek said. 'Let's get down and make sure we give the buggers a bloody warm welcome.'

In the middle of the precinct there was a wide, semicircular entranceway. A long rail of tarnished brass ran around the length of it, and beyond it was the head of a staircase that led down into the solid rock. Odger clutched at the rail and stared down into the entranceway.

'Merosis, Baffin,' he said. 'Go back to the shelter, gather the others and make for the gates. If those Rot Flies are gone from the coast road, then take them out that way and head for the forest. Keep inside the edge of it and make your way to Druhiel.'

Baffin's eyes were wide. 'What about you?' she said. 'You're not coming with us?'

Merosis grabbed his arm. The wind whipped at her hair. 'We're not going to leave you behind.'

'You need to take care of the others, especially Watkyn and Aybel,' he said. 'They're just children, they shouldn't have to stay in this awful place any longer.' He took Merosis' hand. 'I owe you my life,' he said. 'I would have given up weeks ago if it hadn't been for you, but I need to know what happened to them. To Melita, to my son.' He looked at Gotrek and Amara. 'I'll get you down to the harbour, and if you're going across to Wither Island then I'm going with you.'

'You'll get no argument from me, lad,' Gotrek said.

'Odger…' Amara said. She nodded to the open sea as it crashed and surged below them. 'You know that this is going to be dangerous. Even if we make it over to the island, we might not make it back alive.'

'Speak for yourself,' Gotrek grumbled.

'I know,' Odger said. 'But I've done nothing for too long, and it's not enough for me just to survive any more. I have to do something. I have to find out what happened to them, even if it kills me.'

Merosis squeezed his hand, and after a moment they embraced.

'Take care,' she said. 'And good luck, Odger Pellin.' She smiled. 'You were the best steward Kranzinnport market ever had.'

'High praise indeed,' he laughed.

Baffin drew the pendant from beneath her tunic and slipped it over her head. 'Here,' she said, passing it to Odger. 'Sigmar be with you. May his hand be over you, and may he give strength and courage to your heart.'

Odger looked at the golden pendant lying there coiled in her hand, and for a moment Amara thought he was going to refuse it, or that he would snatch it up and fling it over the edge of the cliff. Then, with just the faintest hint of a reverence she didn't think he possessed, Odger took the chain and slipped it over his head. He tucked the pendant away beneath his grubby white shirt.

'Sigmar be with you both too,' he said. 'With all of you.'

CHAPTER FOURTEEN

THE BEASTS BENEATH

The entranceway led to a flight of metal stairs that coiled down into the darkness, so wide that Amara couldn't have reached both sides of it with her arms spread. Lamps were set into niches at the sides, but the only source of light came from the weak shaft that fell down from the plaza above them.

There was a smell in the air of rotting seaweed and brine, and it grew sharper the further down they went. Amara, with Odger in front of her and Gotrek behind, clutched the rail and tried to still her nerves. Dagoleth was a city of the plains and wide open spaces, and the idea of being under the earth in any capacity made her nervous. For the duardin, of course, it was second nature – Gotrek was utterly unperturbed.

They reached the base of the staircase after a few minutes. In front of them was a rusted iron gate that reached from floor to ceiling, the bars bent out of shape as if something had tried to batter its way through. On the other side a black corridor stretched off into the shadows. Amara saw bones scattered on the ground, and there was a smell in the air of raw sewage. Odger took a dead torch from a basket at the foot of the stairs and lit it with a tinderbox. The flame guttered in the cold breeze that whispered through the bars of the gate.

'From now on,' Odger whispered, 'you must be absolutely silent. There are things down here...'

Amara nodded. Gotrek spat on his palms and unslung his axe. Odger swallowed and took a long iron key from inside his tunic. Carefully, his hands shaking, he unlatched the padlock.

The flame of the torch threw a wavering light against the walls as they headed in. The tunnel was banked with white brick and the floor was a tiled mosaic of blue and green coral. The stench of sewage was stronger now. Amara could hear the hollow boom of the waves somewhere far down below, as if they were caught in some enclosed chamber. There were smears of filth on the ground and long ropes of dried slime gathering dust against the walls. Here and there she saw more lengths of human bone, broken skulls, dried scraps of what might have once been flesh.

Before long they came to a break in the tunnel and a high-ceilinged chamber on their left-hand side, the walls of which were studded with brightly coloured shells. A stream of light fell from some hidden aperture far above. In the middle of the chamber was an open well at least twenty feet across, with two lengths of thick cable attached to a pulley or winch that was set high above it. The cables dropped down straight into the well. Amara risked a look over the edge, but the bottom of it was hidden far down in the shadows. Again she could hear the boom of the waves, the sound of them echoing up from what must be the base of the cliffs far below.

'This is part of the cage lift system,' Odger whispered. 'Brings the cargo up from the trading ships down in the harbour, although I wouldn't dare risk it now. The raiders use it, but if we're lucky we can slip by them once those ships come in to the wharf. The tunnels lead all the way down too – hard work bringing up cargo when the cages are out of order, but our best hope now. While they're coming up in the cages, we can head down by the western stairs, and with any luck our paths won't cross.'

'Why don't you just cut these damned things, stop them getting up?' Gotrek said. He gave a test swing of his axe, lining it up against the base of the cables where they were coiled around a brass drum twice as high as Gotrek himself.

Odger silently stayed Gotrek's hand, a look of horror on his face. 'That's Kharadron make,' he whispered. 'It's triple-woven tensile steel. You wouldn't make a dent in it, and the noise would be deafening.' He gave a nervous glance from the pulley chamber back out into the tunnel. 'Please, trust me on this. Do you think we haven't already tried it?'

Gotrek grumbled his assent and drew his axe away with a disappointed look on his face. Odger held up the torch and hurried them on.

They jogged carefully down the length of the tunnel as it curved off towards the west. Every few feet Amara saw more crusts of slime or mounds of dried excrement. The smell, especially here in this enclosed space, was making her head spin. She could feel the bitter tang of the seaweed tea she had drunk that morning flooding her mouth again. At one point even Odger stopped to be sick, hunching over and spewing onto the tiles, wiping his mouth with the back of his hand.

'I'll never get used to that stink, as long as I live,' he said. 'I could be an old man a thousand miles from this place, and that stench would still be thick in my nose. How can such things smell like that and still live?'

Amara said, 'I wouldn't call it living. I wouldn't even call it surviving, it's just...' She shook her head as the words failed her. In her mind came again the image of the Slaaneshi army charging down the slopes of the valley, the perfume-musk of them, the chains and barbs and whips, the flayed skin open to the elements to produce the most exquisite agonies. 'Life is hard, for everyone,' she said. 'But I cannot imagine the hardship that sends ordinary folk to embrace such horrors.'

'It's a ripe enough aroma,' Gotrek admitted. Amara was glad that for once he was keeping his voice down. He took a deep breath and hefted his axe. 'And getting stronger.'

'Come on,' Odger said warily. 'There's another flight of stairs ahead, down to the mezzanine tunnels. Once we reach that, the harbour's only one more level below us.'

The mouths of other tunnels stretched away from them on the right, circles of black shadow that Odger's torch flame didn't touch. Water trickled down the sides of the walls and dropped from the ceiling. Amara saw other grilles and gates covering the openings, the bars similarly bent or torn aside. The scraps and offal seemed thicker underfoot, and the smell was getting richer and more pungent.

They came to the last flight of stairs, which coiled down into the darkness. Odger held up his torch and peered into the shadows. Amara could see by the strain on his face how much all this was costing him. She wondered again at his courage. He had been an ordinary man with a family and an ordinary job, living in a city off the Everspring's beaten tracks, forced now to become a scavenger and a renegade. Everything had been taken from him and he was still going, still striving to keep his friends safe. He may have taken Baffin's pendant, but he didn't seem to care a curse for the gods either.

'Those ships we saw should be reaching the harbour soon,' he whispered. He tossed the torch to the ground, where the flame guttered and sparked. 'It'll get lighter as we reach the bottom, but be as quiet as you can, I beg you. We may have to hide a while until the raiders have passed into the cages, but they shouldn't leave more than a skeleton crew on the ships, and we can sneak past easily enough. There are fishing smacks and rowboats tied up on the western wharf, so that's where we're going to head.'

Amara felt a knot tighten in her stomach. Gotrek said nothing, but she couldn't imagine for a moment that he would be content to hide if there were enemies in front of him.

'Sounds a good enough plan to me, lad,' Gotrek said. He gave a savage grin. 'Row out there, see what's what, and kill what we have to. Sea aelves or no sea aelves, something's going to die, I can promise you that much.'

'Seems a fool's errand to me, right enough,' Odger muttered.

'I'm sure you've been on more than a few in your time, Gotrek,' Amara said.

The duardin's eye glittered. 'Ha! True enough, lass. True enough.'

Odger hurried down the stairs, treading lightly, his spear extended before him. Gotrek followed, Amara behind him. After a few feet the shadows seemed to swarm up and envelop them, and the faint orange light of Odger's discarded torch seemed far behind. Amara felt that dread of enclosure creeping over her, but she gritted her teeth and continued. She could just make out Gotrek's massive bulk ahead of her and she focused on the slab-like shoulders, the teetering crest of hair, ignoring everything else. Down the stairs turned, twisting round and round on themselves as they corkscrewed deeper into the cliffs. She could hear the sound of the water in the harbour slopping up against the stone, the wild sea beyond slamming against the rocks.

'How you doing, priest?' Gotrek murmured in front of her.

'Fine. I'm fine, I'm…' She swallowed, tried to control her voice. 'And you? Can you see in this murk?'

'Clear as a summer's day,' Gotrek said. 'Strolling through tunnels is like coming home for my kind.' He ran his hand over the patterned mosaics of the wall. 'Even if the workmanship leaves a fair bit to be desired.'

The stairs came out at last into a long, ribbed corridor which stretched away in front of them, heading east. The rough-hewn ceiling was no more than an arm's breadth above Amara's head, and she saw that the stone was smeared in filth. The corridor itself looked long abandoned. On the right-hand side of the corridor there was an open archway guarded by a low stone banister, marked by three wide pillars holding up the ceiling. Amara crouched behind one of the pillars and looked down into the harbour.

It was a massive natural cave over a hundred yards high and wider than she could guess. It had been carved out of the cliffs by the long process of erosion, and extended on either side by the ingenuity of the men and women who had founded Kranzinnport back in the distant past. The cave mouth was a blinding circle of light after the darkness of the tunnels. Amara could see two wings overlapping on either side of it, projecting out to sea and forming an entrance channel that contained the wilder waters beyond. There were five massive berths on the near side of the cave, directly underneath the archway where Amara crouched. They were linked by a long boardwalk that ran the full width of the cave from side to side. Each berth was separated by wooden walkways that were strewn with broken barrels, coils of rope and discarded rubbish. The sea air, sharp and clear, cut in from the open cave mouth and blew some of the pervasive stink away.

'There are no signs of the ships,' Amara said. She couldn't see them through the mouth of the cave, plying the winds on the open sea, but that didn't mean they weren't there. They were probably sweeping around from the east, aiming for the open channel where the western harbour wall overlapped the eastern wing and the tide was calmer.

'We'll head down to the far side there,' Odger said. He pointed to the far end of the boardwalk, off to the right, where a handful of fishing boats were tied up to wooden hawsers. They bobbed gently in the water. 'Hide behind those barrels and crates there until we can make our move.'

'Then untie a boat and row out to the island?' Amara said.

'It's the best I can think of,' Odger told her. 'At least it'll be quiet. With the mist rising over the waters here, we should be able to get there unseen.'

Gotrek snorted – but then he froze, his axe raised. His eye went wide.

There was a bubbling, gurgling chuckle from somewhere in the shadows at the other end of the corridor. A slithering sound like a sack of flesh being dragged over rough ground crept from the darkness, and there was a smell that seemed to reach out and grab them. It was as wild as a stagnant swamp, as rich as a butcher's yard. Amara felt the vomit burning in her chest. She covered her mouth, gagging too much to speak. She saw Odger with his teeth bared, his spear up, a look of absolute horror on his face. And then she saw it, as it lumbered from the dark.

She had been a warrior priest by Sigmar's command for a decade of her life. She had fought in skirmishes and battles to defend her city, against orruks and beastmen and Chaos cultists, and she had watched everyone she had ever cared about cut to pieces in the valleys of Thyria. But she had never seen anything quite so horrifying as what emerged now from the shadows ahead of them.

It was like some grotesque, engorged slug, bulkier by far than any of the aurochs that ploughed the fields outside Dagoleth – and they stood more than eight feet tall from hoof to shoulder. It slopped its huge, bloated belly out in front of it, and the blubber was beginning to split under the strain. Even as it shuffled towards them the glistening organs began to bulge out, a wobbling mess of purple and red. The creature's mouldering flesh was greener than the grave, slashed here and there with open wounds that leaked a curdled yellow ichor, and the great boils and buboes and suckers that covered its skin were raw and weeping. It had two vestigial arms, the flesh sagging and flabby, the grey claws fused together, and its head – if it was a head – was crowned with fleshy, wavering fronds that looked like intestinal tubes. Worst of all was the expression on the thing's face. Amara would have been prepared for bestial rage or ravenous hunger, but the beast's bulbous, mismatched eyes were as eager as a demented toddler's. It huffed and panted like some monstrous, catarrhal dog, puking out a string of viscous slime. The mouth hinged open in a ragged grin and the long, slobbering tongue flopped out onto its belly.

'For Sigmar's sake!' Odger cried, lashing out with his spear. 'Don't let it touch you!'

Amara reeled back from the stench as the beast shuffled closer. It made a guttural bark and tried to clap its bloated hands together, straining so much that the skin of its belly split into a web of mucous, the rotting organs tumbling out onto the ground. Odger fell back, his arm thrown up against his mouth.

'Run, get back to the surface,' he choked.

He stabbed in again with his spear, trying to force the beast back. The blade plunged into the creature's flesh, but it made little difference. The beast bounded forwards with a loathsome chuckle and tore the spear from his grasp. Odger stumbled and fell backwards, sprawling on the tiles. Amara rushed to his side, throwing herself in front of him as the creature bore down, her arm up in a desperate attempt to hold it back.

'Khazukan Kazakit-ha!'

Gotrek's war cry was deafening in that enclosed space, louder than the waves that crashed against the cliffs beyond the harbour. With a roar he leapt directly at the beast, his orange crest brushing the ceiling as he brought his axe in one huge round-house swing to try to hack its head from its blubbery shoulders. The brazier in the rune-axe trailed a tail of fire. The blade bit into the beast's flesh – there was a twist of grey smoke, and a gout of black blood splashed onto the tiles. A wavering cry spiralled from its throat. Gotrek chopped in again, gnashing his teeth, his face purple with fury. The beast quivered and reared back, hooting in distress. The axe blade sunk in deep, tearing out a flapping chunk of skin and muscle, but it was like trying to carve jelly. So grotesquely bloated was the beast that it seemed to absorb the blows. Gotrek, howling with rage, clambered up onto the monster's back as Amara rushed to pick up Odger's spear, slipping in the spilled gore as she snatched it up from the tiles. She tossed it to Odger as he got to his feet. Bracing himself with both hands, he stabbed the blade into the jumbled mass of its organs.

The long tentacle of the beast's tongue, raw with blisters, snaked out to grab the spear. Odger was thrown aside, rolling to the edge of the archway and the drop down to the harbour below. He cried out, scrabbling to stop himself as he tumbled between the stone pillars of the banister. As he fell over the side, Amara dived across the tiles, her hand just managing to clutch his wrist.

'Don't let go!' Odger cried.

'Stop bloody struggling then,' she muttered.

She snatched out with her other hand, grabbed his arm and started hauling him up. Odger, his face flushed with the effort, flung his leg up to gain some purchase on the edge of the archway. The wharf was a long drop down, at least half the height of the cave itself, and he would have been lucky to come away with anything less than a broken neck if he'd fallen. Inch by inch, Amara hauled him back up, until they were both sprawled there on the tiles. Risking a glance behind, she saw Gotrek balancing on the monster's hump, hauling back with his axe, still roaring to himself. He plunged the blade deep into the beast's skull, splitting its head open from side to side. There was a slop of brains like a tide of rotten vegetables, a slick of blood that came thundering onto the tiles. The beast howled – a grotesque, chilling sound. The bulbous eyes rolled and wept, quivering in their sockets – and then each half of its head peeled away and flopped to the side.

The beast's slug-like frame shuddered as it collapsed. The arms shook and the bloated tail slapped and twitched on the tiles like a beached fish. Gotrek leapt from its back as it slumped to the ground and hammered his axe again and again into the monster's trembling flank, yellow ichor spraying up into his face.

'Ha!' he roared, frothing at the mouth. 'My axe will drink its fill, you sack of snotling brains!'

'Incredible,' Odger whispered. He was still sprawled on the ground. He looked at Gotrek with awe as the duardin hacked the corpse to pieces. 'I've never seen anything like it. He should be dead a dozen times over. These things have killed scores of our people. Civilians, trained soldiers – anyone who's tried to fight their way through them has been killed in moments!'

Amara couldn't think of anything to say. It was true enough. More than anyone she had ever met, Gotrek seemed devoid of fear, and he threw himself into fights so recklessly it was as if he knew no force in the realms could stop him. It was more than confidence. It was… Gods, it was a kind of faith. And she had seen what effect his presence alone had had on Odger and the others. Hope had kindled there when he appeared. Hope, where before there had only been despair.

'Wait a minute,' she said, as she helped Odger to his feet. The wet crunch of Gotrek's axe was the only other sound in that filthy corridor. 'Did you say "them"?'

There was a huffing roar at the far end of the tunnel, a blast of sewage-stench, and another slobbering beast hauled itself from the shadows. Its solitary eye gave an eager blink, and the tendrils on its head quivered with excitement as its belly split into a yawning mouth ringed with shards of bone-like teeth. As it loped towards them it left a trail of stinking slime behind it.

'Don't be shy!' Gotrek said, turning towards it and planting himself in the middle of the tunnel. He raised his axe above his head. 'Come and play, little one!'

Just then, cutting across the air, came a long and mournful blast. There was something solemn about it, like the sorrowful boom of a stranded whale.

'What in the hells is that?' Amara said.

Odger threw himself behind a pillar. 'It's them,' he said. 'It's the raiders from Wither Island – they're here!'

CHAPTER FIFTEEN

PIRATES OF THE PLAGUE

'Why do you blow on that cursed thing?' Lord Cholerax grumbled from the gunwale. He scowled across the deck at the Blightking who had pressed his diseased lips to the mouth of the ivory horn, which had pride of place on the forecastle of the *Diphthemious*. 'Do you mean to alert every last mortal in the city to our presence, hmm? Damn your eyes for a pirate!'

He should have flown this distance on Thrax, his Rot Fly, rather than sink to the level of these scum. He could see Thrax resting on the quarterdeck, aft of the main mast. The bloated fly had tucked its wings behind it and squatted on its abdomen, its legs folded underneath it and its tripartite eyes staring as bright and bloody as three clustered rubies.

'Quickens the sport of it all, my lord,' Captain Pertussis said as he sidled near.

He clamped the rail with his lobster claw and stared with his solitary eye at the cave of Kranzinnport's harbour. The ships were slipping in along the edge of the cliffs, taking advantage of the calmer waters on the other side of the harbour's wider wing. Glutinous tears leaked from the captain's eye, called out by the fresh salt wind. The mouth in his stomach yawned wide, strings of mucous stretching out between the teeth. The purple tongue lapped at the breeze as if tasting it.

'We are not here for sport,' Cholerax fumed. He could feel something writhe and wriggle in his throat and hacked twice to clear it, spitting out a maggot into the interior of his helmet. 'Bilgeous Pox desires fresh meat for the pot, and it is our task to provide it.'

And provide it a damned sight more efficiently than you have done so far, he thought.

'Take my word for it,' Pertussis said, 'the horn gets the fear right up 'em. All scrambling about and shouting and that, not thinking straight, and then we comes right in and sorts them all out. Har har har!'

He laughed long and loud – a grisly, guttural roar. Around him the other Blightkings joined in, snickering as they flitted between the ropes, drawing down the sails and shouting orders to the cultists chained to the benches below decks. Soon the oars were all slipped through the riggers on the lower hull. The sails were taken in, and the schooner began to slowly pivot towards the mouth of the harbour. The cliffs slipped by on their right, as grey as slate. Down below, the oars lifted and dropped from the hull, cutting smoothly through the water. To the left, three hundred yards away across the bucking sea, the *Rust Scythe* drew down its sails and dropped back to follow the *Diphthemious'* path.

'Tradition, lad,' Pertussis said, in a confidential tone that was only partly undermined by his gurgling voice. 'My ships have done ever thus, from the Amnios Sea all the way to Smuggler's Haven, and don't you forget it. There ain't a village, town or coastal city

we haven't terrified with one blast on that there horn!' His cyclopean eye shone moistly, as if recalling happier days. 'Kranzinnport
though, this has been a nice little earner and no mistaking it.
Chock full of slaves, all of them bowing down to our power –
it's all our paydays come at once. Isn't that right, boys?' he cried.

The pirate Blightkings roared their approval, laughing delight-
edly, raising their cutlasses and tossing their tricorn hats into the
air on the end of cannular tentacles and bifurcated claws. One
fired a blast from a black-powder pistol into the air, the bullet
clipping the face of the lookout in the crow's nest to much merry
laughter from his fellows.

Pertussis turned back to the gunwale and the sea beyond, as the
prow cut and rose through the waves. There was a jovial smile on
his wrenched, elongated mouth and he reached up to pat Cholerax on the shoulder with his claw. The Blightlord stiffened. The
affront, it was too much. Cholerax was as cheerful as any fol-
lower of the Grandfather, but he was a military man at heart. He
was Lord of the Underswamp. He commanded a troop of the finest
knights in all the Maggotkin armies, and he would not be taken
on such familiar terms by a common bloody pirate!

'Well,' he said, dressing himself in all his dignity, 'remember, this
is no mere raid for pillage and plunder. Bilgeous Pox has charged
us all with a holy task, to the glory of the Grandfather – and the
Grandson that will be. Your own desires should not come into
this, sir! No, not at all I say.'

He hawked again and spat out a gobbet of fibrous catarrh into
his helmet. It dripped deliciously down his chin. Cholerax's goitre
ached, and there was a fresh tumour brewing in his knee. He could
feel the belly-mouth under his armour champing and slurping,
eager to be released. In the Grandfather's name, how he longed
to reveal it! How he yearned for the miasmic air to wash over its
fangs, and for the tuberous rope of its tongue to slobber free. It

was only a strange and so far unexamined fastidiousness that had made Lord Cholerax keep the mouth under his plate. The maw was a new development, a recent burgeoning of the gifts he had already received from Papa Nurgle, and (although he couldn't quite admit it to himself) he was shy of what the sorcerer and his minions would think of it. Not to mention Pertussis, with such a notably fanged and chomping maw of his own.

Often Cholerax found himself giggling at the feel of the mouth's jaws snapping beneath his armour, his whole frame shuddering with each empty bite. It cheered him up so much that he could not bear the thought of anyone thinking it was somehow… less impressive than their own. He was Lord Cholerax after all, conqueror of the Blistered Isles and tyrant of the Relentless Plains! He was no common thief or reaver, out to stuff his purse with spoils.

'Grandfather, Grandson, it's all the same to me,' Pertussis said, with a leering half-smile. He leaned on the gunwale. The harbour was near now, and he signalled for the rudder to make the turn into the high cave mouth. They'd done this half a dozen times already, and the manoeuvre was second nature to his crew. 'Let those who bother the gods make their plans and prayers, and I'll see to my own enrichment.'

'Damn you for a heathen!' Cholerax cried. 'This is blasphemy!' He turned savagely on him, raising his scythe. He could scarce believe it. His tentacle reached for his sword, and for all the fury in him then he would have cut the pirate down on the deck of his own ship. Pertussis moved not a muscle though, and did not take his eye from the choppy waters as the ship sloped in towards the harbour. The rudder turned and the schooner heaved to starboard as the cave came near.

Cholerax glanced up and realised that two dozen pirate Blight-kings stood on the forecastle, their swords drawn and their black-powder pistols raised. For all the cheerful grins and chuckling mirth they normally showed, they were in deadly earnest now. Cholerax had never lost a battle in his long and violent life, but he knew when discretion was the better part of valour. His tentacle drew back from his sword hilt and he lowered his scythe. After all, he admitted to himself, they were supposed to be on the same side. Weren't they?

Pertussis clacked his lobster claw and chortled to himself, still leaning on the gunwale.

'You're a passionate fellow, my lord,' he said reasonably. 'I can see that. Committed. Zealous. I respect that, truly I do. And make no mistake, me and the boys are as god-fearing as anyone you'll find in the Jade Kingdoms. I love old Papa Nurgle, and there's not a day goes by I don't raise my eye and thank him for all my blessings.'

He straightened as the ship smoothly turned into the booming cave of the harbour, signalling for his men to prepare the hawser ropes.

'But our sorcerer back on the island there,' Pertussis continued. His eye gave a watery stare as the maw in his gut chomped on the gunwale. 'He's something else, is Bilgeous Pox. There are many ways to serve the Grandfather in these wide and wonderful Mortal Realms. He chooses his, and I chooses mine.'

'You don't believe he can raise the Grandson? The greatest Unclean One in history, an aspect of the Grandfather himself? You have seen the first fruiting of the Garden on that island, have you not? What in Nurgle's holy name makes you doubt him?'

'Oh, I don't doubt him,' Pertussis chuckled. 'Not in the least. But there's raiding and pillaging in the Grandfather's name, and a very pleasant business it is. And then there's holy war, which is something else entirely if you get my drift. Tends to be harder and less rewarding work, shall we say.'

Cholerax stood tall as the ship broached the harbour, the cave roof high above even the crow's nest of the mainmast. His armour plates clacked and clattered, and when he spoke it was as if he were already mounted on Thrax, addressing his knights as they were garbed in all the panoply of war.

'A holy war is exactly what I want,' he said. 'When Bilgeous came to my court in the Underswamp as a pilgrim and a wanderer, I gave him shelter as was his due. But when he told me of the Grandfather's vision and what he had been commanded to do, I felt new faith stir in my chest.'

'Could have just been the maggots?' Pertussis offered. Cholerax ignored him.

'I would follow him to the very Gates of Azyr,' he said. 'When the minions of the God-King crushed our hopes in the Everspring Swathe, centuries ago, they sowed the seeds of their own destruction. For all that rots and falls into decay will grow again, in new and abundant life, and our humiliation will be avenged.'

'I believe it will,' Pertussis said, with a cynical laugh. 'Yes indeed, I truly believe it will.'

The ship cut smoothly across the still waters of the harbour. Pertussis commanded the *Diphthemious* to moor at the berth on the right-hand side, while the *Rust Scythe* docked to the far left. Ropes were thrown to loop the hawsers. The anchors were dropped, and the crew, with much eager laughter, began to set the gangplank down to the wooden wharf. Cholerax looked up to the ceiling of the cave, high in the shadows above, and the archway that looked down onto the docks. The dockyard itself was a mess of wreckage. Barrels and crates were scattered haphazardly across the wharf, along with coiled lengths of rope, casks of pitch and tar for caulking the ships' keels. There was even a brazier that still smouldered in the corner, the flames painting a wavering red light against the walls.

'Come, captain,' Cholerax said as he strode across the deck to harness Thrax, his Rot Fly. 'Let us make this quick and round up the last of these stragglers. The rite must be completed before the last day of the dead moon, before it begins to grow once more. By tomorrow's dawn, we will see the Grandson walking on the surface of the Mortal Realms, to the greater glory of Papa Nurgle, and Kranzinnport will be no more than a memory.'

A titanic roar split the hollow silence, slamming and echoing from the walls. Cholerax whipped around, his flab quivering and his scythe raised. Pertussis, lobster claw clacking, scanned the shadows in the far corners of the harbour; and then, from high up on the archway above the wharf, where the mezzanine tunnel ran crosswise to the stairwells, there was a crash and a cloud of dust as something pummelled its way through the stone.

Faster than they could see, it came plummeting down towards the deck of the *Rust Scythe* fifty feet below, a blur of green and grey and orange. There was an almighty crash as this struggling mass punched through the decking, a high whine of screaming wood, and then uproar as the crew of the *Scythe* charged from their stations.

'We've been holed below the line!' one of the Blightkings cried across the wharf in disbelief. 'We're taking on water, captain, the whole damned ship's going to sink!'

Already the schooner had pitched very slightly to the right, the hull crunching up against the wooden walkway and shearing it away from the hawsers. Great bubbles of air popped and crackled around the keel, and then the ship unmistakably began to list at the stern, as if it were trying to dive head first to the bottom of the harbour. A fountain of black water billowed out of the hole in the ship's deck, and then there was a foamy tide surging across the harbour and rocking the *Diphthemious* from port to starboard.

'We're under attack!' one of the pirate crew cried from the forecastle of the *Scythe*.

'Man the guns!' another called, his bulbous arms flapping with diseased flesh, his eyes bulging. Blightkings lurched and hobbled across the deck, stumbling over as the schooner pitched forwards. 'Cannons! Rockets – must be!'

'Arm yourselves, you sons of dogs!' Pertussis shouted to his own crew. He hawked up a gob of maggoty phlegm and spat it down into the water, then sidled crabwise towards the gangplank. 'We'll cut these scum down if they dare to stand against us! Cutlasses! Muskets! Axe and buckler! Look lively!'

It was the strangest thing, Cholerax thought as he jogged heavily towards his Rot Fly. It hadn't looked like a cannonball or a rocket at all.

In fact, he could have sworn it seemed more like a half-naked duardin straddling a dead Beast of Nurgle.

CHAPTER SIXTEEN

FORCE OF NATURE

Gotrek cleaved chunks from the creature as it lapped at him with its sinuous tongue, drawing him closer and closer. It seemed to Amara as though it wanted nothing more than to give him a hug. He raged and writhed against the tendril, his arms pinned to his side, the snapping maw getting ever closer.

Odger charged in with his spear and pierced it in the shoulder. The spear blade sunk deep into the flesh, and even though the monster barely seemed to feel it, the distraction was enough for Gotrek to get his arm free and chop the tongue off at the root. After that, the duardin went berserk. Amara threw herself aside as he flailed at the creature with manic fury, slicing it to pieces as it hooted and whined at him. Chunks of wet flesh fell like rain, and the rune-axe streamed out a burning tail of fire.

Amara watched him crash through the stone banister of the archway, gripping the back of the monstrous beast. His axe was planted deep in whatever passed for the creature's brain, and Gotrek wrenched the blade from side to side until it went charging blindly through the pillars. Its pestilent bulk easily smashed them aside – and then down they went, tumbling end over end, the duardin's demented bellow ringing out in the hollow space of the harbour even as the two Nurgle ships came planing in across the water to settle at the berths.

Gotrek and the beast struck the deck of one of the ships, crashing straight through the planks and leaving a ragged hole behind them. Amara threw herself to the edge of the smashed archway, staring down at the masts as they shivered with the blow, the ship heaving to the side and crashing its prow into the walkway. It was sinking fast.

'Come on,' she cried to Odger. 'We've got to get down there before he drowns!'

'No one could survive that,' Odger cried. 'And anyway, what by Sigmar's mercy do you think we can do against *them*?'

He pointed at the crew of the other ship, who were charging down the gangplanks with their weapons raised. They were roaring and chanting what sounded to Amara like a sea shanty. Amara had never seen such terrible, bloated fiends. They were thickset warriors at least a head higher than a normal man, all of them dressed in rusting chainmail and corroded plate. Some of them had tricorn hats crammed onto their deformed heads, while others hid themselves behind full-face steel helmets that were pitted with holes. For all the streaks of rust and corrosion on their weapons, the swords and axes they bore looked deadly enough.

On the other side of the wharf, the crew of the wrecked ship were leaping from the deck into the water. The boat pitched even further to the side as it quickly began to sink. The masts splintered as they crashed into the boardwalk and the sails billowed out like monstrous petals on the surface of the sea.

Amara peered into the shadows at the eastern end of the harbour. She could see a ladder that led up from the wharf to some point at the far end of the tunnel. At the base of the ladder there were a few scattered drums of pitch, and a brazier still fuming with a low and angry flame.

There was no sign of Gotrek. Fountains of water still surged up from the wreck of the sinking ship, spilling over the smashed walkway, but neither Gotrek nor the beast had floated up to the surface yet. Damn it, she thought, he could be trapped in the hull as it took on water, pinned beneath a spar of wood or by the corpse of that awful thing. If he hadn't drowned already, he soon would, and there was nothing she could do.

A great Rot Fly floated up from the surface of the intact ship. Straddling it was a Nurgle warrior more terrifying even than the pirates who crewed the boats. Thickset and well-armoured, his grey necrotic flesh was marbled with purple veins and his black armour was stained with verdigris and rust. He bore an immense scythe at least eight feet long, and he leaned forwards on the pommel of the saddle as if barely restraining himself from a charge. His face was hidden behind the black shell of an iron helmet. He guided the droning fly over to where the other ship was bubbling in the waters as it sank, hovering over it as if searching for survivors.

The Nurgle crew hadn't seen them yet at least. They were charging along the boardwalk towards the other side of the cave, where the rapidly sinking vessel had crushed the walkway. It should be possible, Amara thought, to sneak down there without them noticing. They had to do something. Even if Gotrek was somehow still alive and managed to get himself to the surface, the pirates would cut him to pieces before he could haul himself out of the water. She looked at the brazier and the barrels of pitch.

'This way, come on,' she said. 'I've got an idea.'

She grabbed Odger by the arm and pulled him up. Together they crawled past the broken archway until the wall of the tunnel hid them from view, and then sprinted for the head of the ladder. The tunnel extended on into the complex beneath the cliffs, and Amara only hoped that there weren't more of those grotesque beasts trundling their way towards them.

It was easy enough to slide down the rusted rungs of the ladder. Odger clutched his spear to his side and shot nervous glances over to the other end of the harbour, where the Nurgle crews were milling together as their ship went down.

'I want the filth who did this!' one of them was screaming, a disgusting, bug-eyed freak with a hand that looked more like a lobster's claw – no doubt their captain. 'Not all Sigmar's navies could sink the *Rust Scythe*, damn them all, and I'll have my vengeance for it, you see if I don't!'

Like the beast Gotrek had killed, he had a slurping maw in his stomach with dozens of yellow, decaying teeth and a thick, rubbery tongue that curled and flopped up against his chest. He raised a fist, which was relatively normal compared to the monstrous claw on his other hand, and shook it at the distant ceiling.

'Spread out!' he cried. 'Hunt them down, the dogs, and bring them to me alive! I'll skin the hides from them and make myself a new pair of boots!'

Amara reached the walkway, landing silently from the bottom rung of the ladder. She crouched and slinked past the stands of barrels and crates until she came to the brazier and the buckets of pitch. The shadow of the other schooner fell against them and made her shudder. The hull, not more than six feet away from the edge of the walkway, dripped with slime, and the wood looked so blighted and decayed that it was surely only some dark magic that made the thing stay afloat. It was pitted with green barnacles that blinked at her like a thousand tiny bloodshot eyes. From the waterline the hull stretched up above them at least twenty feet, a gloomy cliff of rotten wood. She could see its name, picked out in nacreous pearl: *Diphthemious*. She looked at the barrel of pitch at the side of the walkway, where the flames lazily curled, still alight. And what was better for burning away corruption, she thought, than fire…

The pitch was as tough as leather, but there was still some give in it. Grabbing a spar of broken wood, Amara stabbed it into the treacly black substance and managed to coat the end of the stick. She dipped the spar into the brazier and the pitch caught flame. Odger saw what she was doing at once, and within moments he was rummaging about the broken slats of wood for a brand of his own. Together, they flung the burning spears high up towards the deck of the ship.

'Move fast,' Amara said. 'The moment they see what we're doing, we'll have to fight for our lives.'

Odger's brand only stuck to the hull, but the flames soon caught hold all the same. Amara's spar of wood went sailing up like a spear before dropping down onto the deck, and before it had even had time to fall she was twisting another plug of tar onto the end of a broken oar and setting fire to it on the brazier. She flung it up with all her might, hurling it like a javelin. The oar sailed cleanly over the gunwale and stabbed down onto the deck. Already she could hear the flames roaring across the boards. A rolling ball of smoke lifted up from the deck and the fire crackled like dry leaves in an autumn forest.

''Ere, captain!' came a glutinous voice from the other side of the wharf, pausing as he pulled one of his mutated comrades from the water. 'The *Diphthemious* is on fire!'

Amara risked a look, peering around the sodden prow of the ship. As the flames took hold above them, writhing quickly across the deck of the boat, the shadows drew back. In moments they were clearly exposed. As she crouched behind a stack of crates, Amara saw the captain of the Nurgle vessel waving his lobster claw in the air while his cyclopean eye bulged from his head in fury. The slobbering maw in his gut gnashed its teeth.

'You ruddy bilge rats!' he screamed. 'I'll rip yer guts out for this, I will!' He thrashed his crewmates with the haft of his trident. 'Into them, you damned swabs! Cut them down for saboteurs and ship wreckers!'

The Maggotkin pirates, their heavy flesh bulging from their armour plates, their rusted chainmail ringing, stamped across the walkway from the far berth. The wooden slats sagged beneath them as they drew their weapons. Some roared blood-curdling battle cries. Others cheered and laughed with the sport of it all, as jolly as ever.

'Oh Sigmar, save us,' Odger muttered. He threw a last burning slat up onto the deck of the ship and grabbed his spear. His jaw was set. 'I'm glad to have known you, Amara Fidellus,' he muttered. 'I only wish… I only wish we could have made a stand sooner. Perhaps Kranzinnport would have held.'

Amara allowed herself a bitter smile. She had refused to spill blood in the name of the gods, and now her blood was about to be cast onto the waters in the name of a god so loathsome he was a byword for filth and corruption across the realms.

'Better I had died that day,' she whispered.

Odger braced his spear. 'It's not a day we can ever choose,' he said. 'It comes to us when it will.'

The stink of the Maggotkin pirates preceded them, billowing along the slatted walkway. The fire roared and crackled on their left as the great schooner went up in flames, the heat of it beating against their skin. Amara could hear the screams of the crew below decks as the fire reached them, no doubt slaves chained to the rowing benches with nowhere to go. There was a stench in the air of cooking meat and burning tar. The masts had gone up like torches, smuts and ashes streaming from them like smoke from a candle wick. The wall of the cave rose up on the other side of the walkway to their right, but there were no handholds in that wet stone, nowhere for them to climb to escape what was charging towards them.

The boardwalk shook as the diseased warriors came near. Clouds of flies alighted from them, and the stench was stomach-churning. Rotting flesh dripped from their bones; pustules burst and wept on their cankered skin. The walkway was only wide enough for them to run two abreast, and they jostled against each other in a good-natured fury, each of them eager to be the first to hack these saboteurs down.

The ground shook. The flames thundered. Odger prayed, his arms shaking – but he still held his spear. Amara stared unblinking at the pirates – the slack-jawed drooling madness of them, the grotesque mutations that twisted their flesh into some dark mockery of life, the green decay, the maggots that writhed on their skin and the buboes that suppurated and wept. They were everything she hated, creatures that had chosen the madness of the gods above all things.

The water erupted at the side of the boardwalk in a froth of spray. The wooden slats rocked to the side, and some dark, bulky mass hauled itself up out of the foam in front of the charging Maggotkin, fuming with rage. The pirates stumbled to a halt, weapons at guard.

'Gotrek…' Amara whispered.

In the light of the flames from the burning ship he looked like a daemon that had clawed its way out of some hellish underworld. His mohawk had collapsed in the water and dripped down the side of his head, and he was slathered in black slime and mud from the bottom of the harbour. His massive shoulders were covered in livid red weals, and blood was pouring from his lacerated face. His beard was sopping wet, tangled with lengths of rotting seaweed and slime. The rune on his chest glowed with an angry red flame, but it was a mere spark compared to the fire of rage in Gotrek's black eye. He glanced briefly at Amara and Odger, but it was like he looked straight through them. They were nothing to him, just another thing to kill.

'Sigmar, save me!' Odger choked, backing away.

'Gotrek, please,' Amara said, trying to keep her voice level. She raised her hands to him. 'Listen to my voice, it's–'

'What are you waiting for, lads?' cried the pirate captain as he rushed up the boardwalk behind his crew. He spat on the boards and chortled richly, and his laughter sounded both grim and jovial at the same time. The lobster claw clicked and snapped. 'Brush that stunted little duardin aside and get those ruddy ship wreckers! I'll strip the flesh from their bones before I'm done with 'em!'

Gotrek slowly turned to face the pirates. Amara felt the heat of his rage withdraw, and it was only then that she realised she'd been holding her breath.

The fire rekindled in the brazier of his axe. His great shoulders trembled and his face was purple with rage. The rune flared.

The scream that Gotrek gave was like the bellow of a god, and it shook the very walls of the cave. The Maggotkin pirates took a step back – but then Gotrek was on them, charging like a steam tank down the length of the boardwalk, the slats shaking under his boots. He leapt at the last moment, clearing near six feet off the ground as he crashed into the column of pirates with his axe swirling around his head.

It was like an explosion. Screams, the clash of metal, the rending cry of armour plate carved aside. Bodies went tumbling into the water at the side of the boardwalk – bloated corpses without heads, severed limbs, flapping tentacles. A cascade of guts went splattering into the air. Shattered swords and axes were cast aside. Gotrek, as if speaking in tongues, let loose a war cry of unintelligible rage, his axe rising and falling in a blur of gold and silver.

'Fight, damn your eyes!' the captain cried. His voice gurgled like a broken sewer.

He waved his trident in the air, but the press was too dense for him to move forward. The narrow channel of the boardwalk funnelled the pirates straight onto Gotrek's axe, and blood and filth were sheeting through the air as the duardin clambered his way past. Every stroke of his blade carved a tranche through the foe. Skulls were crumpled, helmets split asunder. For those warriors who managed to parry a blow or make a thrust of their own, Gotrek turned their weapons aside in a crash of splintered steel. A knife slashed across his ribs but he barely seemed to feel it. A tentacle thrashed at his face but he cleaved it aside.

Amara and Odger followed in Gotrek's wake, Odger pausing to spear the wounded in the face as they passed. Bodies bobbed in the black water, face down, leaking green fluid into the harbour. Others, still half alive, were tugged down to the depths by the weight of their armour, gurgling and crying out as they drowned. The flames of the burning ship roared, and the masts came crashing down in a gout of fire and smoke. Even the boardwalk was beginning to smoulder now. In moments the whole harbour would be an inferno.

At last, Gotrek carved his way through the rancid crew, slashing the last few of them apart until the captain was the only one left. The duardin, red with fury, clambered over the corpses that were strewn across the walkway, gnashing his teeth, his beard streaked with blood. The battle had made him even more furious, if that was possible. It had stoked his anger until it seemed unquenchable. The rune on his chest flared like a blacksmith's forge.

'Get back, you dog!' the captain cried. Despite his terror, he gave a hearty, catarrhal laugh and held his trident on guard. 'I'll make you rue the day you took on Captain Pertussis, you scoundrel! You see if I don't!'

A hollow buzz murmured across the cave, rising to a whining pitch as the warrior on the Rot Fly soared across the water. The fly reared back with a gust of sewage-stink as the warrior swung his scythe at Gotrek's head, and as the great rusted blade clashed into the haft of Gotrek's rune-axe, the duardin was thrown backwards off his feet. He slammed into the cave wall on the other side of the wharf.

'You fight well, duardin,' the rider said. His voice boomed inside his helmet, and he gave a horrible, high-pitched, snickering laugh. 'I'll give you that. But now you shall pit your skills against me, scum. I will carve the Grandfather's rune on your back, to match that blasphemous rune on your chest!'

'Cholerax, you fool!' the captain cried, scuttling back along the walkway. 'Get us out of here!'

'You would demand anything of me, pirate?' the warrior mocked. The Rot Fly bobbed in the air, the tattered wings a blur of motion. 'Lord Cholerax does not retreat from combat!'

Gotrek, snarling, got to his feet. He snatched up his axe, spittle flecked on his lips, his eye blazing with fury.

'Remember the ritual,' the pirate whined as he retreated along the boardwalk. He was almost pleading. 'You would risk that for your honour?'

Odger flung his spear at the Nurgle warrior with a gasp, but Cholerax tugged the pommel of his saddle to one side and the Rot Fly banked to avoid it. As if this had made up his mind, the Nurgle lord swooped back along the wharf with a strangled roar. The gangling legs of the Rot Fly scooped up the pirate captain, who gave a defiant shake of his trident. Gotrek leapt forwards, snarling with rage, but they were well out of reach of his axe now. Surging off across the surface of the harbour, banking to avoid the flames of the burning ship, the Nurgle lord and his passenger passed through the cave mouth and headed out to sea. Soon the Rot Fly was no more than a black speck against the trembling mist that rose from the island in the distance, and all around them was fire and smoke.

A day out from Xil'anthos and he found the remains of the camp-fire, tucked into a spur of ancient ruins. There was thick green grass underfoot, a cool breeze whispering from the plains. A sheltered spot, somewhere to rest up and gather your strength.

He found a patch of ground where someone had lain down for a while. Crushed reeds at the side of the pool where someone had dipped their head to drink. He felt the grass with his gloved fingers, pushed back the hat on his crown, stared up at the wide spread of the blue sky. Xil'anthos was still visible there in the distance, a discoloured smudge against the grasslands, not far from the epic sweep of the forest. Hard land for someone travelling alone, as he well knew.

He sat there for a while and thought, looking back the way he had come. His knuckles still ached, but the bruise on his jaw was beginning to fade already. He'd left payment for the damage, and enough to pay for a bottle or two for those he'd questioned. It was only fair, and he always paid his way. He'd got the answers he needed in any case. Always did.

He shrugged the saddlebag off his shoulder, wondered if he should rest for a while here himself. He'd been travelling for some time, always a step or two behind. Ahead of him there were only the downs falling to the edge of the plains, and the plains studded with what looked like diasporgum, even what might have been a herd of yethars in the distance. Dangerous animals, especially if you came upon them unawares. He could skirt it, loop round till he came out by the western edge of the forest, but then that was a long trek down to the coast, along the coast road and back up. He scanned the ground again on the far side of the dell. The tracks were still visible, just. No rain these last few days at least. Kept them fresh.

He sighed, took out a pipe and stuffed the bowl with the ruby Ghyranite tobacco he kept telling himself he would give up. Sparked his flint, smoked a while as he thought over what he'd learned. Far up and across towards the south, he could see the flat black shapes of jade eagles quartering the land. He wondered what they'd seen out here. If only they could tell him. No point putting the question to them. Shame.

He thought about what he'd learned in Xil'anthos. Hadn't expected it, he had to admit. This new addition, not what he had anticipated. Strange. Always made him uneasy, an extra complication like that. He wondered what the story was behind it all. Figured he'd find out soon enough. He always did. In the end it didn't make any difference.

Later, he passed through the fields of diasporgum, pushing them aside, his pistol drawn. Always hated the smell of them. Perfect spot for an ambush, but nothing challenged him as he came out onto the flat green fields on the other side. He holstered the pistol, stopping to drink from his canteen.

On the ground, sprinkled through the grass, he found the crushed remains of harrowbugs. Thousands of them, mangled, splattered, scraped off in a fit. No corpses, though, no sign of anyone succumbing to the creatures. Good, he thought. Would feel somehow pointless for it all to have ended here.

He stared off towards the forest, a mile distant. Druhiel of the Pines, the hidden city. The tracks pointed to the cusp of the treeline. There was still a trail to follow. Still a moment when all this came to a head, when the punishment was administered. He wondered if they were still there. Probably not. Still, there would be more folk he could question, more answers he could get.

By the authority vested in me, *he thought. A slow smile, just the hint of it on his lips.*

He set off for Druhiel. High above, the jade eagles screamed. Ahead of him, the forest trembled.

PART THREE

PART THREE

CHAPTER SEVENTEEN

OVER THE SEA

The flames from the burning ship lapped along the boardwalk, although the sodden planks of wood kept them at bay for the moment. The other vessel still bubbled as it sank to the bottom of the harbour. No more than the aft of the ship was visible now, and there were fat black rats scrambling to escape it, plopping down into the water and swimming off into the shadows beneath the walkways. Amara wondered what kind of rats felt comfortable infesting a Nurgle ship. She shook her head – it didn't bear thinking about.

The whole cave trembled in the fire, and the heat forced them along to the berths on the western side. Gotrek was slumped there on the slats, still gripping his axe, huffing to catch his breath as the rage leaked out of him. The rune flickered to a sullen gold. Gotrek clutched at it with his hand, his face wrenched with what Amara was shocked to see was pain.

'I'm not another weapon you can use,' he mumbled, his good

eye squeezed shut. His fingers once again curled around the rune as if he would tear it out. 'Damn you, I won't be, I swear...'

He coughed and shivered and ran his hands through his sopping hair, spiking it up again into some approximation of his familiar mohawk.

'Gotrek,' Amara said, crouching beside him. 'You're injured, you need to rest.'

The weals on his shoulders were a fiery red, and the lacerations on his face had puffed out into white contusions that leaked a thin gruel of blood and slime. She rummaged in her knapsack for bandages, but she'd used the last of them on the survivors up in the city. All she had left was the tub of ointment she'd bought in Druhiel for the harrowbug bites. Not knowing what else to do, she rubbed it on the contusions, hoping it would make a difference. Gotrek flinched.

'Get off with that damned stuff,' he grumbled. 'I don't need any bloody help, damn you.'

He staggered as he got to his feet, leaning on his axe for balance. Amara could see his eye swimming into focus.

'He's infected,' Odger said. 'By all the gods, I've never seen someone fight like that, but you can push your luck only so far, duardin. The plague is in you now.'

'Damn the bloody plague,' Gotrek huffed. 'I've had worse colds. And worse hangovers.' He stretched his neck until the vertebrae cracked, then shrugged his shoulders to get the knots out of them.

Amara looked down at the splattered limbs and coiled guts that were strewn around the boardwalk or bobbing in the water. Gotrek had gone through the Maggotkin pirates like a bolt of lightning. She offered to let him lean on her, but he shrugged her off and followed Odger as they made their way to the far end of the wharf, where a few small fishing boats were still tied up on their hawsers. She looked back at the burning ship where it spat and crackled with flame. The screams of those who hadn't been able to escape were silent now, all of them burned to death in the inferno below decks as the ship went up like a torch.

She had vowed not to spill blood in the gods' names. She had been true to her word, she supposed. But how many had she just killed by consigning them to the flames instead? This was a violent world, as she knew only too well. Could the answer to that violence ever be anything other than more violence?

They reached the berth where the fishing smacks were tied up – half a dozen small craft that looked better suited to cutting across the harbour than taking to the open sea. Gotrek flopped down into the one nearest the cave mouth and slumped beside the tiller while Odger untied the boat from its hawser.

'We'll have to row,' Odger said. He glanced to the waters beyond the cave mouth. 'No breeze to speak of, I doubt a sail is going to be much use.'

'Let's get it over and done with then,' Gotrek slurred. 'Gives them less time to prepare.'

The duardin looked absolutely terrible. There was a sluggish look in his eye, a drawn cast to his face, and a tinge of green around the wounds on his chest and shoulders. How was he possibly still going? To have killed two of those terrifying beasts, and to have survived a fifty-foot drop through the deck and bottom of a twin-master to the harbour floor, and to then butcher his way through two dozen of the hardiest Nurgle warriors Amara had ever seen… Kranzinnport had suffered weeks of the most unutterable horror, and in a day Gotrek had freed the survivors from their prison and shattered the raiders who had made their lives such a misery.

She looked at the rune, at the deep flicker of coruscating light that seemed to blend with the very gold.

'Krag Blackhammer's master rune,' she said as she stepped into the boat. Odger pushed off and Gotrek passed over the oars. Odger fitted them to the riggers and slowly paddled them out of the berth. 'That's what you called it. What is it really?'

'Buggered if I know,' Gotrek said with a shrug. 'Blackhammer was the Runemaster of Unback Lodge, in Aqshy.' He tapped the rune with his axe blade. 'Maleneth tried to steal it when I first... When I first met her.' He laughed sadly. 'One minute I was in the Realm of Chaos, the next I was walking this world. I thought it was all a trick, another damned ruse of the gods.' He clutched the rune again and winced, as if it caused him pain. 'How it ended up in me, well... that's another story.'

'You fought in the Realm of Chaos?' Amara said, hardly believing the words she was saying. 'Gotrek... what *are* you?'

'The last of a dying breed, lass,' he muttered. 'A dead breed. The last *dawi* in the Mortal Realms.'

Haltingly, as if groping for the words, Odger said, 'The Realm of Chaos...' He shook his head and looked at the duardin. 'When you came out of the water and fought them, those raiders, it was as if... I saw you, Gotrek, but it wasn't you. Or it was *more* than you. We have some dealings with the Fyreslayers from the Mistral Peaks, trade and the like, and I've seen their banners when they march. A golden mask in the form of their god. That's what I saw.'

He took out the hammer pendant that Baffin had given him and kissed it.

'By Sigmar and all the gods,' he said. There were tears in his eyes. 'They have heard our prayers at last, and they have sent you to end this horror.'

Gotrek said nothing. He frowned, his hand tightening on the tiller of the boat. He did no more than stare out at the water as they slipped through the mouth of the cave. It was as if Odger's words had depressed him somehow. Amara watched him carefully. It was all she could do – she could not take hold of her thoughts, they moved so fast. The wounds on his face and shoulders were still tinged with green, but he seemed to have overcome the fatigue of whatever had infected him. She couldn't imagine the natural hardiness that made such a thing possible; even an ordinary duardin, as tough as they were, could not have shaken off the diseases of the Plague God like this.

All of this had made more sense to her when she was a priest. It was the one thing she missed, that feeling of certainty. Hammer in one hand, *Intimations of the Comet* in the other, and the foe in front of you. A warrior priest needed to sign up to only two credos in the faith: the enemies of Sigmar were legion, and Sigmar was wise and just. That's all there was to it. But now? What did she have to hold on to any more, but anger and regret and sorrow. How to carry on, when that was all you had?

Unbidden, the image came to her mind – a hand in hers, the burnt grass, the smell of death on the breeze. She closed her eyes, felt the tears prickle against them. It was only with the sternest will that she kept them from falling.

Odger cut the oars, his back to Wither Island while Gotrek peered across the sea and guided the boat. The raiders had come in seagoing schooners, and the rowing boat was being pitched and tossed on the waters, but still they managed to struggle on. The island itself was masked by a growing mist that slithered across the water towards them – a clammy, foetid brew that smelled of sour breath and seemed to squeeze all the light out of the world. It could only have been late morning, but the sky above them was equally gloomy, as if they were rowing through the dusk.

'It's not natural,' Odger said quietly. 'That smell. Foul, isn't it? Like the stench of corpses, or dead flowers.'

A bell rang somewhere in the distance, a low bronze clang that rolled across the misty waters. Odger met Amara's eye and they both looked at Gotrek, but he said nothing. He pushed the tiller a fraction to the left. All they could hear now was the low splash of the oars, the gulp of the water as they entered the mist. Amara wondered what Gotrek could see through the murk with his duardin eye. His axe still lay at his side and she took some comfort in that. Wither Island had looked around twenty miles across the sea from the coast, and she doubted they had covered more than a couple of miles so far – although with the swirling mist it was almost impossible to tell.

Gotrek saw her looking at his axe. 'Still foreswearing violence in Sigmar's name, then?' he said. 'You burned that ship easily enough at least. If you've made your peace with death, then you have to be prepared to fight when we get to this island.'

'It wasn't in Sigmar's name,' she bristled.

Gotrek shrugged his massive shoulders, wincing against the pain of the red weals. There was a sheen of sweat on his forehead, Amara realised. He was still fighting off the infection. He coughed long and loud, spat a lump of something gristly and black into the water. He thumped his chest with his fist, his good eye screwed up tight.

'Gotrek?' Amara said, leaning forwards. 'Are you all right?'

'Right enough,' the duardin choked. His lips were pale. He cleared his throat and started rummaging about in the strongbox beneath the bench he was sitting on. 'And if I know fishing folk as well as I think I do...'

He gave a bark of triumph. From the depths of the strongbox he pulled out a ceramic bottle and gave it an experimental slosh. He pulled out the cork stopper with his broken teeth and took a long and luxurious swig.

'Ha!' he cried, smacking his lips. 'Here's a cure for what ails you! Not bad for human grog. Milder than I would normally like, but it's the only damned medicine I've ever needed!'

He passed the bottle to Amara, who gave it a suspicious sniff.

Firewater, she reckoned. She took a mouthful, swallowed it down and felt it burn like lava in her chest. She passed it to Odger, who held off the oars for a moment while he tipped it back.

'Gods!' he coughed. 'It's like swamp water mixed with coal tar!'

He tossed it back to Gotrek, who drank it off and cast the bottle far out into the water.

'Gets cold out here, if you're a fisherman,' he said. 'Got to have something to keep the fires burning in you, and a spot of skaven courage never does any harm before a fight.'

His eye burned and he shakily got to his feet.

'Give me the oars, lad,' he said. 'Sooner we get this over and done with, the better.'

CHAPTER EIGHTEEN

THE DANCE OF DEATH

How many years had it been? Waiting, praying, turning over in his mind those moments when they had all progressed with such joy and delight into the waters of a new world? The Everspring Swathe, an emerald paradise thick with vapours, rustling with beast and virus as they waded through the thickening broth. Rotwater Blight, the paradise that was, and is, and will be again…

He had thought of it often during those long and lonely months while he hid in the Thyrian swamps. Every morning, if such a thing as morning could be said to dawn in that foetid place, Bilgeous had shuffled from his reed shack with prayers on his lips. Hunched into his robes, he had fondled the scrolls of canker and blight and read through the sacred words he had written, the holy texts he was composing about the days when Nurgle's Garden had appeared in the Mortal Realms for that dim and gloomy moment many years ago. All through the centuries he had kept his vigil, cheering himself with the new diseases that fermented in his skin, walking the bounds of the stagnant pools and muddy streams where he had made his refuge.

Sometimes, when the Grandfather thought to bless him, Bilgeous had found mortal trappers and hunters wading through the marsh in search of swamp boars and leopard eels. It was a simple enough matter to still their hearts with a sorcerous blast, or to hack them down with the hook on the end of his staff. It was a comfort to him to watch their corpses melt into the waters of the swamp: the way the skin puffed out and went slack against the flesh, sloughing off in greasy folds and ropes; the way the yellow fat curdled to a rancid green, the meat growing black and boiling with maggots. He delighted to watch the bones emerge, peeping from the slurry, until the corpses were no more than splayed skeletons sinking into the mire. Where life had once been, there was only death, and where death had once been, there now came new life. The maggots began their glorious change, rising from the filth as blue and amber flies. Plants and swamp flowers grew from the compost of the corpse. The richness of change had been all around him; the bounty of decay.

Could he have stayed there forever, content to haunt the margins of that place? The swamps soon accrued an evil reputation, he knew, and became a place where mothers told their children not to play. The hunters and trappers avoided it in the end, for it was said that if you ventured too deep into them, you would become the prey of the swamp fiend, Old Slough, who picked his way through the mire on stilts made of human bones, and who had to clad himself in human skin lest his rotting organs spill out onto the ground. Bilgeous had chuckled at these legends, but they had saddened him in some way too. In those long and lonely years before the visions of the Grandfather had sent him from the swamps, he wondered how many of his comrades in the great crusade of Rotwater Blight had fallen to a similar fate. Scattered by the armies of the God-King, forced to seek refuge in the dim places of the realm, they had slowly become no more than myths and legends – little bits of folklore to scare children before they went to sleep. He could have been Old Slough for all the days that remained to him, his moment of glory in the Rotwater Blight forgotten as it was subsumed in the tide of the centuries.

But no, that was not to be his fate. Bilgeous Pox had been gifted the visions that had sent him creeping with joyful certainty all the way to the Rocanian Coast, to the wide body of water where this shard of the Grandfather's toenail had settled in the deep. It was given to him to achieve what Bolathrax and all his daemon armies could not do. It was Bilgeous Pox who would plant the seeds of Nurgle's Garden in the Mortal Realms once more, and who would stand as midwife to the coming of the Grandson.

He stood on the lip of the pit now, leaning on his staff and staring down into the corpse-mulch as it gurgled beneath him. Here and there he could see the suggestion of a half-melted face, the skin slipping from the bone like a cloth mask. Dead eyes had sunk into grey sockets, teeth were bared in silent snarls, mouths like black caves opened in noiseless screams. He saw limbs poking from the mess of it all, bloated and green. Hands raised in salute or surrender. Hair strewn like weeds across the surface of the lake. Bubbles of corpse gas rose and popped in the humidity with a stench of bile and excrement. Bilgeous breathed it in. He tapped his staff excitedly on the edge of the pit and continued to peer down, where all the bodies were rotting into a vivid soup.

Carefully, with a luxuriant groan, Bilgeous crouched down and dipped his hand into the pit, gathering up a palmful of the viscous liquid. Like a chef cautiously sampling a new recipe, he lapped the filth up with his tongue, rolling the zestful taste of it against his palate. He frowned, parsing the flavour. If only that fool Pertussis would bring his damned ships back to the island so they could make sure! Another few corpses should do it beyond all doubt – fourteen or so, or perhaps twenty-one… But time was running out.

He looked to the sky, a blank grey sheet that rippled with green light, choked in the vapours that rose from the pit. This last day of the dead moon, here in this realm that was so alive with the energies of life…

Pulling himself to his feet, leaning heavily against his staff, Bilgeous unlaced the weave of magic, drawing the threads of reality aside so he could pluck at the strings of sorcery. He closed his eyes, sank into himself, let the colours of Ghyran bloom before his eyes. The colours of the Garden, the colours of the Grandfather.

He felt the broth in the pit start to vibrate. Under the surface, deep in the stew, the waters trembled. Here on this shard of the Grandfather's toenail, and there in the twisted avenues and walkways of the Garden, reality surged and made ready to clasp itself to the skein of the infinite. Bilgeous muttered the words of his spell and felt them fall from his lips like dragonflies and maggots, like ripples of light, like streams of pestilence and decay. Beneath the shroud of his mouldering hood, he opened his eyes and stared out onto the green scum of the lake.

There, where the surface shuddered in the centre…

He held out his arms, raised his staff, felt his voice lurch into a new configuration as the words of the spell shook through him. The pressure behind his eyes was immense, as if they would burst from his head in a spray of ichor. His whole body quaked, and the surface of the pit was alive with dancing flame – streaks of iridescent vapour, threads of green mist, the hiss and sparkle of rot like a marbled flank of dead flesh slowly falling into its long decay.

There! He cried out – and slowly, unfolding from the mulch of corpse and vomit, came the rising face of the Grandson, wrenched with all the agonies of birth. The great eyes were closed, screwed up against the pain that was translating it from the aether. The long, ragged mouth champed and cried in silent ecstasy, the tusks gnashing at the skin of the world, the claws trying to pierce the caul that held it back. The face pressed against the surface of the pool, corpulent, diseased, and so huge it nearly filled the fifty yards of its radius from edge to edge.

Bilgeous sobbed to see such beauty and wonder, and soon his weeping turned to a joyous laughter. But then the threads of the spell began to fray in his hands; the weave of magic grew dark and thin, and he could feel it begin to split apart. Slowly, the great face of the Grandson sank back into the mire, the corpulent brow smoothed out to a saddened resignation. Where there had been a shimmering, humid lens that looked onto the fecundity of the Garden, there was now only a sordid, murky pit, thick with filth and buzzing with flies. Bilgeous collapsed to his knees, dropping his staff, pain lancing through him in spears and arrows of fire.

The Grandson was gone. It was not enough. He had not done enough, and it was only his arrogance that made him assume his powers were enough to compensate.

'Pertussis!' he screamed. He coughed long and loud, spitting out a quivering lump of flesh; a mouthful of blood and bile.

Old Slough, he seemed to hear. He saw himself hobbling through the stagnant ponds, muttering to himself, clutching at his mouldering scrolls, a sad old creature lost in dreams of glory. *Old Slough, where the reeds are thick and the mist lies heavy on the water... Don't go down to the swamps, or Old Slough will get you!*

'Pertussis,' he cried again. 'Bring me my captives!'

The air, normally thick with the gentle buzz of insects, was suddenly split by the Bilepiper's drone. It was coming from the other side of the harbour. Discordant, frantic, the mad tootling spoke of danger and threat, and it was a sound Bilgeous had not heard in all the long weeks since he had raised the island from the waves.

He staggered to his feet and hobbled his way along the path from the pit, the pommel of his staff slurping into the mud as he walked. Disturbed, he could hear the plump, gurgling voice of Lord Cholerax, the agitated buzzing of a Rot Fly, the raging screech of Captain Pertussis.

When he came out of the stands of fern, pushing his way through the overhanging vines, Bilgeous could see Pertussis sprawled on the ground by the stony wharf, clutching his eye. His trident had flown from his hand and was lying in the dirt beside him, and Lord Cholerax, seeming more bloated than ever, was standing over him with his scythe raised. By his side, shivering and making small, agitated leaps into the air, Cholerax's Rot Fly flapped its wings and snuffled in the muck.

'You're no more than a snivelling coward,' Cholerax cried. He crashed his tentacle to his breastplate, his helmet quivering with rage. 'If your incompetence has condemned this ritual, then I will not be responsible for my actions!'

'Curse you for a puffed-up Bloat Fly!' Pertussis retched. He staggered to his feet and scrabbled for his trident. 'What use would it have been for us to die back there, answer me that!'

The goitre on Cholerax's neck shook with his rage, and as Bilgeous limped onto the wharf he was sure the warrior was going to slice the pirate in two with his scythe.

Pertussis held his trident across his chest and sidled back across the rocky ground, preparing to defend himself. Bilgeous saw that the berths where the pirate's vessels were usually moored were now empty, and all he could see on the wharf were the milling crowds of cultists nervously grasping their weapons, perturbed that there were no captives for them to thrash along the trail to the pit. Bilgeous placed himself between the two warriors, and a grim foreboding curled its way across the back of his neck. The sea beyond the harbour and the prow of Wither Island was smothered in a low blanket of grey mist, and Kranzinnport as it hunkered on the Rocanian Coast was hidden from them.

'What is the meaning of this?' he demanded. His voice croaked in the dead air. 'Captain Pertussis, where are your ships? Where are the captives from Kranzinnport? What mockery is this, that you would risk our holy venture here at the last moment?'

His sight blackened, as if a sheet had been thrown over him. Bilgeous reeled, throwing his weight onto his staff. The ritual had drained him; he had been a fool to attempt it before the mulch was ready. A fool, arrogant and impatient, capering about like a Nurgling keen on mischief, when the solemnity of the moment should have shut his mouth with prayer!

He coughed, felt the fit withdraw, a string of drool hanging from his chin. Bilgeous wiped it away with the back of his bony wrist. *Grandfather,* he thought. *How much of myself have I drained into this moment? The swellings and the bloat of your favour have been burned away and replaced by this feeble desiccation…*

'My ships?' Pertussis cried, his voice crackling with phlegm. 'My ships are at the bottom of Kranzinnport harbour for all the good they do me now, and my crew hacked to pieces with not a Blightking left alive amongst them! We've been the horrors of the oceans for a century, and not a port along the coast of Yska and Thyria has been free of our attentions, and now what? Am I to be a lone captain, with not a ship to call his own, and nary a crew to command? Fie!' he cried. 'Damn your holy venture, sorcerer, for you have cost me everything!'

Bilgeous looked with horror at Lord Cholerax.

'Is this true?'

'True enough,' the warrior rumbled. He snorted out a high-pitched screech of laughter, although he sounded far from amused. 'The raid was an utter disaster because of this pirate's incompetence! This is what happens when you trust to such rogues.'

Pertussis rounded on Cholerax, jabbing out with his trident to emphasise his points.

'It was this fool's Rot Fly that brought us news of the forces that had come to Kranzinnport, was it not? We were led into a trap, an ambush! They had a hundred troops at least, hardened warriors all. They had cannons, rockets, incendiary devices of terrible and unknown arts!'

'Lies,' Cholerax spat. He swiped at the pirate with his scythe and Pertussis stumbled backwards, snapping his lobster claw. 'It was no more than a company at best, led by one savage duardin who carved his way through your feeble crew as if they were Rot Fly droppings!' He faltered, turned to Bilgeous as if trying to plead his own case. 'True it was though that this duardin seemed possessed of a mighty strength. I confess I don't understand it, but he burned with such a fury–'

'Duardin?' Bilgeous shrieked. 'Fury? In the name of the Grandfather, you mean to tell me that our forces have suffered a mortal blow, and we have no captives for the rite?'

He stared up at the clouds, the billowing mass of mist and vapour that shrouded the island. There, just faintly visible as the day began to turn, was the light of the last thin rind of the dying moon.

'I care not if it was one possessed duardin or a thousand,' he snarled. 'One company or all the regiments of Hammerhal Ghyra! The armies of the God-King himself could be massed on the Rocanian Shore, ready to sail their way to this holy island, and it would make not a single jot of difference! Blast you for heathens and fools! We must complete the ritual by nightfall or the Grandson will slip from this reality and will not be seen for another hundred years!'

Pertussis, giving Cholerax a nervous, hateful glance, ran his hand over the slobbering tongue of his belly-maw.

'Then what do you suggest, sorcerer?' he said. 'For without ships, I have no more means of gaining you captives.'

'Bilepiper!' Bilgeous called.

He beckoned with his staff, and the daemon skipped near from the spur of the wharf, where the granite wall stabbed out into the silty water. Its solitary eye glared at them from beneath its tattered leather hood, yellow as pus. From its grinning, fang-filled mouth unfurled a sinuous blue tongue, and from its bloated green belly hung a loop of rotting guts. The daemon carried in its hands an intestinal sac, like an air-filled bladder. Poking from it were a trio of pipes carved from bones, and whenever the creature squeezed the bladder, a thin, wheedling sound fluted from them. In its other hand it held a jester's marotte, a screaming head wearing a ragged cap and bells. The daemon, locked to the energies of this holy land, seemed to flicker and contract in the dim light – one moment it had no more substance than a parchment sketch, the next, it leered there in meaty solidity, stinking of offal.

'Play for us, Herald,' Bilgeous commanded. 'Let us hear the wondrous music of the Garden. Play those melodies that drive men mad with joy, and we will salvage something from this wreckage.'

He turned to Cholerax and Pertussis. Both warriors quailed before his wrath.

'My lord, ready your knights for combat, for I doubt these forces – whoever they are – will leave this island unmolested.'

Cholerax, slumped and heavy, slammed the pommel of his scythe on the ground. Behind his belly-plate, the mouth he was so keen to hide gave a chomping snicker. He stilled it quickly with his tentacle.

'It shall be done,' he said. 'The Knights of the Underswamp will ride to battle in the Grandson's name, and all shall rue the day they dared stand against us!'

As Cholerax lumbered away to regain the saddle of his Rot Fly, Bilgeous turned to the pirate captain. 'Pertussis?'

'Aye,' he said. He narrowed his bulging eye and tightened his grip on his trident.

'You will have a chance to redeem yourself, and I swear you shall sail oceans undreamed of when this is done.'

'Is that so?' Pertussis said suspiciously.

'The waning of our hopes is only ever the compost from which new hopes may rise,' Bilgeous said. He gestured to the Bilepiper. 'Now come, let us see what may be done to call the Grandson forth.'

There was a shrieking wail, piercing in that misty silence as the sea slopped against the harbour walls. The Bilepiper squeezed the fleshy bladder and puffed through the scabrous reed, its talons dancing over the fingerholes of the pipes. Skirling and screeching, the tune unfurled – a mad and jaunty melody that loped and skittered about the island, rising and falling and sliding and skimming, until all who heard it felt their hearts lift in happy abandon. Bilgeous Pox tapped his ancient, sandalled foot against the wharf and tried to hum along. Pertussis bobbed his head and chuckled, and on either wing of the harbour walls, the cultists seemed to snap to attention as the notes of the melody drifted over them.

They were mortal still, those men and women who had joined the Cycle of Life. Some of them had been gathered into Bilgeous' care when he first stepped out of the swamps of Thyria and made his way to the Rocanian Coast, drawn by the visions of the Grandfather. Listening to the words he had written in his scrolls, they had found their souls responding to the bounty and happiness of the God of Plagues, and they laughed to see their limbs twisted into such wonderful new shapes. Each creeping skin disease or intestinal infection was a source of joy for them, and they had taken up weapons in his service as they crept their way towards the empty waters beyond Kranzinnport. Some few had chosen to lend their aid to Nurgle's cause when they were brought here as captives from the city. Those young enough that their souls had not been fully poisoned by Sigmar's lies, or old enough that they feared Sigmar's judgement when death at last overwhelmed them, had begged to be admitted to the Grandfather's ranks. Fewer than Bilgeous would have liked, but even so... Yet more had been taken from the merry slaves in Pertussis' ships, to make up the numbers should battle be forced upon them. All in all, there were perhaps two hundred cultists manning the slipways of the harbour, or tending the new growths in the jungle, or acting as grooms and squires for Lord Cholerax's knights. More than enough for what Bilgeous had in mind.

The piper skipped from the wharf, still puffing away on his reed, and slowly, as if tugged on an invisible line, the cultists began to drift over from the harbour. Men and women, their skin thick with boils, came laughing out of the jungle. Mortals, so twisted with disease they almost looked like the holy Plague-bearers of Nurgle's Garden, trotted up from the rocky headlands. The Bilepiper capered to the mouth of the path that led through the jungle and all the human denizens of the island followed him, prancing in the muck, leaping and dancing and laughing as the music filled their ears and swelled their souls. Round and round they danced, linking arms and tentacles, their heads thrown back in such gladness that it made Bilgeous smile to see them.

Even now, in the shadow of this new threat from Kranzinn-port, there was such happiness in the sorcerer's soul that he gave a little caper of his own. Leaning on his staff, holding up the hem of his robes, he shuffled and leapt, and followed the line of dancing pilgrims as they skipped on through the jungle. By his side, Pertussis waved his lobster claw and hummed merrily. He stabbed his trident into the air in time to the rolling melody, but so wild and complex was the Bilepiper's tune, an unruly racket straight from the rotting glades of the infinite, that none could hope to match its madness.

Even the Bloat Flies and the jungle beasts were drawn to the song. Bilgeous could see bulbous eyes watching them from the undergrowth, strange creatures bobbing and shuffling as the procession passed them. The flies droned merrily through the air, slipping this way and that, some provoked into such ecstasy that they launched themselves at the Bilepiper and splattered themselves into paste against his skin.

Waving his marotte, the shrunken head wailing a raggedy little tune of its own, the Bilepiper brought the procession to the edge of the pit in the middle of the clearing. There, the mulch simmered in the heat, throwing up a green miasma that hung like a dark cloud over the jungle. The rotting flesh sighed beneath them. The fermenting bile squeaked and popped, and deep beneath the surface of the mulch foul things were stirring.

'Round, my friend!' Bilgeous Pox called. 'Lead them round, and we will compass this pit with our dance!'

Nodding, leering, the single yellow eye flickering in and out of reality, the Bilepiper skirled its song higher and higher, until the notes seemed to claw at the very sky. The mortals, so seduced by the Bilepiper's tune that they scarcely knew where or who they were, capered madly around the circumference of the pit. Arms flung in the air, they cavorted round and round, chanting prayers, lending their voices to the melody as it tripped through scales and octaves undreamed of.

Pertussis waved his trident like a conductor's baton, snapping his claw in the air as his belly-maw slurped its tongue against his breastplate. Sidling like a crab, he hopped on the outside of the grand circle and lent his gurgling, congested voice to the song. Bilgeous Pox cavorted beside him, feeling new strength in his rotting veins. But where the pirate captain had given himself over completely to the dance, the sorcerer kept a keen eye on its progression. Once the Bilepiper had led the cultists once, twice, and then seven times around the circumference of the pit, he held up his staff and cried out, 'Enough!'

The notes faded at once. The bladder breathed out a last, almost despairing sigh. The Bilepiper, grinning with its yellow fangs, tucked the instrument under its pestilent arm and gave its marotte a last, rattling shake. Bilgeous bowed to it, and the piper bowed back.

All the mortals, their minds still gripped by the melodies, came to a shuddering halt. They stood there laughing and chuckling, ringing the pit and gazing down happily into the soup of rot and corruption.

'Now, my tunesmith,' Bilgeous called to the piper. He raised his staff and suddenly cut it down, and the piper slathered its tongue to the reed once more and guided it into its mouth.

This song it now played was no merry tune fit for capering. It was a single, penetrating note, sharp as a blade and bright as the moon on a cloudless night. It seemed to stab into Bilgeous' ears, wavering and precise at the same time, and he bared his teeth at the agonies it conjured up in his mind.

Pertussis dropped his trident into the mud and clutched his head. The mortals cried out as one, their mouths distended, their arms raised in holy ecstasy. The note screamed higher and higher, like fingernails torn down a slate. And then, as if at some hidden signal, it cut dead, and the clearing was left in stunned silence.

'Now, my brethren,' Bilgeous said, with reverence. 'The dance is over, and the sacrifice must be made.'

Each cultist armed with a knife snatched the blade from their belt and, without pause, stabbed it up into their throat.

Blood sheeted down into the pit. Bodies tumbled from the edge and flopped into the mire. Cries of delight met screams of agony as flesh melted from bones, and as the caustic soup began to digest its meal. The cultists who had no knives to wield took up clubs and bludgeons and beat each other to death, flinging the corpses into the pit before leaping in gladly themselves. The song of the Bilepiper still rolled through their minds, and some still chanted the melody as death overcame them. The pit bubbled and began to rise, and sprays of filth flecked up from its surface. Green mists wrinkled across its plane. The ground began to shake. Night was drawing near – an unnatural night, called down as the moon faded and regrew.

It was nearly time.

Pertussis looked on incredulously. He laughed once, a choking, hacking guffaw. 'By the Grandfather,' he said, 'I never would have thought of it, sorcerer! Aye, I commend you for a ruthless villain, a man after my own rotten heart!'

He turned to Bilgeous and frowned. Then he looked down at the hook that was plunged into his throat – the hook that was attached to the sorcerer's staff. Bilgeous ripped it out in a great spray of green blood.

Pertussis flung his claw up to his throat and keeled backwards, his eye wide. He choked and spluttered as he slammed back onto the ground, cried out as the hook went in again and again.

'Damn you, Pox!' he retched. He scrabbled for his trident but Bilgeous kicked it away into the pit. 'Treachery! Mutiny!' The claw snapped at his legs, but there was no force in the bite. 'You… promised me… *ships*, you cur!'

'I said you would sail oceans undreamed of,' Bilgeous told him. Pertussis wriggled against the pole of the sorcerer's staff as it was plunged into his chest. 'And so you shall, when whatever soul you possess sails the oceans of the underworlds.'

Bilgeous wrenched the hook to the side and the pirate's eye went dim. The claw flopped to the dirt and the belly-maw gave a last, mournful shudder as its jaws fell still.

He was a great lump of a creature, but Bilgeous had a sinewy strength hidden in his desiccated form, and it was no great trial to drag the corpse to the edge of the pit. He levered the body into the soup with his staff and watched as it foamed in the muck, the weight of the armour slowly dragging it down beneath the surface. So went the terror of the high seas, from Amnios to Smuggler's Haven, from the Tendril Reach to the Hauntcave Coast.

'And I said you would redeem yourself – and so you have.'

The pit shuddered. The great meniscus of slime began to ripple. Fire flickered across the surface. Mist rose into a smothering cloud, and from somewhere on the far side of reality came the tolling of a great bronze bell.

Bilgeous felt the last of the piper's notes fade from his mind. In their place came once more the architecture of the spell. It was a rite he had been constructing not just since he had raised the island from the ocean, but since the day the Grandfather had first appeared to him in his dreams. Old Slough had dragged himself from the swamp and had begun weaving the first faint threads of this magic, and now, as the pit drank its fill and was sated at last, it was time for Bilgeous Pox to take his place by the side of the Grandson.

He wept tears of gladness, and for a moment he could not bring himself to speak. And then he held high his rotstaff and began to utter the words that would change the world.

CHAPTER NINETEEN

TO THE SHORES

The oar slopped hard into the water as Gotrek missed his stroke. It sounded like someone glugging down a bottle of ale, and the sound of it woke Amara from her drowsing sleep. She sat up, knuckling her eyes. There was an ache in her head, although whether that was just from the mouthful of firewater she'd drunk or from her general fatigue, she couldn't say. She was exhausted. She had been exhausted for months.

'You let me sleep?' she mumbled. 'You shouldn't have, I...'

'Just for half an hour or so,' Odger said quietly. 'Didn't want to wake you.'

'Looked like you needed it,' Gotrek said.

Amara stifled a yawn. If anyone looked like they needed some rest it was Gotrek. There was a green tinge to the duardin's skin and the lacerations on his face were fringed with black. That indomitable strength still kept him sitting upright and plunging the oars back and forth into the water, but she could tell that his constitution was being pushed to its limits. His eye was dull, and the master rune had lost some of its lustre. There was something slack and listless about him now.

'What about you?' she said to Odger. 'You should take the chance to shut your eyes, get some sleep yourself.'

The man looked utterly frayed, as if he'd passed beyond the end of his tether some time ago. His eyes were sunken and grey, and there were heavy lines carved into his face. She couldn't imagine what was keeping him going. And then she remembered, and wondered how even the certain knowledge of a loved one's death could be a kind of comfort in the end. Odger didn't intend on coming back from this, she knew. Wither Island was going to be his grave, one way or another.

'I don't need it much any more,' he said. 'Sleep, I mean. Too many things hiding in the dark for me now. Too many memories that only come out in the shadows. I'd rather leave them be.'

The air was still around them. A thick mist had billowed up across the waters and nothing could be seen beyond a few feet from the boat.

'How do you know we're going in the right direction?' Amara asked, peering into the gloom. 'We could have cut past the island altogether and be heading for the rim of the realm. Or back to Kranzinnport harbour, for all we know.'

'I don't,' Odger said. 'But he does.'

Gotrek chopped the oars down, heaved back, raised them from the water again in a diamond spray. His brow was furrowed and a darkness seemed to have settled on him again. He raised his head and breathed in.

'Following my nose, lass,' he said. 'Even through this murk I can smell it.'

Amara inhaled. There, on the very edge of the sea-scent, she could pick up a faint trace of rot.

'Wither Island,' Odger said. He kept his voice low, as if there was a chance they would be overheard. 'Not long now.'

Amara peered into the mist. Was it a trick of the light, or was there a darker shape out there, a mile across the water? She had no idea of the time now, but it felt as if the whole world had been smothered by this fog, and the bright afternoon had given way to a permanent dusk.

She looked to the dark water beneath them. There was a layer of weird, gelatinous slime across it, like a carpet of algae. The further through it the boat moved, the more the smell of raw sewage began to thicken in the air. Amara could see things rippling through the slime: worms or maggots, darker shades like flense fish somewhere just beneath the surface, and even darker things further down.

There were flowers growing on it, she realised. Further out, where the walls of mist billowed and contracted, she could see pale blooms opening on the carpet of slime like water lilies on the surface of a pond. Except these flowers were no bright and fragrant things; they stank, and their petals were like the tattered wings of flies. The stamens that flopped from bell and cup were like little tentacles, diseased fronds that wavered in the air, sniffing for sustenance.

Odger saw her looking, saw the disgust on her face.

'Sigmar alone knows what's been happening here,' he said softly. 'Since the day Wither Island rose from the sea, there's been dark goings-on across the water. No one able to get close enough to find out, though. One old fellow, lived out near the spur where the stairs lead down into the tunnels, he had himself a duardin macroscope. Said he'd got it from a Kharadron trading vessel in his youth. Trained it on this place one day and his face went white.'

'What did he see?' Amara asked.

'Never really said. Just that there was jungle growing out here, strange plants he'd never seen before, and… *things* moving on the foreshore. He packed up that day, left for the Living City as far as I know. Took his macroscope with him. And then the raiders came on their ships, and there weren't no one brave enough to make the attempt since.'

'So no one's been on this bloody place then?' Gotrek said. 'We've no idea what to expect or who might be waiting for us?' He chuckled richly. 'Sounds about right.'

Amara turned from the side of the boat.

'The pirate with the claw,' Amara said, remembering. 'He said something about a ritual, that it was at risk if he stayed to fight. That's why they both flew away, back to the island.'

'Aye,' Odger said. 'I remember. I didn't think of it at the time, I just thought we'd got lucky.'

'Lucky?' Gotrek scorned. 'It's luck that kept them away from the edge of my axe, and they won't be so bloody lucky next time, I can tell you.'

Amara looked down at the water again. The carpet of slime was marbled with strings of white mucous, but even as she stared at it, it seemed to flicker and fade. She blinked her eyes. No, there it was, as rich and silty as before. The creatures that slithered across it, the worms and maggots and ticks, seemed to glint in and out of existence if she stared at them directly – just for the briefest moment, so quickly it may have been either a trick of the light or the strain in her tired eyes.

'None of this is real,' she mumbled. She reached out to touch the surface of the water.

'Don't touch it!' Gotrek barked. She felt his strong hand on her shoulder, drawing her back. 'You don't know where it's been.'

Amara shook her head, clearing her thoughts.

'I've seen this before,' she said. She rubbed her eyes. 'Not this exactly, but… In the valley, when the crusade was ambushed. The

Hedonites, they were mortal followers of the Dark Prince, but they had… things with them. Daemons, creatures, like shards of unreality bleeding through into the real world. They flickered like this, like they were made of mist and smoke, but they became tangible, more solid, the stronger they got. As more of us died.'

'It's like something puked out of the Realm of Chaos,' Gotrek said. 'All of this – the slime, the creatures, the mist even. Dream stuff no more real than a nightmare one minute, and then harder than stone the next. I spent aeons knee-deep in this kind of filth, fighting things you can't even imagine. Aye, lass, I reckon you could be right.'

'What do you mean?' Odger said. He looked up from the water in alarm.

'This isn't just disease or infection,' Amara said, her voice level. She felt a twist in her stomach, the raw knot of fear. 'It's some aspect of Nurgle's realm bleeding through into Ghyran. Onto Wither Island, onto the Rocanian Coast itself.'

Gotrek gave a hearty laugh and slapped the haft of the oar.

'Best quicken the pace, then,' he said, 'for we're sailing straight into Nurgle's Garden!'

Odger looked like he was going to be sick, although to his credit he put his hand back to the tiller all the same and set the boat heaving on through the sludge.

'It makes no difference,' he said, wiping his eye against his shoulder. 'I know they're gone. I only want the chance now to die where they died, and to take as many of these pestilent scum with me as I can.'

'That's the spirit, lad,' Gotrek said.

'Odger…' Amara reached for him. 'When we get there, you can row back to the city. You don't have to throw your life away. You can leave Kranzinnport, head to Druhiel, to the Living City even. This doesn't have to be the end for you.'

'But it does for you?' he said. His face was torn with anguish. 'Look at us. You both grieve for something or someone as much as I do. A priest who hates Sigmar and a duardin who... Gods, Gotrek, I don't even know what you are. But I can see the pain in you as much as I can see it in Amara here. Don't tell me either of you think this isn't suicide.'

'He has a point,' Amara said to Gotrek. The duardin smiled – a wry, cynical thing. 'We don't stand a chance. You've been infected, Gotrek, you must be able to feel it. I won't fight, and Odger doesn't even have a weapon.'

'Ha!' the duardin laughed. 'A right set of heroes, we are!'

'This will do me,' Odger said. He fished under the seat and pulled out a boathook. 'My spear might be at the bottom of Kranzinnport harbour, but this should take a couple of them with me.'

'Here,' Gotrek said. He leaned from the oars and rummaged around in the lockbox where he had found the firewater. After a moment he pulled out a hammer. It was a solid tool, something a mason would use to break up old stone. 'Hardly what you're used to, priest, but it'll do in a pinch.'

'I told you, I'll defend myself but I won't kill if I can help it,' she said.

Gotrek gestured with the hammer, but when he spoke his voice was tired and resigned.

'Then what use are you?' he said. 'You should have stayed in Kranzinnport and made a run for it with the rest of them. There are plenty of ways to die in this world rather than wait for one of these diseased buggers to try to snatch your life away from you. Snatch it from them first, lass, before they've got a chance.'

Amara folded her arms. 'Regardless,' she said, 'I stay by your side until my debt is paid.'

'Until you save my life, as I saved yours?'

'Indeed. It is the way of my people, and I cannot change it.'

'And how do you expect to do that if you'll barely raise a weapon in its defence?' Gotrek sighed. He tucked the hammer into his belt and gave a last, heaving tug on the oars. There was a crunch under the keel of the rowing boat, the slush of sand and pebbles. Amara could see a slope of dark shadows beyond the mist, a wavering line of trees. A shingle beach stretched away from them, the stones oily with black slime. The smell was thick in the air – the stench of rot and decay, the cloying scent of pus and vomit and disease.

What a place to die, she thought.

Across the misty vapour came the tolling of a bell. Odger helped Gotrek tuck the oars to the oarlock and gripped his boathook. He was the first to stand.

'Whatever we're going to do, let's do it fast,' he said. 'Before they realise we're here.'

He leapt from the boat and splashed through the last few feet of black water onto the beach. Gotrek hauled himself up and rolled his shoulders, coughing and spitting as he followed. Amara was the last to leave. She looked back at the stretch of sea they had crossed, but there was no sign of Kranzinnport in that murk. It felt like they were on the edge of the world, on the very rim where all the tides of magic coalesced.

'What do we do then?' she said to Gotrek. 'We don't even know what we're fighting here.'

'Where there's a ritual, there's a bloody sorcerer,' he spat. 'Find the bugger and introduce him to my axe. Job done.'

'That simple?' she said. Despite herself, she smiled.

'Always is.' Gotrek winked and strode off towards the line of jungle where it frothed onto the shore, his axe on his shoulder.

CHAPTER TWENTY

THE KNIGHTS OF
THE UNDERSWAMP

The canopy of the jungle snapped at the undercarriage of his Rot Fly, blades of creeper and vine slashing at its gangling legs as Lord Cholerax guided it from the harbour. Chuntering to himself in delight, eager for battle and gripped with ardour, Cholerax swept the fly smoothly over the forest and skirted the flank of the island. He guided the creature towards a stand of huts and hovels on the far side, hidden from sight of the harbour and the wider sea beyond it, where he had set up his camp all those weeks ago. The miasma of the pit, a foul cloud bank that flickered with yellow light as it billowed over the island, broke apart as he swung through it. Down to his left, faint in the murk, he could see the cresting waves of the sea as they broke greasily against the shore.

The water was thick with sludge, a frothing viridescence that bubbled like the surface of the plague pit where Bilgeous Pox was casting his rite. Cholerax, as he swooped in low, could see strange creatures tumbling in the tide – beasts and fish wriggling with feelers and tendrils, dragging themselves from the line of the jungle and disappearing into the waves. The fronds of weird plants lashed at the rocks and nourished themselves on the mulch. All was in change. Everything was rank with flux and instability, surging into virulent life and dying back into entropic rot once more. And as the strength of Pox's ritual increased, so too did the spread of growth and death and regrowth. All would be as the Grandfather desired, and as the Grandson expected.

Cholerax felt a twinge of jealousy in his guts – although it could have been the maggots, true enough. Pox had actually been there, in those far away days of legend. He had walked with Bolathrax when the Great Unclean One strode forth to take command of Alarielle's realm, when the filth of Nurgle had stained the blue waters and turned them virulently green. Aye, what he wouldn't have given to have been there in those glorious moments, fighting the good fight, giving his life in the struggle! He was envious of no one, and in his long and terrible career as Lord of the Under-swamp, Cholerax had accrued more glory to himself than many a Ghyranite warlord. But he had not walked with the gods, as Pox had done. He had not kept the faith through all the long years of disappointment, waiting for the new growth to gift him certainty when all about him seemed lost.

Say what you liked about Bilgeous Pox, Cholerax thought, but the sorcerer certainly had *vision*!

The maw beneath his armour plate champed its teeth. Cholerax shivered, patting the tip of his tentacle to his belly.

'Soon, soon, I promise you,' he whispered. 'You will feel the air of the Garden on your teeth and your tongue, I swear.'

He felt a ripe thrill rush through him at the thought of revealing it. On this holy day of all days, his enemies should tremble to see the blessing he had been given.

Cholerax could hear the crazed, skirling melody of the Bile-piper's song as he flew across the surface of the jungle, but although the music conjured up strange images and feelings deep within him, he knew that the song was not designed for his ears. He blocked it from his mind and called out as he flew, bellowing a long and gurgling war cry that cut across the canopy. Planing in low, the wind from Thrax's tattered wings hazing up a storm of dead leaves and dust, Cholerax drew closer to the camp. Soon he heard the answering calls of his knights as they rode out from where they had been stationed, some buzzing in from clearings deep in the jungle, others swinging in wide from patrols far out to sea. All had planted their pennants and colours in the camp, the devices on their banners rippling in the humid breeze. As Cholerax settled his Rot Fly on the ground and flopped from the saddle, he saw the flags of Lords Lepro-sis and Sy'phalix, of the Baron Gryppe and Sir Anchein, and of the Masterless Cho'reah, who had pledged his sword to Choler-ax's service until the Grandson was raised, and not a moment longer. All were Blightlords of the most exceptional name, val-iant and thrice-blessed in all the beneficent diseases the God of Plagues could gift to his most favoured sons. Knights of the Underswamp, they gave fealty to their liege lord and would follow Cholerax anywhere.

'My lord,' Sir Anchein rasped as he drew near. 'Where are the damned squires? Am I expected to stable my own Rot Fly! An outrage if so – I shall have them flogged for this!'

He dropped into the centre of the camp from the saddle of his Rot Fly, a corpulent beast with a trio of mad pinprick eyes and a dangling trunk that dripped purple ichor onto the dirt. The dull brass of his armour was flecked and corroded with rust, his half helm masking most of a wide, underslung jaw. His strain-ing stomach, swollen with corpse gas, was marked with the three holy buboes, and the fingers on his left hand were slowly fusing together into a gnarled and blistered club.

'Did you not hear the song, Sir Anchein?' Cholerax said. He grinned widely beneath his helmet and strode on as the others landed, beckoning to Lord Sy'phalix and Baron Gryppe as they swooped around the circumference of the camp, looking for a place to settle. 'I fear our squires have gone the way of the deck-hands and the harbour rats, and every mortal cultist who joined themselves to our cause, to say nothing of the hordes we took from Kranzinnport.'

'And what way is that?' the Masterless Cho'reah said, in a liquid, sneering voice. 'Mere arrow-fodder, I doubt they have the courage to desert. And in any case,' he said, swinging his pouchy arms wide, 'where exactly can they go?'

'Into the pit, I expect,' Cholerax said with triumph. 'A master-stroke on the sorcerer's part, I confess.'

He stared at his gathered knights, the weapons of his will. They dropped from their saddles and stood there proudly, firm of purpose all. Cholerax felt a great swelling of satisfaction.

'Alas,' he said, 'after so many weeks of raiding at will in the streets of Kranzinnport, the pirates of that imbecile Captain Pertussis have at last found their match. We were beset in the harbour, and the good captain's ships now decorate the sea floor.'

There was much outrage and upset at this – more for how the disgrace might reflect on their own reputations than because any of them had any great respect for the pirates. They might have followed the same god, but the lackadaisical style of Pertussis' crew, their slapdash piratical ways, meant they were no real broth-ers in arms. The Knights of the Underswamp had altogether more exacting standards.

'Defiance!' Baron Gryppe cried. He shook his scimitar and the rusting bars of his faceplate cut deeper into the malodorous folds of his skin. 'We shall give them such a hiding that they shall never forget it!' He leaned closer, as if in confidence. 'Who were these rebels, exactly?'

'Outsiders,' Cholerax confirmed. 'Not the trash of Kranzinn-port, but more professional warriors who have come to their aid.'

He strode to his own tent and unshackled the rusting brass pole of his personal banner from where it was displayed. With much contorting, twisting and cursing of the absent squires, he managed to harness it to his back, where the dirty crimson cloth sagged in the mist.

'Pertussis thought we were beset by all the engines of war, yet I believe our foes to be no more than a company of bold adventurers. Dangerous for all that, but no match for the combined arms of the Knights of the Underswamp.'

There was an adenoidal roar of approval from the gathered knights. Weapons were shaken, voices were raised, and unshackled folds of mouldering skin were quivered. A great stinking haze rose up from the warriors, released from under their armour plates and their tucks of sweating flesh.

'Fix your banners!' Cholerax roared. 'Harness your flies! Ready yourselves! If these devils don't sweep across the sea to confront us, then we shall ride across the bay and cut them down in the streets of their ruined city!'

His goitre shook and he slapped at his breastplate with his tentacle. Was this the moment? Should he do it now, to inspire his knights to even greater feats? Yes… he would show them exactly what the Grandfather had seen fit to grant to their commander. Let them gaze at last on the true quality of their lord and master!

Nervously his tentacle plucked at the edge of his plate – and then, with one grand and sweeping gesture, Cholerax tore the armour aside and let his bloated stomach flop out into the air. The maw in his belly gnashed its teeth with mad abandon, the tongue flicking out like a serpent's to taste the breeze. Cholerax, swapping his scythe to his tentacled arm, patted his gut with his right hand, preparing himself for the wave of awe and congratulation that was surely his due.

But it never came. Lord Sy'phalix, his cyclopean eye staring at some point over Cholerax's left shoulder, cleared his throat and with almost fastidious care spat out a lump of gristle into the sand. The waves splashed and burbled on the shore. The flies buzzed in the choking stands of the jungle. Cholerax looked down.

Where he had expected to see a vast and distended mouth, lined with razor-sharp fangs and taking up the entirety of his prodigious gut, Cholerax saw instead a feeble little aperture, more like a toad's flabby muzzle. It gave a fluting screech. The tongue, bottle-green, curled out and quivered in the air.

'To arms!' Baron Gryppe cried, breaking the silence. His comrades roared merrily alongside him, clashing their weapons, shaking their scythes. 'To the banners! To the Rot Flies! To war!'

Cholerax watched them take up their pennants and drag themselves up into the saddles of their beasts. After a moment, and with a final, bitter glare at his breastplate lying there in the sand, he followed.

'I demand restraint in only one thing!' he called, as he mounted Thrax once more. 'If you see a duardin in this company, then leave him to me.'

CHAPTER TWENTY-ONE

CHARGE OF
THE ROT FLIES

Far on their right was a spur of black stone, a rocky headland that opened out into a wide, natural harbour. The walls on either side had been built up and reinforced, and two long slipways had been constructed from banked slabs of rock to form berths for the pirate ships they had destroyed in Kranzinnport. The seawater sloshed back and forth against the harbour walls like the dregs of a latrine.

Everywhere Amara looked she could see the creeping attention of the jungle. Purple vines, as fleshy as intestines, snaked out of the treeline and coiled themselves around the hawsers on the wharf. Mats of ground ivy, each bladed leaf blistered with lichen, crept down towards the beach, as if trying to cover the sea. There was a fibrous breed of yellow moss growing between the great blocks of granite and sandstone on the harbour walls, as furry as an animal's pelt. It wriggled with mites, and everywhere they put their feet they felt the crunch of beetles or the soft, pustulant squash of slugs and worms. Sallow Bloat Flies bumbled through the air, and the air itself was thick with vapour.

Everything stank – from the ground underfoot to the creatures that slithered across it; from the plants that flourished in such mad and unnatural profusion to the rotting sludge of the undergrowth as it died beneath them. The sea was a rank soup and the air was a sour miasma. It didn't feel like they were standing in the real world any more. They were somewhere else entirely.

'How could any of this be?' Odger whispered. He clutched his boathook to his chest, a haunted look in his eyes. 'How could they bring people here, ordinary people, taken from their homes? What evil twists in their minds that they turn to the worship of Chaos?'

'Hard to fathom the madness of these folk,' Gotrek said gruffly. 'No point even trying, take it from me. None of it makes a bit of sense.'

He stalked on across the width of the harbour, his boots crunching on the beetles that scuttled along the wharf. Amara followed him, Odger bringing up the rear. The boathook in his hand looked a pitiable weapon, but she supposed it was better than none.

She looked to Gotrek, stomping over the wharf with the sea breaking against the stone beneath him. That tinge of green had spread across his face now, and the weals on his back and shoulders were pale and weeping. He was going to die, she knew. He should have died a dozen times over since she had met him, and yet he was still going. Even the illness that was slowly sickening him, as unnatural as it was, couldn't stop him. The axe up on his shoulder, the cannonball of his head held up proud, the muscles coiled and ready to fight... Gotrek wouldn't stop for anyone or anything. He had barely paused since they had heard about Wither Island back in Druhiel.

Evil had raised its head, and Gotrek's first thought was to cut it off. *The hand reaching out for her. His voice calling, as the dawn began to break. Screaming as the dusk fell down, and the hills boiled with the foe...*

Amara forced herself onwards, pushing the images from her mind.

'It's quiet,' Odger said. He stood on the wharf and stared back across the sea, out to where Kranzinnport was hidden in the mist. 'I thought... I don't know, but I thought somehow they'd be expecting us.'

'Would you rather they were?' Gotrek said.

'No,' Odger admitted. He looked at Gotrek's axe, the ferocious cast of his face. 'But I bet you would.'

'There are those two buggers who got away on that flying monstrosity,' Gotrek growled, 'and I'll have their heads at the very least.'

He jogged towards the line of the jungle, his axe up.

'There's a trail here,' he called. 'Well-trodden too, by the looks of it.' He crouched to the side and rummaged in the grass, pulling out a rusting manacle. 'This is where they were taken,' he said. 'The folk from Kranzinnport. Look.'

Odger took the manacle from Gotrek's hand. His jaw trembled for a moment as he stared down at it. He ran his fingers over the cruel iron, and Amara knew he was tormenting himself with the thought that this same cuff had been encircled around his wife's wrist. Had his son held her hand as they were dragged into these shadows beneath the trees? Had she tried to calm him with soothing words, telling him that everything was going to be all right? Had she lied to him, and hidden the terror in her own eyes so he would not be scared when the end came? Had she stood there on the cusp of ruin and prayed to a god who would not help them, would not help any of them?

...Reaching out for her... Calling...

Odger looked at her. He brandished the manacle, and the torment was like a mask that had descended on his face.

'You'll still not take the fight to them?' he shouted at her. 'You'll not make them pay, even after this?'

With a savage cry, he flung the rusting manacle far out into the water. His face was set now. His eyes were like stone. Amara could not look on him.

'Come on,' he spat. 'If any of those monsters are still here, I'd see them in the grave before the day is out.'

'Now you're singing my song, lad!' Gotrek said. He laughed, but the laughter turned into a choking splutter that doubled him over. He leaned and spat out another gobbet of black mucous, reeling to get his balance.

'Gotrek, you need to rest,' Amara said. She rushed over and helped him to stand. There was a smell coming off him, even more pungent than his usual reek of sweat and stale beer. His skin felt as hot as a furnace and there was nothing left in her knapsack that could help him now. 'You're no use to anyone if you're too sick to fight.'

'We'll see about that,' he said, wiping a hand across his eyes. He glowered at her. 'Seems you need someone to fight for you after all, doesn't it?'

The breeze picked up suddenly, the wind blowing harsh across the slimy pebble beach and the wings of the harbour. The water, fuming under its sheet of slime, rucked against the stone. The canopy of the jungle bristled – and then Amara could hear it, a pulsing drone that rose higher and higher, until it made the teeth rattle in her jaw.

Six Rot Flies came screeching around from the other side of the island, cutting fast across the waves. Their wings shivered with a dull sheen of oily green light, and in the saddle of each of them was a Nurgle warrior with weapons drawn. Hollering thickly, waving their swords, the riders banked their steeds and sent them droning down towards the harbour.

In their lead was the Nurgle lord who had been at the harbour in Kranzinnport, his tentacle wrapped around the black shaft of his scythe and his other hand gripping the pommel of his saddle. Even behind the pitted helmet that covered his face, Amara could sense the thrill of battle in him. He marked Gotrek at once and leaned forwards, the great rusty hook of his scythe swinging out as he came soaring in, the stench of the flies billowing across the wharf towards them.

'There they are! Cut them down, my knights!' he bellowed. His laughter was as unctuous as the seawater that beat greasily against the walls. 'Leave the duardin for me. I will have his rotting head on my skull-rack before the day is out.'

CHAPTER TWENTY-TWO

THE JOUST

The pebbles and sand skimmed up from the beach as they flew in. Amara threw herself to the ground. She felt the whistle of a scythe cut just past her head, looked to see Odger thrown back as he desperately parried a blow with his boathook. The force of the impact sent him sailing over the edge of the wharf and crashing down to the slipway below.

The Nurgle lord may have commanded them to ignore the duardin, but his knights were too keen for glory to obey. One of them, a corpulent brute with a barred faceplate that pressed deeply into the sagging folds of his marbled white face, waved a scimitar and shot forwards. Outpacing his master, the warrior shifted in the saddle and prepared himself for a stroke that would have cut Gotrek in two.

The duardin didn't even move. Laughing uproariously, gnashing his teeth, he crouched with his axe at the ready and his glittering black eye fixed on the foe that was sweeping towards him.

'Baron Gryppe, damn you!' the Nurgle lord cried as his Rot Fly was outpaced. 'The duardin is mine!'

'Do not sully your scythe on him, my lord!' the other shouted. He pulled back for the swing, the sand and dead leaves of the treeline billowing up around his steed as it dragged its gangling legs in the dirt. 'I will deliver his head unto you!'

The other beasts shot over Amara's head. She rolled to the side, just in time to see Gotrek duck the blow of the warrior's scimitar and grab hold of one of the fly's rear legs. Dragged back by such an anchor, rearing and droning in a frenzy, the fly bucked to the side as it launched itself higher into the air, with Gotrek still clinging to it. As the Rot Fly went barrelling madly up into the mist above the sea, the rider tumbled from the saddle and crashed heavily onto the stone wharf, the sword skittering out of his grip.

'Grandfather's holy ailments,' he groaned.

His helmet had been cracked open by the force of the fall, and something that looked very much like his brains hung in a lumpy tangle from the rent. Still lying sprawled on the wharf, he reached up and pushed them back into the crack. He scrabbled at his face-plate, trying to prise it loose.

Amara was only a few yards from him, flicking her eyes up to scan the air for the Rot Flies as they banked round for another pass. She couldn't see Gotrek anywhere. Either he had fallen from the creature and plunged into the jungle, or he was still somehow holding on to it as it gained height. Either way, he had disappeared into the mist.

'A priest, eh?' the Nurgle warrior slurred, glaring at her. 'I'll have at ye, priest. I've killed your kind many a time, each one a prayer raised up to Papa Nurgle! Damn Sigmar's beard for a coward.'

His yellow eyes and their pinprick red pupils were glazed. The brains slopped out of his helmet again. The brute rolled onto his side, slapping his empty scabbard for his weapon. Amara crouched, backing off. She could rush him, snatch up a stone and crack his skull before he could get up. She could run, lead him into the jungle and try to lose him. She could–

But it was all immaterial. She had no weapon, and the warrior was slowly heaving his bloated bulk to his feet.

She saw Odger rushing up from the slipway and vaulting onto the wharf only a few feet behind the Nurgle warrior. He had his boathook in hand and there was blood on his face.

'I'm no priest!' she shouted at the warrior, hoping to distract him. She spread her arms wide. 'I'm not even armed. But I'll see you in the ground all the same, you rotting freak.'

'Ha! More fool you for facing me without a weapon.' He lurched closer, one hand still up to clutch his leaking head. 'For I am Baron Gryppe, master of the Foetid Woods, chief of the Noisome Sward, and I hold my fief in honour from Lord Cholerax himself. And I will see *you* in the–'

Odger swung the boathook clean into the back of the brute's thigh, ripping upwards with all of his strength. The flesh sagged open and the grey muscle flopped out. Although he barely seemed to feel the pain of the wound, Baron Gryppe stumbled and collapsed backwards as his leg folded up underneath him.

'Stab me in the back, would you?' he gurgled. 'Dishonour! Shame!'

Odger, without even breaking his stride, slammed the hook down into the bulging grille of the warrior's helmet. As the brute thrashed and screamed, Odger dragged him over to the edge of the wharf. Amara rushed over to lend her strength, and together they sent him pitching down into the slime.

'Where's Gotrek?' Odger panted. He wiped the blood from his face, looking up to scan the sky. Amara could see the black flecks of the Rot Flies as they cut and scattered in the air, hundreds of feet above them. She pointed.

'Up there.'

'Then Sigmar help him...'

Even as they watched, the black specks spread and crossed each other, haring back and forth in the mist. Where the banks of fog were heaviest all they could hear were disembodied shouts, the frantic buzzing of the Rot Flies and the clash of steel. Amara realised she was holding her breath. At any moment she expected to see him tumbling through the air and crashing down onto the rocks, or plunging deep into the bowers of the jungle. She wasn't sure even Gotrek could survive such a fall.

The squadron of flies, a knot of swarming bodies, began to straighten into a line. Soon, one of them buzzed into a clear lead, quivering to left and right, the other five chasing keenly to catch up. Amara watched the lead fly hurtle back down towards the shore on the far side of the island, near where they had beached the rowing boat, at the last minute pulling up and then dashing towards the wharf. Gotrek had buried his axe blade deep into the creature's skull, and while he clutched onto the saddle with his knees he yanked at the axe's haft as if pulling on a ship's rudder.

'How do you stop this bloody thing?' he roared.

He wrenched the blade to the side as the other riders caught up with him, sending the Rot Fly careering through the upper branches of the jungle canopy. Slick with a putrid gruel from the rotten leaves, Gotrek was becoming incandescent with fury.

Somehow he managed to haul the Rot Fly around. The beast gained height as Gotrek pummelled the shaft of the axe, then looped into a roll that had it facing the way it had just come. Gotrek's laughter was terrifying as he thrashed the creature on towards the pursuing Nurgle warriors.

'Gods,' Odger breathed. 'It's almost like he's enjoying himself.'

'For Gotrek,' Amara said, 'I think this is as good as it gets.'

They sprinted on down the slimy beach to follow, both of them trying to fix onto Gotrek as he charged. The flies jostled and swept near twenty feet above them, and the stinking wind from their wings choked them as they ran.

'A joust is it, sir?' the Nurgle lord cried out. His voice boomed in the misty air. 'Very well, let it be a joust, but do not expect the mercy pass from me!'

He had a fanged mouth high up on his belly, little more than a slobbering pouch, and it gnashed its teeth as he levelled his scythe. Gotrek came on fast, snarling, his beard streaming out behind him. He wrenched the axe blade from the fly's head with an audible slurp. The creature whickered and droned, its spindly legs flopping about grotesquely in the wind.

It happened almost too fast for Amara to see. At the last minute, with only feet to spare, the Nurgle lord pulled aside with an oath. Gotrek leapt from the saddle, raking his axe through the air, missing him by inches. His dead Rot Fly, brains and blood flickering from its head, plunged towards the ground. As Gotrek fell, one of the other riders, moving too fast to pull away, crashed into him.

The Rot Fly spun, wings ripping through the air. Amara saw Gotrek grappling with the rider, who was trying to bludgeon the duardin with a blistered, club-like fist. Holding his axe short at the haft, Gotrek punched it again and again into the warrior's face. The rider fell back, his slobbering jaw hanging by a thread from the rim of his half helm. Green blood ribboned into the air. With one last, contemptuous blow, Gotrek flung him from the saddle, and he dropped like a sack of rotting meat into the sea.

'Bring him down!' the Nurgle lord screamed as he banked round again, but Gotrek had thrown his hijacked steed deep into the enemy's formation. Wings scratched against each other, steel clattered against steel, and the drone of the flies twisted higher and higher.

Another warrior fell to Gotrek's axe, a swollen monstrosity with a yellow cyclopean eye. Two ivory horns spiked up through his bronze pauldrons, and on his back he had a trophy rack decorated with rotting heads. Too close to use his scythe, the warrior fumbled for a dagger strapped to his saddle, but in moments his severed head was spinning off into the jungle far below. Not content with this, Gotrek was soon hacking the fly beneath him into pieces, screaming with battle-madness. The blade shone gold and silver, the brazier sparkled, and soon chunks of rotting flesh were splattering into the canopy as the fly dropped.

'He's going to crash,' Amara said. She grabbed Odger's arm. 'Come on!'

The canopy shuddered. There was a crash of splintered branches and torn leaves, a cry of transcendent rage, and a high-pitched, droning scream. Amara plunged into the undergrowth, her arms up to shield her face, Odger following. She waded through the slop underfoot, crunching through maggots, batting aside the tendrils with puckered mouths that snaked out like vines towards her. Odger cut down the oozing creepers that hung like curtains between the trees. Things skittered and crept away from them, scurrying into the scrub. Ankle-deep in filth, Amara followed the sound of Gotrek's roaring anger as the remaining Rot Flies circled the trees.

CHAPTER TWENTY-THREE

THE DUEL

She found Gotrek standing in a small clearing deep in the jungle, a mess of guts and organs at his feet. He was panting for breath, his axe clutched in both hands. The Rot Fly was a shredded mess beneath him and a great ragged hole had been torn through the canopy above. Leaves and splintered twigs shivered on the ground at his feet. Even as they watched, they seemed to flicker and contract, and whatever web of magic and ritual kept them together began to slacken its grip. The leaves melted into a slick black paste, and there was a stench in the air of burning flesh. Whatever this place was, whatever foul magics had conjured it, for the moment it had only a tenuous grip on the skin of reality.

There was a crash in the undergrowth somewhere behind them. The sweep of a scythe, the sound of iron boots wading through the muck.

'They have despoiled this holy place,' a voice cried out, muffled by the trees. 'Find them, cut the blasphemers down!'

'Gotrek, there are still three more,' Amara said quickly. 'If there is some sorcerer behind this, then we need to find him fast and end it.'

He didn't seem to hear her. Pain flashed across his face and he staggered, thumping his fist to the dormant rune on his chest. A lurid shade of seafoam green had thickened about his eye. The disease was ripping through him now, sapping his strength, drowning him in a deep confusion.

The ground shuddered beneath them. The jungle whispered, and the air trembled like the first fingers of a storm were rushing through its branches. From far away over the conjured trees came a rolling, guttural roar that felt like the ocean itself had been heaved aside.

'Merciful Azyr, what is that?' Odger whispered.

Amara looked for a trail through the scrub. Flies rattled through the leaves and something lank and sinewy slipped through the muck at her feet.

'I don't know,' she said. 'But whatever it is, I'll wager that's where we need to be. Help me with Gotrek, he's the only chance we've got.'

The undergrowth crunched and rattled off to their side. Faster than she could blink, the shroud of the illness thrown off in an instant, Gotrek raised his axe overhead and flung it into the trees. It spun end over end, a gold-and-silver comet, and crunched into the breastplate of one of the Nurgle warriors as he emerged through the vines, practically splitting him in two.

Gotrek bounded after the blade, snatching it up from the ground. In two well-practised swings he had decapitated the warrior. He punted the severed head through the trees with a snarl.

'Here he is, Lord Cholerax!' a gurgling voice called out. 'Damn him for a villain, but he's just killed Lord Leprosis!'

'Into them, Cho'reah,' the Nurgle lord commanded, as he burst through the trees. He pointed with his scythe, the maw on his belly snickering with amusement. 'Cut down his companions while I deal with this duardin brute.'

The one called Cho'reah lumbered across the cramped space towards Amara and Odger. He laughed long and high, with a sound like a drain choked with dead leaves. The armour plates strapped to his shoulders, green as corroded copper, were slathered in filth. He bore a long, serrated blade in one puffy, swollen hand, a brass buckler in the other. His face was hidden behind a flared helmet, and the helmet's wings were shaped like screaming mouths in profile.

'Stand and fight, dogs,' he muttered, his voice rattling in his throat. 'The Masterless Cho'reah desires your heads for trophies. I will eat your eyeballs and use your flayed skin for a handkerchief. I will bathe in your entrails and use your sinews as the strings for my minstrels' lutes. I will–'

Gotrek's axe tore through his shoulder, near cutting his arm away. Cho'reah grunted as the blade tore free, his sword dropping into the mire at his feet.

'There,' Gotrek snarled to Odger. 'Think you can deal with him now?' He hooked a thumb at Cholerax. 'I'm going to chop this bugger a new mouth in his belly.'

Gotrek launched himself at Cholerax as the Nurgle lord thundered across the clearing. Muck and filth sprayed up from his boots. The jungle itself seemed to hold its breath as he swung in with his scythe. There was a deafening clash of steel, but then Amara drew back as Cho'reah grunted and shook, flinging off the last sinewy cords of his severed arm and letting it flop into the mud.

'May the Grandfather grant me new gifts to replace that!' he cried.

He swung out with the buckler. Amara tried to block it with her arm, but the blow crashed against her breastplate and threw her backwards. Even with one arm he was insanely powerful, his corpulent form filled with the strength of his foul god. She saw Odger cutting down with his boathook, ripping the steel through Cho'reah's wrist, but the Nurgle warrior barged him aside. Amara kicked out at his knee, rolling aside as he slammed the buckler down to try to crush her skull.

Odger came in again with the boathook, stabbing the spike into Cho'reah's thigh. The warrior chortled and knocked it from the wound. A rank green sludge trickled down his greaves.

'Even disarmed as I am, you are no match for me, you mewling scum,' he said. Laughter bubbled up from his chest as he batted Odger aside. 'Cease your futile struggles, and let me feed you to the Grandson. You'll thank me in the end, I promise you. When he rises it will be as if Papa Nurgle himself walks free in the Mortal Realms, here where his holy feet once trod.'

Amara felt a flash of cold fear in her gut – but then there was something else, a warmth that seemed to spread through her, a sense of strength and power. Her fingers had curled around something hidden in the muck – the hilt of the hammer Gotrek had taken from the boat. He must have dropped it when he was falling from the Rot Fly. She grasped it tightly, and felt for a moment as if her hand had been guided to this very spot.

'Whatever this Grandson is,' she spat, 'he'll never walk free on Wither Island, I promise you.'

He loomed over her with a stench as strong as a latrine. Behind the slits of his helmet, she could see weeping yellow eyes, blazing with jovial madness.

'Wither Island? Is that what the mortals call it?' He guffawed, his head thrown back. 'This is a shard of the Grandfather's toe-nail, child, and the Grandson is an aspect of Papa Nurgle himself! This is no mere island, you foolish girl. It is a place of growth. It is fecundity and fruitfulness. It is fertility and–'

Amara snatched up the hammer and smashed it into his jaw.

'I get the idea,' she said.

With a cry of rage the warrior stumbled backwards, green ichor pouring from his chin. Amara reeled. She flicked the slime off her hands and tried not to vomit at the stench, and then saw Odger charging in with the boathook raised. He leapt and slammed the spike deep into the back of the Nurgle warrior's neck.

The brute fell forwards, howling. He slammed into the ground and Odger, screaming, insensate, stabbed the spike down into his skull, splitting the plate. Face down in the mire, the warrior choked and burbled. At last, the swamp scum thick with his blood, the diseased body fell still.

Amara staggered to her feet. Odger fell back from the corpse, his chest heaving.

'For Kranzinnport,' he panted. 'For Melita and Clovis, and for everyone you murdered there, you bastard!'

On the other side of the clearing, Gotrek and Lord Cholerax still duelled, hacking in at each other without mercy. The Nurgle lord was a monster, seven feet of rotting, marbled flesh and corroded steel. The tentacle of his right arm coiled sinuously around the shaft of his scythe, giving him an even greater reach as he swung and cut. The blade of the scythe itself was near five feet long, and Gotrek had only a fraction of his reach. In his weakened state it was all he could do to batter each blow aside, prowling the clearing while he looked for an opening of his own.

Amara could see how weak he was now. Every time he leapt forwards, it took more out of him. Each blow of his axe had a little less power behind it, a little less of the explosive force she had seen him use before. When Cholerax struck back, slamming the boss of the scythe into his chest or hacking down in a great whistling sweep, Gotrek staggered under the pressure. His shoulders sagged, his skin was green and sallow. Only his eye still seemed to blaze with that same hot fury.

'You cut through those pirates easily enough, duardin,' Cholerax chortled, 'but they were no more than a crew of idle roustabouts, more used to terrorising children and old folk in the ruined streets of their cities.' He snapped out with the butt of the scythe and caught Gotrek a blow across the temple. The duardin grunted and backed off warily, blood dripping from his forehead. 'Here, I suspect, you have met your match. I have never lost a duel, in all my long years. Can you say the same?'

'Aye, I bloody can,' Gotrek sneered. He ducked and launched himself like a cannonball into Cholerax's gut, knocking the Nurgle lord off balance. 'And I've fought bigger and uglier things than you and all!'

He cracked the axe blade deep into Cholerax's side. Cholerax gasped, hacking down with the scythe so the point pierced Gotrek's shoulder. Locked together, snarling at each other, each fighter pressed home their weapons. Blood sheeted down Gotrek's back.

Odger ran up with the boathook, slashing out at the Nurgle lord's tentacle. Amara snatched up a clammy length of vine from the mire, shuddering at the feel of it. She flung it round the folds of Cholerax's neck and tried to choke him from behind. The Nurgle lord's gurgling roar rang out across the clearing.

'Gotrek!' Amara gasped. 'I know what they're doing – they're going to summon some aspect of Nurgle himself, unleash it on the Everspring Swathe, on the whole of Ghyran. On the Mortal Realms themselves!'

'Time to cut this bloody dance short then,' he muttered.

His broken teeth bared, the veins standing out on his forehead, Gotrek dropped his axe and grabbed hold of the jaws in the Nurgle lord's stomach. With a grotesque, wrenching snap he pulled them apart and reached in up to his elbow, his arm cut to ribbons by the maw's needle teeth.

Cholerax screamed. His blubber shook and his tentacle whipped at them all. Odger was batted aside, the flank of the tentacle smacking into his face. Amara lost her grip on the vine and it slithered through her hands. But then Gotrek, grunting like a butcher cleaving a side of meat, tore out a string of putrid organs from Cholerax's chest. Heart and lungs and liver all came slurping through the maw, all the offal packed into that rotting cavity – a rancid stew that Gotrek flung with disgust over his shoulder. As Cholerax staggered backwards, arms flailing and an outraged cry rattling from behind his helmet, Gotrek scooped up his axe and planted it with a roar in the Nurgle lord's face.

The helmet split apart. The skull shattered, and the wild, staring face was sliced in two.

Gotrek collapsed in the mud. His chest was heaving and his eye fluttered with exhaustion.

'Grungni's beard,' he groaned. 'Feels like… Feels like I've got a hundred of my worst hangovers all at once…'

'It's the infection, Gotrek, you have to fight it,' Amara said. She knelt by his side, cradling his head as it sunk down onto his chest. 'We need to find this thing and stop it before it's too late, and we need you. Do you hear me?'

His eye flickered shut and his jaw went slack. Amara drew her hand back and slapped him across the face as hard as she could.

'Gotrek! Damn it, we need you! *I* need you, do you hear? There…'

She squeezed her eyes shut, then opened them again to see the duardin's battered, brutal face staring up at her own.

'There's nothing left for me without you,' she said.

A slow, gap-toothed smile spread across his face. A sliver of golden light flashed across the surface of the master rune. A touch of colour came back to his cheek, the smallest flush of red beneath the sallow green.

'There's plenty left for you, lass,' he mumbled. 'You might be half-cracked, but I can… I can see the anger in you… The will to fight on, for what you've lost.'

'I have lost everything,' Amara said.

'Not… Not your memories. Never let them go, you hear me? That's what you fight for… For what you once had. And to stop other folk having them taken away…'

Once again came that apocalyptic roar, deep in the earth, booming across the livid stands of the jungle. The ground trembled beneath them. The trees shook.

Gotrek groped for Amara's hand. Cautiously he got to his feet. He groaned as he bent to pick up his axe, but the rune was flickering with light now. He ran his fingers over it, set his jaw with what Amara thought looked something like regret.

'No,' he muttered. 'I'll do this under my own steam or not at all.'

The rune flickered once and cooled, like a hot ingot plunged into cold water. Gotrek wiped the blood from his face. His skin remained pale and yellowish, but there was some strength left in him still.

'Right,' he said, hitching up his belt. 'If I can't kill Nurgle, then let's at least go and kill his grandson.'

CHAPTER TWENTY-FOUR

THE GRANDSON

Bilgeous stood on the fringe of the steaming pit, inhaling the deadly vapours. He looked beyond the tattered fronds of the jungle plants that surged into reality from the roots cast deep into Nurgle's Garden. He saw past the fume of mist that rose from the pit, past even the flickering presence of the Bilepiper as it prowled the clearing. He looked beyond all this to where the rags of his previous spell lay scattered in the black grass, fronds of emerald and acid yellow invisible to all but those who had trained their sight to the perception of the arcane. The lines of the old spell were dying, but as the Grandfather had long made clear, death and decay were no more than the necessary conditions of new life.

The staff was heavy in his hand but he raised it high. He cast his mind back to the words of his spell, felt them unfurl like sickly vapour on his tongue. First the framing prayers, the calls for fecundity and grace. Then the statement of intent, the thrust of the rite barked fearlessly into the air. Finally, as Bilgeous felt the weight of the rite settle across his shoulders like a familiar old blanket, warm and comforting, he began to gather up the scraps of the spell once more.

The energies of the earth, this island, this festering sliver of the Grandfather's toenail, rose up around him. His head thrummed with power, and before long the words he spoke seemed to come from somewhere outside space and time. Bilgeous raised his staff higher and higher, his arms trembling. He saw the architecture of the spell form in the unreal space around the clearing, the ladder of his chanted words plunging down into the pit and up into the roiling murk of Nurgle's Garden, where all that died would grow again, and all that grew would one day fade into fertile decay.

The crust that lay across the soup of rotting corpses and vomit began to shudder. Like a scab shrivelled over a gaping wound, it began to flake apart. Splits appeared in the film of that broad meniscus, and from each gap a gurgling, viridescent light spewed out violently into the air.

The earth rumbled beneath him, so powerfully that it almost threw him off his feet. Bilgeous raised his voice, shouting his words into the air and into the aether that lay a hair's breadth away, on the other side of reality.

In the scum of the lake, a face began to gather. Claws, each one as long as a man, pressed at the caul. Two racks of many-pointed antlers pierced the veil. A gaping mouth choked in the filth, roaring with a sound like the end of the world. Three eyes flashed open in the depths of the slime, red as flame and each near three feet across. A hand surged out of the foul stew and gripped the edge of the pit.

Slowly, like a world being born, the Grandson began to lever himself into the Mortal Realms.

Bilgeous, weeping tears of blood, a pallid gruel pouring out of his nose and ears, shook violently as the spell came to its conclusion. He fell to his knees, leaning all his weight on his staff.

He looked up in reverence and terror at what he had wrought, clasping his hands in holy ecstasy.

'Grandson!' he cried. 'Lord, I have yearned for this moment for centuries! Let me partake of your holy illness, lord. Let me drink the ichor of your sacred buboes!'

The daemon, hollering as its skin fumed in the light of the real, hauled itself further from the pit. The great blades of its antlers tore up the turf as it wrenched its way free. The chest, a massive slab of rotting muscle, was flecked with blisters and subcutaneous infections. Each of its sagging arms was more than twenty feet long, and maggots swarmed in their folds. As it pulled itself from the aether, heaving its gnarled and infected gut over the rim of the pit, its exposed organs steamed in the clammy air. The surface of its skin glistered like some bright mirage. The red eyes, clustered in the form of Nurgle's tripartite mark, glowed with a rarefied, unearthly light.

It was a Great Unclean One, drawn from Nurgle's Garden – but it was somehow part of Nurgle's Garden too. It was the warp and weft of the bladed ferns, the carpet of fecund sludge, the towering hirsute trunks of the bloated trees. Where the light fell through the cover of the mist, the Grandson shimmered like the surface of clear water. Where the shadows fell across its skin, the daemon seemed to be no more than a sketch of life scribbled on the page of reality. All around it the grass withered and died. The fruitful scrub at the treeline beyond the clearing shrivelled into a brown husk. Yet even as Bilgeous watched, shielding his eyes from the majesty of it all, the withered scrub was engorged with new life. Green sap surged, bursting in a paste from stem and leaf. The trees lurched higher, their trunks fat with corpse gas. Bloat Flies skimmed excitedly over the green scum of the pool, landing on the Grandson's skin to nuzzle it with tuber and beak, and laying their eggs beneath the crust of its flesh. Almost immediately those eggs burst open and the maggots munched their way to the surface, wriggling on the cankered skin and dropping down into the filth of the pool.

The Bilepiper thrashed the weeping sack of its instrument, skirling out a frantic melody. Capering, leaping, dancing for joy, it skipped around the pit as the Grandson slopped its great belly onto the turf and lumbered from the muck.

In one vast hand the Great Unclean One held a bronze bell flaking with rust. In the other it wielded a hooked blade that was ten feet long from point to hilt, the blade itself decorated along its spine with malformed, screaming faces. In its gut, slashed across the surface from side to side, was a maw of unparalleled magnitude. The pointed teeth, ridged with encrusted calcium, snapped together with a sound like the clashing of steel. The gums were riddled with sores, and the flabby tongue was torn here and there with open wounds that glistened with maggots. In all his dreams and nightmares, Bilgeous Pox had never imagined that something so awe-inspiring could be gifted to the arts of his spellcraft.

'Pox!' the daemon boomed, voice thundering across the glade. It clattered the bronze bell, which tolled like the last defiant peal of a doomed cathedral in a city cast down to ruins. 'Pox, my servant – you have done well. Let the blessings of the Grandfather be on you.'

The daemon huffed and spat out a gobbet of slime, which drenched Bilgeous from head to foot. The force of the expectoration threw him backwards. Sprawling in the dirt, the sorcerer felt his limbs swell, his chest and belly expand with fluid.

'Master!' he cried, writhing on the ground. 'Your humble servant thanks you!'

The straps of mouldering leather split across his chest. His greying robe was torn where his belly sagged against it. He felt like a globe of rotting juices, like a fruit plucked from the tree and allowed to ripen. Rolling to his feet, strange liquids leaking from between his toes with every step, Bilgeous Pox paid reverence to the Grandson.

'My arts are at your command, lord. By the visions of your Grandfather are you brought into being, here to bring his gifts to the common folk crying out for his favour.'

'Then let us spread this filth into the waters of the sea,' the daemon intoned, clashing its bell once more. 'Let us bring holy distemper to the lands. The Everspring Swathe will be choked by our glorious infections. Ghyran's rivers shall run green and black with putrefaction. The Mortal Realms shall be brought into the folds of the Garden, and the Garden shall expand to cover all.' It gave a deafening chuckle, the laughter wobbling the cankered flesh from its belly to the folds of its neck. 'All will taste the fruits of decay. All will be given the gifts of Nurgle, and the Melody of Life and Death shall cover the worlds from end to end.'

Gotrek hacked the scrub aside, chopping through root and bower with the blade of his axe. Brakes of plump weeds barbed with spikes seemed to lunge across their path. Coverts of bladed palm leaf sprang up around them, the edges as sharp as knives. Vines trailed down in trembling loops from the canopy above, where a flinty grey light fell to illuminate the brackish muck they were forced to wade through. Virulent lichens leaked spores into the air around them. Corpulent gourds shivered in cups of leaves, as pale as corpses, splitting open to reveal strange half-formed creatures that looked to Amara like skinned piglets or boiled puppies. Everywhere was fungus and reed, weird algae, rotting verdure that stank of fish and sour fruit, and yet none of it had the tangible grip of reality. Creepers melted in their hands. Bark puffed away into a glittering, aetheric mist. Even so, the deeper they cut their way into the jungle, the stronger everything seemed to become. Dreamlike and unreal, it soon grew more densely physical.

Odger slapped a Bloat Fly against his cheek. 'It's getting worse,' he said. 'Can you feel it? The air's like… Like when a storm breaks out at sea, and all the spray comes thrashing back to shore.'

'It's like the Realm of Chaos itself is trying to break through,' Amara said.

'If the madness of that damned place breaks through here,' Gotrek muttered, 'then all the Mortal Realms will be at risk.' He chopped his way through a jagged clump of saplings, the broken stems spraying out a sap that looked and smelled like days old porridge. 'There's nowhere more depraved in all creation. Although,' he mused, 'when it comes down to it, daemons are just like anything else. They still tend to die if you hit them hard enough.'

Odger passed a shaking hand over his face. 'Sigmar's *blood*…' he whispered.

The booming toll of that bell rang out again, and behind it came a thickened rumble of nightmare speech. Amara felt it deep in her gut, the words shaking through the canopy and shivering through the earth, and although she could hardly make them out, they still put a rank fear into her. She clutched the hammer tightly, trying not to think about what she was going to do with it when the time came. In whose name did she wield it now? Sigmar's? Her own? Or perhaps even Gotrek's…

The undergrowth began to thin out at last, the creepers drawing back like the veils of a curtain, the stands of sapling and shrub petering away until a vast clearing opened up before them. Gotrek splintered his way through the last few overhanging trees and stumbled to a halt, and as Amara staggered into the clearing behind him, she didn't at first realise what she was looking at.

In front of her there was a mass of ravaged turf, a stream of some cloying dark liquid washing up against a cliff of lumpy green rock. The water was thick with the remains of human bodies, she realised – arms and legs poking from the soup, half-rotten faces leering into the air.

And then the green cliff face began to move.

It shuddered, and the liquid danced beneath it. Amara looked up. Her breath died in her throat.

'Grungni's *arse*,' Gotrek snarled. 'Now there's a big one.'

'Oh, Sigmar protect and save us!' Odger cried. His voice shook, and he clutched his boathook as if it were a holy icon that could protect him from the horror that loomed over the glade. He fell to his knees.

Top to bottom, it must have been a hundred feet tall. The spears of its antlers stabbed up above the trees. The spread of its arms, rolling with great folds of fatty tissue, reached out at least fifty feet from side to side. High on its stomach champed a grotesque, slavering mouth, the gums riddled with weeping sores, the teeth like sharpened ivory. Its eyes were like three clustered buboes, red as fire, the white pupils dancing with a pale amusement. The daemon's massive jaw hung slack below a mouth that grinned from ear to ear, the lips like rolls of curdled fat. The teeth in that mouth were the stones of a shattered graveyard, a rack of grey fangs slathered with drool.

Amara found a prayer on her lips, a form of words beseeching Sigmar for benediction that she had not spoken in months. It was only the shock of it that snapped her out of her horrified daze.

'What do we do? What in the name of–'

'The only thing we can do,' Gotrek spat. Despite his tone, despite the horrors that faced them, he still charged forwards with a look of elation on his face. 'We fight!'

CHAPTER TWENTY-FIVE

GLADE OF RUIN

Gotrek crossed the clearing in a rush. Gambolling along the edge of the pit, in the shadow of that monstrous daemon, was one of its lesser brethren – a leering, gangling thing with a swollen belly and a sack under its arm that looked like a grotesque set of bag-pipes. The lesser daemon tootled on the instrument as it skipped towards the duardin, shaking a stick on which a tiny, shrivelled head was screaming. Gotrek barely paused. A quick sweep of his axe, a sidelong glance, and the thing was falling onto the grass in two separate halves, the notes of its melody wheezing into a dis-cordant drone. Sundered from the world, even in the slurry of a place where Nurgle's will was strong, the creature faded into a black paste on the grass.

Amara's hands shook. It took every ounce of her self-control to take that first step into the clearing. She could feel the breath catch in her throat, her heart stutter in her chest. She was too terrified to know or care what deep resources she had drawn from, what residual faith or animal need to fight, but she had the hammer in her hand, a scream on her lips, and a rage stoked high in her heart. Odger, praying to himself, followed her. His face was like stone, as lifeless as the dead. Amara didn't need to ask what had made him charge into that fiendish glade. He had seen the pit. He had seen the corpses floating in the mire, melting and disarticulated. He knew now what had happened to his family.

The greater daemon was utterly beyond them. Most ordinary folk would have been driven insane to be merely in the presence of this monster, and Amara was almost shocked to find herself still moving forwards. The stench was like a physical thing trying to hold her back, and the ice of fear was cold enough to stop her heart, but still she went on. 'Sigmar's grace protect us!' Odger cried, and for a moment Amara was forced to agree. Perhaps Sigmar was with them after all...

Over on the far side of the pit she saw what could only be the sorcerer who had raised the beast. Staff in hand, his skin so swollen it looked like it was about to burst, the mage shrugged back his grey hood to reveal a face blistered with infection. A string of lank hair dribbled from his lumpy scalp. His mouth was like a slit carved into a wooden mask, and his eyes had receded so far into his head that Amara thought at first that he must be blind. Then he turned towards them as they charged across the slickness of the grass, and that mouth ripped wide into a yellow-toothed grin.

Gotrek had thrown himself at the greater daemon, this 'Grandson' as the Nurgle warrior had called it. The sight of the duardin with his matted orange beard and spiked mohawk leaping at near a hundred feet of cancerous blubber was so ridiculous it almost made her laugh. He just wouldn't give in. Even something like this, from which normal people would flee in abject terror, was just another target for his axe. There was no...

She struggled with the thought. It wasn't just confidence, was it? It wasn't battle madness, or some nihilistic desire to die fighting.

Amara thought of something then that she had not considered in many months, that she had pushed from her conscience whenever it crept near. It was an image, nothing more. It had been front and centre in her mind when the bodies began to fall around her. When the last of her comrades had died, when the sword blade had cut across her scalp and knocked her unconscious in the Thyrian wilderness. It had been the last thing she imagined – the golden light of Sigmar's warriors, the Stormcast Eternals, slamming to earth in a flash of lightning, meting out Sigmar's justice to the blasphemers. Unstoppable. Righteous. Grim with faith.

Please, she had cried then. *Send your champions down to protect us, God-King!*

But the God-King had not answered…

She looked at Gotrek, howling his duardin war cries, slashing his axe deep into the creature's toad-like leg. The red fury in him, axe blazing like a burning brand.

…Or had he?

There was no more time to think about it, or to worry about Gotrek. Amara saw the mage snap out with his staff, a sorcerous blast fuming on the tip. She shoved Odger to the side and dived to the dirt. The blast screamed past her, a gibbering flash of power that exploded against the treeline. The air shook. Across the clearing, the jungle seemed to swell. It thrashed higher and deeper, thickening in some foul parody of growth. There was nothing natural about this, nothing like the clean, organic growth of Ghyran. This was the frantic, unstoppable expansion of a tumour, mindless and diseased. The more power the daemon accrued to itself, the more the fronds of Nurgle's Garden were leaking into reality – and they would not stop here.

'If you are the same fools who sunk the ships in Kranzinnport,' the mage cackled as he stalked near, 'then I regret to tell you that you are too late. The rite is complete. The Grandson has been born into the world at last, and the world will tremble to his tread!'

Amara, slumped in the mud, risked a glance at Gotrek. He was clambering up the sagging folds of the daemon's belly as it heaved itself across the clearing, hacking in with his blade like a mountaineer hammering in a piton. What he thought he could possibly do when he reached the chomping jaws of its belly-mouth, she had no idea. High above him, craning its flabby neck to watch, the monster chortled in amusement.

Odger rolled to his knees and threw the boathook like a spear. The sorcerer knocked it from the air with his staff, the distraction giving Odger enough time to rush him. He threw himself forwards, fingers like claws, screaming, wanting nothing more than to rip the sorcerer apart with his bare hands.

The mage, so bloated now that his skin was beginning to split apart, and clearly drained by the rigours of his ritual, still managed to whip his staff around and crack it into Odger's jaw. He went sprawling, eyes slack. The sorcerer pivoted the staff, raising the rusty hook high to claw it down into Odger's chest.

Amara scrambled up, slipped in the muck strewn about the clearing, and dived forwards with her hammer pulled back.

Gotrek had been right. She had cleaved to her code – her determination not to kill – only after watching everything she loved die. Could she really sit back and watch another good man perish when she had the power in her hands to stop it? In a world of such horrors, perhaps the only real choice someone could make was to struggle against the darkness, or choose to let it win. That was all.

She brought the claw of the hammer down, trying to hook it into the sorcerer's skull, but the mage was still quicker than she imagined. He may have been drained by his spell and swollen with disease, but he was no creeping, feeble thing. As Amara darted in he swung the staff around and slammed the edge of the hook into her stomach. Doubled over, her weapon falling from her hand and all the breath punched from her, Amara collapsed and choked for air.

A roar split the air as the daemon plucked Gotrek from its chest and flung him across the glade. Amara saw the duardin smash into the ground, carving a trench in the dirt. Spitting dead leaves and pungent grass as he got to his feet, Gotrek snarled with a rage that was the equal of the daemon's chortling amusement. He snatched up his axe and sprinted back, flinging himself again at the Grandson's sopping, corpulent bulk.

'A tide of filth spreads from this island across the sea,' the mage hissed with delight. He raised the hook above her head. 'The Rocanian Coast sickens, the trees of Druhiel will wither and die, and soon the Living City will be counting their dead in the thousands. The *millions*. The Grandson walks... and he will not be stopped by some ragged band of heroes, no matter how valiantly they fight.'

Odger, spitting blood, flung himself across the grass and stabbed in with the boathook. The spike plunged into the sorcerer's side with a spurt of rancid pus. The mage staggered, a flash of pain across his face.

'We did nothing to you!' Odger cried. He looked possessed, all the horror of the last few months shaking through him. 'We weren't warriors, damn you! We weren't Stormcast, or any kind of threat you could possibly imagine! We were just ordinary folk!'

He swung in with the hook again. The sorcerer managed to block the blow with his staff, but the fury of Odger's assault was pushing him back.

'Does the gardener ask the waste he rakes into the compost for permission?' the mage laughed. 'Do the beetles and the worms have a say in the plans of the gods? And yet, they are part of the Garden all the same.'

He caught the boathook on the shaft of his staff, twisted, tore it from Odger's grip.

'If your family was one of those taken from the streets of Kranzinnport, then allow me to reunite you – I'm sure you have missed their embrace!'

He stabbed out with the staff, and a streak of sallow lightning flashed from it. The blast hit Odger in the chest, and instantly the flesh began to wither on his bones. In moments he looked like a month-old corpse, shrivelled and desiccated, and yet still held in the cruel grip of a life that would not leave him. Odger screamed and fell back, staggering to the edge of the pit. The soup of rotten corpses bubbled beneath him, and then, with a last disdainful flick of his wrist, the sorcerer sent him tumbling backwards straight into it.

'Odger!' Amara screamed.

She fumbled for her hammer. The sorcerer, his eyes glowing like swamp gas, turned towards her. The fumes of the pit rose up behind him like a curtain on a stage, shimmering and mephitic. Slowly, he pointed the staff at her. Threads of green magic crackled along the shaft like corposant.

She had faced death many times in her life. As a warrior priest, fighting for her city. As a lonely wanderer in the wild, spreading her angry gospel of the callous gods. Her own violent extinction was something she had long accepted as the likely end of her journey, wherever it took her. But Amara did not think she had ever been suffused with as much anger and hatred as she was now.

Her fingers found the hammer from where she had dropped it. Slowly, she got to her feet. The robes were a threadbare remnant of what she had once worn as a priest, but she felt a flicker of that same certainty in her now, a spark of that same unyielding faith. It rushed through her veins like a drug and made her grind her teeth. The hammer hung slack from her fist. Her eyes were like still pools, infinitely deep, and she did not draw them from the sight of the mage who faced her. She readied herself to step out once more from the grey world into the harsh purity she had tried to leave behind. She felt the power of Sigmar draw near; as near as it had ever been.

'I can't fault your courage,' the sorcerer laughed. 'But for such bold adventurers it was perhaps unwise to arm yourself with mere household implements. Boathooks? Hammers? Am I a nail you wish to fix to the wall, my dear? A boat you wish to scull across deep waters? Foolish, very foolish.'

'I was a priest of the God-King,' she said. She raised her weapon. 'Do you know why warrior priests are armed only with warhammers? It's an old belief, one that stems from a more pious age. In those days it was thought that the priests who expounded the Word of Sigmar should not sully their souls by spilling blood. A blade cuts deep, they say, but a hammer only bludgeons and does not break the skin.' She smiled. 'Of course, that all depends on how hard you hit.'

The mage chuckled richly to himself. The skin on his swollen chest had split open now, and the muscle and sinew, engorged with blood, was beginning to protrude. His eyes, so buried in folds of marbled skin, were like glinting pinpricks. He pointed his staff.

'When your corpse has shrivelled away to no more than a withered bundle of bones,' he said mildly, 'I think I will have you affixed to the Grandson's banner. As our legions march, we can cheer ourselves with the knowledge that Sigmar's Word marches with us – as false as it has always been.'

'The truth cannot wither,' she said. 'And Sigmar's justice cannot wane.'

The mage cackled as if he had expected nothing less. He levelled the staff – and then, churning up from the muck behind him, lurching from the pit, a withered claw snatched at his leg and threw him off balance.

The blast of necrotic energy shot past Amara's head. Odger, what was left of him, moaned in pain as he hauled himself dripping from the pit. More than anything she wanted to run to him, to try to help him in his agony, but Amara knew she only had this one last chance as the Nurgle mage staggered. She hauled back with the hammer and brought it crashing down, smashing it into the shaft of the sorcerer's staff and splitting it in half.

Yellow fangs bared, mouth like a stinking tunnel into the depths of an overflowing sewer, the mage hissed at her. The skin on his face peeled back as he howled, splitting around his mouth to reveal the wet ligatures of his rotting muscle.

There was a force in her now, guiding her hand. She could feel it thrumming through her arm, down the shaft of the hammer into the flattened iron head – Sigmar's strength, crackling in her veins. She swept the hammer down with more than her strength alone, and all the pain of those months since the crusade had been destroyed flared up in her soul. It was like a red mist was on her, and she felt the hammer crump solidly into the very centre of the sorcerer's skull.

His breath, as rank as corpse gas, choked in his mouth. His purple lips were spattered with blood. Amara slammed the hammer down, again and again, crouching over him as he fell. The crack of bone, the wet slop of brains. Was she screaming now, or was she crying? It was like she stood beside herself, watching the hammer smash the mage's head to pieces. She hooked the claw into his skull and ripped it apart like a melon. His hands, the fingers leaking black fluid, scrabbled at her wrists. She shucked the hammer up and smashed it down, again and again, muttering through gritted teeth.

'That's the other problem with wielding a hammer,' she snarled. 'After a while, *everything* looks like a nail.'

Hacking down, battering his brains into the grass, she hit so hard the shaft of the hammer snapped.

CHAPTER TWENTY-SIX

BLIGHTSLAYER

The sorcerer's arms flopped into the dirt. The bloated chest heaved once and fell still. Amara slumped to the side, spent. The red mist swirled in her eyes. Light sparked and flashed around her. She felt a bubble of nausea rising in her gut and turned to spew into the grass. She saw Gotrek, incredibly, still fighting. He leapt up the flank of the daemon, throwing himself across its folds of skin as it tried to swat him off. The daemon laughed, long and loud, as Gotrek hacked his blade into its belly and kept on with his furious, futile climb. Pallid drool fell from its tusks. The slobbering carpet of its tongue unfurled, purple with corruption.

'Amara...' a voice croaked.

Amara turned to see Odger's shrivelled body lying there on the edge of the pit. His flesh was as tough as leather, his muscles shrunken and twisted like coils of tar-covered rope. His face was little more than a skull, the skin stretched back on the bone, the teeth falling from his blackened gums. His eyes had been burned from the sockets and he could see nothing now; not the pallid vapour in the clearing nor the rancid, surging life of the plants as they tangled across the island and carpeted the sea. Pain was written across him, and Amara could not understand what force kept him alive.

'Odger, gods...' she breathed. 'Try not to... I'll get help, I'll...'

There was nothing she could do. She didn't dare touch him, not knowing what fresh agony she might cause. His hand, like a clutch of burnt sticks, reached up to his throat. The rags of his shirt fell aside, and there around his neck was the hammer pendant Baffin had given him.

It was untouched. Where all else had been scoured away by the acids of that caustic brew, Sigmar's symbol glowed like polished gold. The chain was as fresh as the day it had been forged, and the pendant shone almost with an inner light.

'Take it,' Odger whispered. He tapped the pendant with his burnt fingers. 'You... You need it more than I do now...'

'Odger,' she wept, 'I cannot, I...'

She could hear the wet crunch of Gotrek's axe as he slashed at the daemon on the other side of the pit. Even fifty feet away, across all the wriggling, rustling growth of this dread foliage, she could hear him struggling for breath. He was slackening. His skin was almost as pallidly green as the flesh of the Grandson, the welts rising up on his back like white snakes.

'Foolish duardin,' the daemon rumbled. Its voice shook through the glade like an earthquake, so deep Amara could feel it in her chest, her stomach. It made her want to vomit. 'Slayer from a world long gone, the last of your kind. You have a power in you, true. I can sense it, I can see the threads of it tangled in your soul, but you do not understand a fraction of it, child.'

Odger groaned at her side. He scrabbled at the pendant again.

'Amara,' he choked. 'Please – take it! Call on... Sigmar for aid. He has granted you this strength, you know it. He has never left you, he has... He has never left me.'

He hissed with pain as it lanced through his withered body. Quickly Amara unhooked the chain from around his neck.

'Throw me in,' he whispered. 'Please... let me be with them, one last time...'

She clutched his hand, nodded, though he could not see her. Amara wrapped the chain around her knuckles and clutched the pendant, and then she kissed Odger's brow.

'Be with your family once more,' she said. 'And if Sigmar does not grant you peace in the underworlds together, then I swear I will go to him and demand the answer why.'

The life left him. Amara tipped his body into the pit, and in moments it had sunk. She stood up and clutched the hammer pendant so hard it broke the skin of her palm.

On the other side of the pit, the Grandson chortled richly and flicked Gotrek to the ground. The vast daemon, its three massive eyes dancing in their sockets, smashed the great bronze bell down into the dirt. Gotrek only just rolled aside in time.

'Aye, duardin,' the daemon roared, 'you are like a child peering at a picture you do not understand. The source of what is in you is utterly beyond your ken... Now come! I would swallow you down and have done with this!'

Gotrek pushed himself to his feet, leaning on his axe.

'Then get on with it, you great rancid lump!' he screamed. 'What are you waiting for? Swallow me down and see if I don't choke you!'

The orange mohawk bristled. What it was costing him to stay on his feet, Amara couldn't imagine. He looked half-dead already.

The Grandson lumbered forwards, the earth shaking beneath him. Gotrek stood his ground, the axe planted head down in the grass while he crossed his arms and leaned on the pommel. He turned his glinting boar's eye on the daemon, and for a moment Amara couldn't have said which was the more terrifying sight.

The daemon's laughter shook the world around them. The trees shivered and the jungle itself seemed to froth with increased growth. Polyps and nodules popped in the humid air, belching out seeds that took root the moment they touched the fertile earth. Flowers bloomed and sickened in an instant, their rank petals sloughing from the stem. Flies were so thick in the air that Amara could barely breathe without inhaling them. Everywhere the fruits of Nurgle's Garden continued to grow and spread, the stony crust of the island covered in a carpet of lichen and moss.

The Grandson tossed the bell to one side with a clang so loud Amara clutched her head and fell to her knees. She stared in horror, paralysed, as the daemon reached down and snatched Gotrek up off the ground. The drooling maw in its stomach quivered. The tongue slurped out, green as a Bloat Fly's belly. Gotrek looked like a toy in the Grandson's massive fist, like a doll in the hands of a monstrous child. He gasped in pain as the monster squeezed him, but his eye was undimmed.

'Gulp me down, you great heaving bastard!' he roared. 'I'll wager I'm tougher than those teeth of yours can manage!'

'Very well, dwarf,' the daemon chortled. The great belly shook, the laughter rippling through the slack folds of its rotting skin. 'Let the last of your kind find peace in the depths of the Garden.'

'Gotrek!' Amara screamed.

It was like a nightmare. She couldn't move. All she could do was look on impotently as the daemon stuffed Gotrek into the gaping jaws of its belly. With a last skirling laugh, Gotrek disappeared into that monstrous cave, going to his doom with duardin oaths on his lips.

She hadn't known she was doing it, but Amara's hands were clasped as if in prayer. How many times had she bowed her head as she took to her knees, praising Sigmar or beseeching him for aid? In all her years ministering the Word, how often had her hands sought one another like this? What power was the will when the instinct was this strong?

The hammer pendant bit into her flesh. The chain fell between her hands, the wrought gold shining in that grim clearing like starlight in the firmament. The flies danced around her, seeking her eyes, her mouth, anywhere they could lay their eggs. The air thickened and the clearing became a cloying swamp. Reality itself felt thin, as if it would take only the smallest rip to break through to a place so grotesque it would shatter her mind as quickly as it would infect her body.

The Grandson, sparkling with aetheric light, laughed uproariously. With fingers as thick as tree trunks, it scooped up the bronze bell from where it had rolled into the undergrowth and rang out a lazy, booming peal. Again and again it rang the bell, the bronze clapper tolling out a wave of sound that seemed to shimmer in the air.

'Come forth, children of the fecund way,' the Grandson chanted. 'Fall from the bowels of the Grandfather and step into this world, so rich and ripe for plucking! Plague and epidemic, virus and distemper – the Grandson is calling you!'

The clearing flickered. Around the greater daemon shone a hundred lesser lights. Everywhere the air rippled with unease. A high whine cut across the world, like a million voices raised in ecstasy, but Amara knew the sound came from no living throat. The Realm of Chaos was near. The claws of the enemy were scraping down the walls of the world.

She stilled her breathing, closed her eyes. She felt the pendant squeezed between her palms, tried to concentrate on the sharp pain of the metal pressing into her flesh. She thought of Odger, destroyed by the loss of his family but still fighting on. She thought of the crusade, dying in the wilderness. She thought of Gotrek, sickened near to death but still raising his axe for one last blow – for what was Gotrek, truly, but a sign for all to see that the struggle must still be fought. If they could show the gods that they were still worthy, perhaps, just perhaps, the gods would return to help them in their hour of need.

She thought of a hand, reaching out for her when all was lost…

Let that hand now be yours, she prayed. *Sigmar, lord, if I have ever called on you before, then let me call on you now. I will give my life for this moment, if need be. Strike me down if you must, for I have turned my face from you in anger and sorrow. But do not let this happen. Hear my prayer, I beg you. Let my debt be passed to you, and I will strive every day of my life to fulfil it, I swear. Only let Gotrek live. Let him fight on, for he is indomitable. We need him now as we have never needed him before. If you spared me when all around me died, then let that have been for this moment. Spared so you can hear my prayer now, in this dreadful place. At this moment, please, smite the heathen. Destroy the unclean, I pray.*

The air shuddered in the glade. The points of light surrounding the Grandson stretched out like the rays of dying stars. The daemon snorted, dragging its colossal bulk towards her across the clearing. Jungle trees cracked and fell as his massive flanks pressed against them. The sides of the pit collapsed into the pool of stagnant filth, where the people of Kranzinnport had been sacrificed.

'I feel your prayer, priest,' it boomed. 'I feel the ribbons of your faith flowing up to the God-King, and they are as weak as mouldering rags.'

The voice seemed to echo in her mind as it throbbed in her chest. It was a voice from beyond the material plane. It was a consciousness woven from the madness of Chaos – eternal, incoherent. Amara fixed the daemon with her gaze. It was mere yards away from her now, and the clammy fever of its shadow fell across her.

The air quickened. The daemon roared, drunk with pleasure,

and its laughter was like an avalanche. Its lesser kin flickered into being around her, hundreds of them, thousands. Staring yellow eyes, savage ripped grins, fangs and slurping tongues. Stench, corruption, maggots and flies. The fertile madness of the glade surged in every direction, and she could only imagine how much of the sea had been poisoned now. Did the survivors of Kranzinnport look with horror on that boiling filth as it swept towards them? Did the men and women of Druhiel know how close they were to being overwhelmed?

Amara opened her palm. She looked at the hammer and it glowed – but it was more than the natural glimmer of the gold. Light shimmered across the surface like oil. It was like the light she had seen in Gotrek's rune. It was the light of Order, decency, faith. It was the light of the gods. The light of Sigmar.

'It is not the strength of my prayer that matters,' she said. Her voice sounded like a breeze battling against a hurricane. 'It is the strength of the response.'

The mist, high beyond the choked canopy of the jungle, began to break apart. A clean wind cut in from across the sea, from deep in the sky above. Like threads of spiderweb, the mist was cleaved. Clouds gathered up there, and they were dark. Amara felt the wind haring through the jungle, blowing the stench away. She looked up, raising her face to the heavens, where the clouds roiled and boomed. Light crackled through them, flickering like the flames of an inferno. The air felt like a sheet of steel being struck, again and again.

The Grandson, looming like a mountain above her, showed a flicker of unease.

'The Heldenhammer deigns to respond, does he?' it mocked. The grotesque antlered head craned back on the folds of its flaccid neck. The tusks champed and the eyes stared wide. 'Then let him strike me down, if he can! Come, Sigmar – I await your vengeance, if you dare!'

The flies in the glade buzzed with agitation. Electricity crackled through the trees, skimming over the rotting grass. The dark clouds swirled like water in a drain, flickering with light – and then the sky answered the challenge.

The flash was so bright Amara thought she had been blinded. A split second after came the sound of the world ending, a crash so loud she thought she had been deafened too. She screamed and could not hear her voice, her arm flung up over her eyes. There was a blast of heat that burned her skin, a screeching howl that felt like a billion nails being dragged across a billion pieces of slate. The ground heaved up and tossed her into the undergrowth, and there was a stench in the air of burning abattoirs, boiled vomit and scorched dung.

Crawling in the grass, weeping and retching, Amara blinked against the afterburn of the lightning strike. There was a high, thin whine in her ears and her skin felt like it had been crisped away. Slowly, black shapes formed in her sight. An acrid smoke that smelled of ancient decay billowed across the jungle. She could see a dark mound shuddering in the steam. After a moment of stunned silence, it began to speak. Its voice was slurred, like a drunk deep in his cups trying to order one last drink.

'Is… Is that it, God-King?' it said. 'Is that… Is that all you have?'

As the steam was gradually swept away, Amara staggered back into the clearing and stared up at the charred wreckage of the greater daemon. If she had had anything left in her stomach, the sight would have made her spew it into the dirt.

Every inch of its skin was blistered with burns. The protruding loops of intestine were scorched black. The eyes had melted into a rivulet of pink liquid that streamed down its face, and the subcutaneous fat beneath the flopping sag of its belly had been seared into a golden crackling. The handle of the bronze bell had fused to its fist, and all around it the air shimmered with the burnt grease of the Bloat Flies and the lesser daemons that had stood, for one brief moment, on the firm earth. And yet for all that, the monster still lived.

The laugh started deep in its charred belly. Reeling, the daemon tried to raise its blistered arms.

'Is that all you have, Sigmar? I scorn your feeble works, God-King! I will bring you Nurgle's embrace when I take Azyr. I am the Grandson, the Grandfather's presence in the Mortal Realms! I am the scourge and I am the life. I am rot and decay, and I am the green shoots of a new beginning. I am–'

It lurched, the words faltering on its cankered lips. Although the eyes were now no more than a fluid that dribbled into its yawning mouth, the daemon swung its head as if staring into every corner of the clearing. Amara backed off, every instinct screaming at her to run.

Pain stabbed across the daemon's scalded face. Motes of light sparkled around its monstrous bulk. Amara blinked. She could see a red glow high on its chest, and the more she stared, the stronger it seemed to get.

'I am the holy virus…' it retched, gasping in agony. 'Curse you, priest, what is this? What have you done?'

The motes of light quickened. Here and there the charred skin began to fracture and bleed. The red glow burned brighter, like a flame surging across a stand of dry fuel.

Amara grinned as she realised what was happening.

'Hurts, does it?' she cried. She gave a harsh laugh. 'I think something you ate is disagreeing with you!'

The daemon shrieked. The light burst in a haze of flames from its chest, and as the monster screamed with a voice that echoed from the other side of a sundered veil, Gotrek erupted into the clearing. Hacking his way madly through the daemon's aetheric flesh, his axe blade blazing with fire, the Slayer burned like some duardin god of war. In a spray of rotting entrails, he leapt to the ground as the Grandson broke apart behind him, and the battle cry he screamed would have forced any army in the Mortal Realms to retreat.

Amara fell to her knees, shielding her face. The master rune scalded the light and burned away the foulness of the grass. The flames that crackled through his hair and beard were like threads of lava, and his axe seemed more like a shard of lightning than a mortal weapon. His eyes – and there were two eyes now, she saw – were points of blinding light blazing in the depths of the void. He was Grimnir. He was Grungni the Maker, blessed of Azyr. He was the soul of every duardin that had ever lived, geared to war and lusting for the blood of his enemies, undefeatable.

And then, as the Grandson's daemonic form smeared away with a crack of thunder and a horrified scream, fading into the hidden weave of reality, and as the clearing steamed with its melting guts, Amara saw that the Slayer was none of these things. He was Gotrek Gurnisson – the most brutal, violent and deadly character she had ever met, but a mortal thing for all that. The light left him and the pain of his injuries returned. The unnatural disease that had come so close to bringing him low redoubled its efforts. Gotrek slumped forwards and collapsed, his skin stained that same infected green.

Amara rushed to him. She knelt at his side, her palms on his heaving chest. The rune was dull as brass again, and his breath came ragged from his lungs. His eye twitched, half-closed. His hand slackened its grip on his axe.

'Gotrek!' she cried. She could feel his heart hammering beneath his ribs, stuttering and weak. He was barely breathing now. A dark contagion crept through his veins, marbling them against his skin. He was dying. 'Gotrek, can you hear me?'

She slammed her fist against his chest. She slapped him and

tried to drag him up into a sitting position, but the duardin was too heavy. His frame was too slack. He was spent.

The pendant was still gripped in her hand. The hammer of Sigmar, the sign of his justice, of his mercy. Amara, weeping, held it to the sky. Up there, just faintly visible, she could see the emerging blue as the foul smoke of the pit was blown away. The ground shook. The smoking crater where the Grandson had been struck cracked and a spray of seawater leapt a dozen feet into the air. Wither Island was breaking apart.

'I was a priest once,' Amara whispered. 'And I can be again.' She laid her hands on Gotrek's chest again. She stilled her breathing, tried to feel the flow of his life as it faltered. 'A warrior in Sigmar's name. But to heal is to fight in a different way.'

She mumbled the prayer she had last spoken when she knelt over the body of her son. When the dusk had faded and the pain of her injuries almost eclipsed her grief, she had pleaded with Sigmar to bring him back – her boy, killed in the valley as the crusade died around them. The hand that had reached out to her from the tent that last morning, that had reached for her when the Hedonites descended. Sigmar had not listened then; or, he had listened, knowing only that greater trials lay ahead for her.

Tears spilled down her face. She felt Gotrek's heart stop beneath her fingers.

'Bring him back,' she wept. 'Please, bring him back, for all that he has done.'

Another fount of seawater, another tremble in the earth. The trees of the jungle melted into a stinking paste. The stone and rock of Wither Island was crumbling into the ocean.

Through her fingers she felt the island shiver – and then she realised that it was not the island, but the faintest beating of Gotrek's heart.

Amara held her breath. His eye flicked open. There was a shimmer of light fading from her hands. The master rune flashed with a last effulgence. Gotrek moaned, his skin flushed and ruddy. The green tinge had vanished from him.

'Gods above and below,' he muttered. He pressed his stubby fingers to his forehead. 'My mouth tastes like an orruk's loincloth. I swear, I'm never drinking again.'

'Gotrek, you're… You're alive?'

She tried to keep the reverence from her voice, but she could not help it. She looked at her hands. Had the healing passed from her to Gotrek, or had some hidden power in the rune, charged by Sigmar's lightning, brought him back from the brink of death? The hands of a healer. The hands of a warrior.

'Course I'm bloody alive,' he snarled. 'Although I'd give all the treasures in Karaz-a-Karak to be dead, if it would only get rid of this utter bastard of a headache.'

Whatever had happened, there was no time to think of it now. The island was shaking apart around them. Amara tucked Odger's boathook into her belt and threw Gotrek's arm around her shoulder. She tried to drag him to his feet.

'Move yourself,' she said. 'We have to get out of here. With any luck the boat's still moored on the beach.'

Gotrek groaned again as he picked up his axe. He shook his head clear. He was covered in slime and dried blood, and half his face looked as tender as pulverised meat, but he could walk under his own steam at least. Amara didn't think she'd have been able to drag him.

'Why? What's happening?'

'Wither Island,' she said, as she started to run. 'It's about to sink back to where it came from!'

The boat swung on the tide, smacking up against the rocks. All the pebbles on the beach were shuddering, the sand rippling like liquid as the skin of the island began to crack. The earth buckled beneath their feet, throwing them to the ground, and behind them the trees and jungle scrub were being torn up by the roots. Amara pulled Gotrek up again, but each time a little more of his strength seemed to return.

'Whole bloody place is falling down around our ears,' he said. 'Either Sigmar's lightning holed it below the waterline, or that sorcerer's spell was the only thing keeping it together.'

Amara waded into the sea to grab the gunwale of the boat, dragging it back across the sand. The crust of algae had melted away now to an oily stain across the surface of the water. Where the line of the jungle met the beach, the thickets of putrid brushwood began to melt. Dissolving fluids trickled down onto the sand, hissing like acid.

She flopped into the boat, Gotrek collapsing beside her. She reached for the oars where they were clipped to the lock, but didn't have enough strength to pull them free. Her fingers felt numb and there was a sheet of dark shadow sweeping across her sight. All her strength seemed gone from her, after everything that had happened since they woke up in Kranzinnport that morning. The tunnels to the harbour, the fight against the pirates, the dreadful confrontation with the Grandson. And the prayer she had given up to Sigmar, the prayer that had in some way been answered...

'Rest yourself, lass,' she heard Gotrek say. 'I'll see to that.'

She fell back as Gotrek took the oars, and as she drifted off into an exhausted sleep she found herself wondering how it was possible that he had the strength to continue. After everything that had happened, he should be unconscious at the very least. The water gulped around them as the oar blades struck the surface of the sea. As they pulled away from Wither Island she could hear the great gurgling roar of the ocean surging up to drag it back down, hiding it safely down there in the deeps where, Sigmar willing, no one would ever find it again.

As they struck out into the wider sea, she could hear a thin, high scream somewhere on the breeze, like the call of a bird. It was the howl of something on the other side of the veil, she knew, only a hair's breadth away. The sound of wrath and fury. The sound of defeat.

CHAPTER TWENTY-SEVEN

THE LAST CRUSADE

The plains of Thyria... The crusade into the wilderness, the valley ahead... She dreamed, and remembered.

They had made camp in the plains the night before, the wagons and carts in a ring around the pickets. In the morning they doused their campfires and packed up their gear. The dawn was spectacular, like the first dawn of a new world, rising above the jagged mountains in the distance, their peaks gnashing together like teeth. The sky was a blue canvas touched with fiery reds and oranges, and it stretched from end to end of an infinite horizon. Far in the distance, a hundred miles away, they could see the floating pads of plains-lilies and the rolling progress of the veldt-louses, each of them larger than Dagoleth itself. Each blade of grass was as green as emeralds, thicker than a human wrist, a carpet of jade that ran on unbroken for a thousand miles.

Amara woke early and stood at the mouth of her tent, breathing in the fresh, fragrant air. Everything smelled clean and pure, unsullied even by the smoke of the first campfires or the rich stink of the latrine they'd dug on the campsite's western edge last night. Thyrian air, she thought. The finest air in all the Everspring. It was the smell of promise and new life. In that wide and unbroken vista was the sight of a new civilisation just waiting to be built, wrought into being by the brave hearts and strong hands of the Dawners who'd left Dagoleth on the crusade.

She knelt and took up a handful of soil, rich and loamy in her hand. All the obligations had been paid, she knew. All the debts back in Dagoleth, large and small, had been settled. The commitments had been fulfilled, and every man, woman and child who set off from the gates of the city was doing so with Sigmar's name on their lips. They were bringing hope into the wilderness.

More folk started waking, coming out of their tents and getting the first Xintilian tea brewing on their campfires. The sutlers started banking dry wood around the cook pots, boiling up the remaining rockworms they'd harvested by the Crimson Cliffs. The pickets were dismantled as the soldiers fell into their marching order. Some of the bivouacs and shelters were taken down and packed away. Once everyone had eaten, the wagons would be tied once more to the oxen. Hundreds of people would get ready to move, to make the last stage of their journey. Hundreds had already died on the way, but once they were in the valley the real work could begin. They would toil and clear and build, and before long they would have a place worth defending with their lives – a new settlement cut out of the unforgiving land, a shard of civilisation planted in the wilds.

Amara crouched at the mouth of her tent and softly called his name. There was such a day ahead of them. She would give a sermon before they set off, put the final touch of courage into hearts that were already near brim full of it.

She heard him call for her. She smiled and held out her hand,

and he reached for her; and though she didn't know it then, by the end of the day he would be dead. They would all be dead, and Sigmar would have turned his face from them.

It started as a faint rumbling in the distance, as though a storm were brewing in the mountains. Then she felt the tremor underfoot, the earth shaking very slightly, the drumming of hoofbeats. There was a blast of noise, a note skirling wildly across the grasslands. Amara stood. She felt for the hammer in her belt.

'Arnza,' she said to her son. 'Stay inside the tent.'

There were cries from the pickets. She heard the flat discharge of a black-powder weapon. The rumbling was deeper now, more insistent, and above the wailing notes she could hear yelling, a wild, ululating call that scratched at her mind and put ice in her belly. There was a sudden smell wafting across the air, pungent and sickly, a mix of musk and dead flowers.

Amara ran between the tents, leaping over the ropes, pulling the hammer from her belt. She cut west, sprinting across the clearing in the centre of the camp, where the cookfires were already burning. Freeguild troops were forming up on the far side; other soldiers were running back from the pickets with blood on their faces, their uniforms torn. There were screams in the air, the clash of steel. Still that damned yelling, that frantic, piercing cry.

She saw one of the Freeguild sergeants, a big man with a flaring handlebar moustache and muttonchop whiskers, bark out orders to his men. He pointed with his sword, shouting, exhorting.

'Get them to the armoury wagons,' he cried as she passed. 'Guard the supplies and get troops on the hospital tents.'

The sergeant turned – then fell back with an arrow jutting from his eye.

The troops bunched up, some of them drawing their swords, others swinging round with their handguns, looking for targets. More screaming on the other side of the clearing, the bright clash of weapons. Amara saw men and women running, staggering through the tents with blood sheeting down their faces. Arrows came down like hail, peppering the clearing. Three of the Freeguild troops fell at once, pierced through by arrows fletched with iridescent purple feathers. The ground shook – and then the enemy burst onto them like a tide.

In moments the clearing was a chaotic melee of oiled steel, blood and furious screaming. They were Hedonites, she saw, the depraved, debauched followers of the Dark Prince. She had a swirling impression of shaved skulls tattooed with sickly glyphs, of brutal piercings designed for maximum agony, of savages festooned with feathers and trinkets, drenched in cloying musks and perfumes. They ran and leapt with barbed blades and whips in their hands, lancing in with gleaming spears that dripped with honeyed unguents. Some rode grotesque reptilian creatures barded with glistening silver armour, their spikes and spurs tearing through flesh or lopping off arms and legs as they rode past.

In moments the clearing was overrun. The whole damned camp was overrun, as far as Amara could tell. She smashed in with her hammer, cracking skulls and breaking limbs, screaming for the Dawners to stand firm.

'Hold!' she roared. 'Sigmar wills it! Raise your voices in holy prayer so that he may strengthen our arms this day!'

The crusade had combatted everything Thyria could throw at them since they had left Dagoleth. An orruk tribe, their ugly faces streaked with white paint, had tried to infiltrate the camp one night; their bones still decorated the wagon trains. A pack of bone-gryphs, creatures rarely seen outside of Shyish, had shadowed them for days, until the Freeguild Pistoliers rode out to shoot them down. A field of vast, near-sentient fungus had tried to suck the crusade into its voracious maw, and they had battled more bandit raiders and wandering gargants than Amara could even remember. But even as she fought in the clearing, she knew this was different. Shattering bones with her hammer, bellowing prayers to Sigmar, she had no real sense of how the battle was unfolding. It was all happening too fast.

The Hedonites had swamped their camp like an avalanche, pouring down from the mountains, taking advantage of how few of them were left after their long months in the wilderness. They moved so quickly it was impossible to form a coherent defence. Amara watched the last Freeguild soldiers in the clearing cut down, felt an arrow streak across her brow and carve a line of blood from her forehead. She staggered backwards, parried a scimitar already stained with gore, swung out and saw a leering face crumple under the flat of her hammer. The light seemed to flicker around her, the hot morning bending and twisting into weird, unnatural shapes – daemons, summoned by the Hedonites' foul lusts, shrieking into reality from their own dread realm. She ducked a guy rope and reeled back into the lines of tents and bivouacs, half of them now torn and smoke-stained, the canvas red with blood.

The screams around her were wilder now. Not the shouts of rage or battle madness, but sheer panic. Everywhere she looked there was the flash of silver blades, the gleam of oiled leather, the exposed flesh and flensed nerves of cultists so deranged that even their own terrible wounds were a source of ecstasy to them. Fires had taken hold over where the armoury wagons had been corralled. There was a hard, flat explosion, a gout of smoke as the black-powder stores went up in flames.

She ran on, fighting where she could, trying to rally the survivors. She tried to push all thoughts of her son from her mind. He would live or die depending on their strength now, on their unity. If the Dawners truly broke, then all was lost.

'Turn and fight, damn you!' she screamed. 'Sigmar sees all, and your cowardice will reap his judgement!'

Frightened eyes, wild with panic, rolled away from her. Folk gibbered and cried and ran, heedless of everything but their own survival.

'Only together will our strength prevail!' she shouted. She raised her hammer. 'Face your deaths with gladness in your hearts and a prayer on your lips, for Sigmar asks only that we die in his name!'

An arrow slammed into her thigh. She gasped, the pain flashing through her. A spear came stabbing out of the rolling smoke, and it was all she could do to parry it with the haft of her hammer. She grabbed the collar of the spear point and wrenched it aside, swinging wildly and feeling bone crunch under her blow, and then she was falling backwards into the stained grass.

'Sigmar, please,' she whispered. She started crawling, dragging her wounded leg behind her. Blood was crusting on her face. She could feel the heat of the flames, could smell the spilled blood even above the stench of the cultists' perfumes. 'Hear my prayer. Send your champions down to protect us, God-King! Send the Stormcast Eternals to deliver us from this evil, I beg you!'

On she crawled, and when she heard him screaming she felt something wrench and tear inside.

'Arnza! Arnza, run, my boy, run!'

Hand over hand she crawled. She tried to stagger to her feet, her leg buckling under her. She heard him scream again, heard dark laughter on the stinking breeze.

The tent she had left only a few minutes ago was no more than a tattered rag stained with blood. She heard the scream ripping across the burning campsite, wondering for a brief, dislocated moment who could possibly feel that much pain, before realising that it came from her. She held what was left of him in her arms. She looked to the sky and it was empty. Sigmar had turned his face from them, and when the last blow came she did not feel it. There was only darkness around her, and the body of her son in her arms; and when she woke, the sole survivor left for dead, the darkness was still there. It would never go away, she knew.

CHAPTER TWENTY-EIGHT

ESCAPE

It was dark when she woke. The night sky was filtered through a thread of purple cloud, all the realmspheres soaring through the firmament above them. A strange, pale light danced across the surface of the sea, but after a moment she realised it was just the natural luminescence of the plankton that grew along this part of the coast. The air was still and she could smell a distant trace of woodsmoke. It was the smell of a cookfire, of the homely mortal world.

Gotrek sat at the other end of the boat, the oars resting in the clippers. He had folded his arms, his head brooding on his chest while he stared off into some inner distance.

'You're not rowing?' Amara said as she surfaced.

'Tide's taking us in. I'm letting the sea do the work for me.'

In the darkness she could see the sparkle of lights somewhere off to her right, the black line of a distant coast.

'Kranzinnport?'

'No,' Gotrek said. 'Least, not as far as I can tell. We've come a good distance down the coast. It's a settlement of some kind though, a town or a small city maybe.'

Amara winced as she stretched out, every muscle in her body stiff. Gotrek said nothing, although she could sense the gloom that had settled over him, the strange weariness.

'Your prayer was answered then,' he said. 'I've been thinking about it.' He glanced up at the night sky, the glinting stars. 'Someone up there, in Azyr… Whether Sigmar or Grungni, I felt it. The lightning, the rune… Seems I don't have a choice in using it or not. If I don't, then they'll just use it for me.'

She could feel the anger coming off him in waves. Hunched there in the darkness, squat and muscled, he looked like a carved stone idol, a god of an earlier and cruder age.

'I prayed to heal you too,' she said. 'Someone wants to keep you alive, Gotrek Gurnisson.'

'My life's my own,' he said bitterly. 'My death too. I won't have… *them* sticking their noses in where they're not wanted. Anyway,' he said, the gloom flowing away from him as suddenly as it had settled, 'it was you that healed me, not the gods. Take it from me.'

Amara clenched her hands. She still had the hammer pendant in her fist, she realised.

'Does the power not come from the gods either way?' she said. She looked at her fingers, the dark skin bruised and blistered.

'I don't know,' Gotrek admitted. 'But all I do know is it can't go anywhere without a mortal heart behind it. That's what matters. The gods can jump up and down all they bloody like, but they still need honest flesh and blood to get anything done.'

Amara ran her thumb over the pendant. She took the boat-hook from her belt and wrapped the chain around the head. She thought of Odger and hoped, after all he had suffered, that he had found peace at last.

'You lost someone, didn't you?' Gotrek said. 'Saw it in your eyes the moment we met. Felt it in the prayer you made. The pain, the grief.'

Amara nodded. After a moment she said, 'My son. When the crusade was ambushed in Thyria. I could have left him behind in Dagoleth, sent for him when... But no, the point was we were going to build a new civilisation in the wilderness. I was going to give him a new life. Instead, I gave him only death.'

'What was the lad's name?'

She had not spoken it for months, and it took all of her efforts now to form the word.

'He was called Arnza,' she said. 'He was seven years old.'

'I'm sorry. But you didn't give him death. Know that. It wasn't your fault. You did all you could for him.'

'I know.' She shook her head. 'I fought, as hard as I could. I survived, and for so long now I have blamed Sigmar for letting me live when all I wanted was to die with my son. But he spared me. He spared me for this moment, to save you instead. It seems I had no choice in the matter either.'

They sat there in silence as the tide drew them further in. The breeze skimmed the water and after a while Amara could hear, very faintly, the sound of voices raised in laughter. The lights glinted in the settlement across the sea. It was a cool, clear night.

'So your debt to me is paid,' Gotrek said. 'About bloody time.'

Amara smiled. 'It is paid. I am free of the obligation.'

'Good. Not sure I like having folk feeling so *obliged* to me. And Sigmar?'

'What of him?'

'Are you back to swinging a hammer in his name?'

'I don't know,' Amara admitted. 'There is much that is still unclear to me, much I still need to think about. I cannot say I fully believe in him.'

Gotrek was incredulous. 'Are you soft in the head, lass? Fair enough, I don't like him any more than you do, the gilded great *umgi* moron, but I do believe he's actually there all the same!'

'That is not what I mean,' she said. 'I suspect, Gotrek Gurnisson, that you think the warrior priests of Sigmar's Temple to be unyielding and unimaginative folk, but–'

'Ha! That wouldn't be the half of it.'

'But,' she continued, 'we need to wield theology in our battles as much as we wield a warhammer. To *believe* in something is not to blindly accept its veracity. Belief can mean trust as well.' She looked at him, hunched forward in the boat, his massive arms folded. 'I believe in you, Gotrek. I *trust* you.' She looked to the heavens. 'I believe Sigmar is up there in Azyr, but I am not sure if I fully trust him again. Not yet. There is a long way to go before I feel that once more, I fear.' She glanced at him, the scowl on his face. 'But I have taken the first step.'

'*Gods,*' Gotrek spat, as if no more needed to be said.

Amara settled uneasily in the boat. She meant every word she had said, but she couldn't help but remember the form of her prayer when the Grandson was bearing down on her, Gotrek stewing in its belly.

Let my debt be passed to you, she had prayed, *and I will strive every day of my life to fulfil it, I swear…*

There would be time enough to think about that later. She had spilled blood once more, breaking the vow she had made when her son had died, but she had not done it in Sigmar's name. If anything, she had done it in Gotrek's.

Amara closed her eyes and lay back. The tide tugged gently on the boat and the sounds of the city drifted closer. Let the gods struggle amongst themselves for faith and trust; all she wanted to do now was rest.

'I tell you what,' Gotrek said. She could hear him scratching at his matted beard. He stood up in the boat, and as Amara opened her eyes she could see him peering into the gloom with his one good eye. 'Our luck's in. I swear I can smell a tavern beyond those walls there.' He cackled to himself and grabbed the oars. 'All worked out fine in the end, eh?' he said. 'Can't be called a wasted day when there's good ale on tap at the end of it!'

Amara might have agreed, but she was too tired to say so. The road ahead of her felt very long, suddenly, dangerous and obscure, but she knew she needed to walk it all the same. The light of faith had been revealed to her once more, after she had spent so long wandering in the dark. She tried to imagine the days to come in the company of this strange, taciturn duardin, prone to such violent, brooding moods, but she knew her fate was linked to Gotrek's now. Whatever her place might be in the Mortal Realms, she would only find it at his side.

She turned over and fell back into an exhausted sleep as Gotrek rowed them closer to the shore.

In her dreams she felt a hand reaching out and touching hers. She held it tight. It was a beautiful morning after all. The dawn was spectacular, she thought. The first dawn of a new world.

Easy enough to follow the road from Druhiel. Folk could talk about nothing else, apart from where they had gone afterwards. Barkeep in the Amber Sap complained about his broken furniture, looked like he expected compensation. He stared the fellow down, made it clear no such compensation would be forthcoming. Least not from him.

He had paused to look at the rotting stump in the centre of the town. Looked like nothing so much as a corpse dredged out of a peat bog. Stank too, a brackish smell of stagnant water. Folk said they had burned most of it, but left the roots in the hope it might grow back, bigger and better than before.

Foolish, he thought, but he left them to it. Not his problem. The goddess, Alarielle... Well, he guessed it took all sorts. Better than most gods they could have picked.

He hiked the rough country to the coast in a few days. Didn't find much on the way; a couple of burnt-out campfires, that's all. Had the feeling they were making time, like they were in a hurry.

He couldn't figure it out. Like they were looking for something, or answering a summons.

Outside Kranzinnport he found burned-out farmsteads, abandoned cottages. Fields were laid to waste, city didn't look like it had done much better. He drew his pistol as he approached the gates.

The streets were empty. Buildings looked like they'd survived a siege. Filth in the gutters, strewn about the roads, climbing the walls. Nothing living though. Looked like a jungle had swamped the place and then died back, took all the folk with it. Curious. He'd have to make a report, and the thought soured him for the rest of the afternoon. What happened here? Where did they go?

He stood on the bluff, peered down at the entrance to some tunnels that descended into the cliffs. Foul smell down there, not one he wanted to explore without some food in his belly. As the light died he stood by the rail at the edge of the cliffs and stared out to sea. Dark out there, a slick of something like oil on the water. Folk in Druhiel had talked of Wither Island, some landmass rising up from the deep, but he could see nothing. Yokels getting overexcited about something they didn't understand, no doubt. Went with the job.

He built a campfire in the room of an abandoned house, blocked off both doors, made sure he had an escape route up to the roof. Loaded his pistols, put them within easy reach. He cooked some of the oats he'd bought in Druhiel, read over his papers by the light of the flames while he waited for the oats to cool down.

He couldn't figure the woman out. Some said she was a priest, and he couldn't figure that out either. Not important in the end, he reckoned. The duardin was what mattered.

He ate his oats, rolled up his coat and used it for a pillow as he tried to rest. Couldn't stop thinking about it though. He thought the Slayer would have led him straight to the aelf, but maybe the duardin didn't know after all. Maybe there was nothing in it to start with? The report had come from Kurrigar, out in Chamon, and you couldn't trust Kurrigar as far as you could throw him. And he was a big man.

He pushed it to one side, settled down to sleep. He'd head on tomorrow, set off along the coast road. He'd find them in the end. He always did. And then he'd get the answers he was looking for.

EPILOGUE

The mire was darkest just before the dawn. The moon seemed ashamed of itself as it gripped the western sky, slinking away beyond the horizon and leaving a fading trace of silver against the grass.

The dead trees clattered, dry as bones. The fenland shivered in a breeze as cold as the grave. Threads of mist crept across the dark water and ravelled themselves around the flank of the tower, and inside the tower the shadows shrank away as if afraid.

In a chamber blacker than the night, an eclipse of moths were fluttering through the gloom. Some were as large as birds, their wings like sheets of parchment scraping at the air. Others were no more than motes of grey light flicking from beam to beam. Some were the colour of turned earth, dun and black, while others were filigreed in gold and bronze, their clasped wings patterned with the roving amber eyes of predators. Every few moments one of them would skim the fading moonbeams to the arrow-slit windows and disappear, while another would flutter in from the world outside. From every corner of the realms they flew, bringing word of everything they had seen.

Tunnels and passageways stretched below the chamber, burrowed deep into the black earth beneath the mire. Torches flickered every few yards, illuminating doors of black ironoak bound with bronze. Some of these doors had not been opened in many years, while others had welcomed new arrivals only a few days before. Behind each of them leaked the smell of fear and desperation, the raw terror of condemned things just waiting to die. Sometimes, in extremity, a scream would break out from behind these doors, but it never lasted very long. The doors would open only when he wanted them to, and not a moment before.

Beyond these passageways there was another chamber – a darker, older place, buried deep in the foundations of the sinking castle. It had once been a room of some stateliness and grandeur, where noble guests would be honoured on the occasion of their visit. Sometimes – and this very rarely – such guests were still welcomed, but to his relief it had been many years now since any of his extended family had deigned to travel here. He was to all intents and purposes alone.

Velvet curtains thick with dust hung across the empty windows. Tapestries so stained by time their pictures were unreadable hung on the walls. A four-poster bed hung with a tester of black satin sat in the corner, although of course he had no need of it now. The curtains were riddled with holes from where the moths had laid their eggs, and scattered all across the flagstones were the discarded husks of the larvae's chrysalides. Against one wall there was an oaken table, ten feet long. Legends said it had once belonged to a mortal king, who had ruled an empire that stretched from the mountains to the sea. Legends also said this very castle had once been the seat of his power, from where he had ruled his kingdom. The only one who could have confirmed this either way was the figure hunched over that table now, but he could not recall the truth of it any more. It had been so long ago.

The table was scattered with scraps of parchment: maps, accounts, books of history and mythology, treatises, discourses, proclamations. The figure ran his claws across them all, seeking information. The moths had brought news of Kranzinnport, and it was with great satisfaction that he had heard of the sorcerer's failure. All had gone as planned. The pieces had been lined up and set in motion, and the duardin Gotrek had thrown the minions of Chaos into utter confusion. All it had taken was a rumour here, a small piece of speculation there, and the pieces moved where he wanted them to. Even now, another trail had been set. The fool from Azyr blundered across the landscape, and soon he would cross paths with the Slayer. And then...

At last, he found what he was looking for. The grey claws snatched up the sheet of parchment. He began to read, and when he had finished he began to laugh. It was a sound like cold wind coursing through a ruined city, like death on the breeze.

Yes, he thought. Most appropriate, and it had been so long since he had travelled to the Realm of Light.

The shadows in the chamber seemed to expand. The light from the torches guttered and died, and suddenly, where there had been only darkness, there was now a great flurry of silver dust.

The chamber was empty. The passageways and corridors were deserted. The screams behind the black iron doors went unheard, and over the mire there flitted a terrible black shadow, darker than the night.

ABOUT THE AUTHOR

Richard Strachan is a writer and editor who lives with his partner and two children in Edinburgh, UK. Despite his best efforts, both children stubbornly refuse to be interested in tabletop wargaming. His first story for Black Library, 'The Widow Tide', appeared in the Warhammer Horror anthology *Maledictions*, and he has since written the Age of Sigmar novels *Blood of the Everchosen*, *The End of Enlightenment*, *Hallowed Ground* and *The Vulture Lord*.

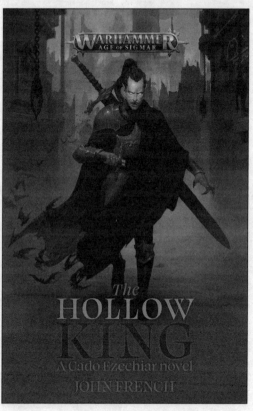

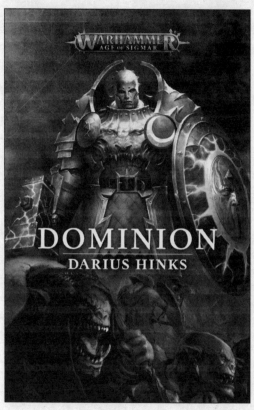